Blinded By Hate

Blinded By Series

Book One

Jaclin Marie

Editing Done by Antonia Salazar from AMS Editing Physical Cover done by After Dark Cover Designs by Ama

ISBN PRINT: 979-8-9881467-6-6
A-ISBN (E-BOOK): 979-8-9881467-7-3

PLAYLIST

BITTERSUITE	**BILLIE ELLISH**
I WANNA BE YOURS	**ARCTIC MONKEYS**
ALL I WANT	**KODALINE**
PERFECT	**SELENA GOMEZ**
MORAL OF THE STORY	**ASHE**
EYES DON"T LIE	**ISABEL LAROSA**
BORED	**BILLIE ELLISH**
LADY KILLERS III	**G-EAZY**
LONG TIME	**PLAYBOI CARTI**
ANXIETY	**JULIA MICHEALS**
AFRIAD	**THE NEIGHBORHOOD**
WILDFLOWER	**BILLIE ELLISH**
SAD GIRL	**LANA DEL REY**
PACIFY HER	**MELANIE MARTINEZ**

Blurb

Maybe we just found forever at the wrong time and someday time will pull us back together again.

———

Hayden Night corrupted my thoughts. Even after four years of going to therapy and trying to rid myself of him he is still in the back of my mind.

He is one of the best boxers in the country, possibly in the world. He always had a talent for fighting, he craved it and fed off of it. He used fighting as a coping mechanism to block out the demons in his head.

But I still found myself going to his wedding, watching him smile at the girl he "loved" and watching him laugh and pretend that what we had in the past didn't matter, but in reality it meant everything.

We were bound to meet again but will this also end in chaos?

*To the girls who are still waiting for their unexpected love,
it's out there. You just have to let it find you.*

Prologue

Jaclyn

Present

No one told me that therapy would take more than five years to recover a damaged heart. At the same time, my heart was never just damaged.

It was ripped in half and broken down to the tiniest piece you could imagine.

There is only one reason I didn't just end it all after that night.

"How's your heart feeling today, Jaclyn?" Patience, my therapist asks.

I force a small smile on my face and try to relax in the leather chair.

I've been seeing Patience for almost three years now. After the first year I moved to New York, I spent a good year rotating through different therapists until I found

Patience. She has been super patient with me, pun not intended. Sometimes her advice isn't why I come, sometimes I just want to cry it all out with no one to watch or judge.

It's hard to cry in front of Junior when I'm always with him.

And crying on the subway home is definitely something I will never do because that's just pathetic and embarrassing.

"It's the same as always. It's healed."

"Are you still getting nightmares?" A guy in a black hood pops up in my mind and I can't help but wince. Patience notices and she nods like she always does whenever she mentions him. "Time heals wounds, Jaclyn. It's only been about five years."

"I'm just done feeling like this," I say, trying hard to not let a tear slip from my eye. "Every time I look in the mirror naked, I feel so disgusting and worthless. I feel empty."

"But then you look at Junior and what happens?"

When she mentions Junior, I look at him on the floor. He's laying down and watching his favorite movie, The Lion King. That little boy is the only reason I'm alive and am still breathing.

If I didn't have him, I probably would have been six feet under.

"I feel like suddenly I'm filled with life again. Like

there's actually something living in here," I say while touching my chest.

Patience smiles at me, it's not a happy smile, it's a sad one.

She knows all the gory details of that tragic night. She, my mom, my uncle, and Brandon are the only people who know.

I remember seeing my mom and I just broke down in her arms, wishing for it all to go away. She cried with me after I told her the details. She made me move back in with her for a good two years and then I moved out to New York when I got offered a journalist position. She always flies out to New York to visit and check up on me. She also calls every day to make sure I'm doing good and remaining healthy. She also loves talking to Junior as well.

We did have a big argument before I left for New York because she thought I wasn't ready. But I still moved because I just needed my own space and to be alone with Junior.

"Like I said, time heals wounds. You have a huge wound, Jaclyn, and you sitting here and talking to me does help. You've grown a lot since you started seeing me. Each day is one step closer to finally moving on."

"I just wish it wouldn't take so long and that I could stop thinking about him and that night. I want the night-mares to go away. I have to sometimes sleep with Junior for those nightmares to go away and when they don't, I scare him sometimes."

"What happens when you scare him?"

A tear finally falls because I hate scaring Junior. He looks at me like he is scared of me and then he will run down the hall to Brandon's apartment to get him to wake me up.

I wake up all sweaty and out of breath and I end up crying in Brandon's arms before grabbing Junior and holding onto him.

"He cries and then tries to wake me up but sometimes I don't wake up. Sometimes he would have to go to Brandon's apartment to get him to wake me up. I try not to sleep with Junior much because of that, because I don't want to scare him," I explain before wiping the tears away from my eyes so that Junior doesn't notice.

He's too focused on his movie though.

"How are you doing with your eating?"

"Better. I eat the same as I told you last time," I lie smoothly. Sometimes I might miss breakfast or lunch because I'm too busy or in a rush. But she doesn't need to know that. "I have talked to my doctor about it, and she always makes sure I'm eating right and my A1C is in range. No more binging and then purging right after. I don't like it when Junior asks me why I'm not eating with him at dinner."

Patience nods her head again.

She does a lot of that, nodding her head at the good things I'm improving on.

"How are you feeling regarding your father?"

At the mention of him I feel nothing.

I know it's shitty for a daughter to not feel anything regarding her dead father but to me, he died a long time ago.

There are always times when I wish I had something better than what my father gave.

"Nothing. I don't know why I never feel anything for him when I think about the news my mother told me."

My father died three years ago, when I moved to New York.

He was speeding on the highway while drunk and he ended up in a car crash where he died on impact.

I mean, that's what he gets for doing that. Putting himself and others at risk while drunk was a stupid decision and he paid for that as well as all the other damage he caused.

All my father was, was a parasite that infected everything he touched.

I mean look at me?

I was one of the unlucky ones that got infected by the one person who was supposed to love me.

But he's gone and I couldn't help but feel relieved about him not reaching out again or talking to me.

I did ask him one night, just to give him a chance, if he wanted to meet his grandson and he told me to fuck off.

I never contacted him again.

"Does that make me a bad person?" I ask Patience.

She shakes her head. "No, Jaclyn. It doesn't make you a bad person. You never saw your father as someone to look up to, so his death wasn't significant to you. You only ever saw him as a regular person." I nod my head at her, understanding and agreeing because she's right. My father stopped being my father a long time ago. "And then what about him? What happens when you hear about him or see him?"

I've stopped crying about *him* every night. It took a good year or so to stop when Junior was born. I had other things to think about when Junior was born so I didn't have time to think about the boy who ruined me.

My heart still aches, like a part of it is missing whenever I look at him or hear his name.

"I'm better than I was five years ago."

"Do you still cry about him?"

I shrug. "I do, sometimes when I feel lonely or miss him."

"And that's normal. Have you gone out recently?"

I shake my head. "No, no dating for me. I want to focus on Junior."

"You know it is healthy to date other people or at least see someone. It could help too, putting yourself out there," Patience explains while I just sit there and stay quiet. "Hayden was your first love and he's the father of your first child. He will always be a constant in your life because of that. But that doesn't mean you should put your life on hold."

"Yea," I mumble while looking at Junior.

Whenever I look at Junior, I always see *him* because Junior reminds me so much of him.

"Junior gives you purpose. Anytime you're having those thoughts, keep looking at Junior. He gives you strength. Usually, mothers who experience something traumatic cling onto their child because you grow a bond. That bond is so strong, and it keeps you going."

I look away from Junior and stare at Patience. "What about the nightmares? I'm scared he's gonna show up in my dreams."

The black hooded man has been in my dreams since before I got kidnapped by Marco. He doesn't leave my mind and with my dreams it's the same thing as always. The hooded man kidnaps me, I wake up in that God-awful room, facing Marco before everything goes black and I start screaming. I have told Patience about this, and she tells me it's just my anxiety and PTSD which she has prescribed medication for.

"I can increase your dosage by five more milligrams. If you need more, I can do another five but that would be the last adjustment before we try other things."

"Okay. We can try that."

"I don't want you to rely on these medications though. Eventually, I do want you to stop taking them because they are very strong," Patience says while writing down something in her notebook.

"Okay."

I'm not addicted or anything, I just need something to get rid of the black hooded guy and all these fucking feelings that just won't go away.

"I also want you to try sleeping without the trazodone for a few nights to see how it goes. We'll follow up next week with another appointment to see how that works out for you. I'll give you the prescription for the new dosage of sertraline but take the exact dosage, no more than twenty-five."

"Okay," I repeat.

"And spend more time with Junior. Take a day off from work and just spend the day with him. If you need a doctor's note, I can give you that but I really think Junior is going to help you heal, as he has been helping you."

At that I look at Junior and instantly feel my heart swell, in a good way.

Junior is my world.

I know that if I didn't have him, I would be six feet under.

He is the only reason I'm still alive and my heart is still beating.

One

Jaclyn

Light shines through the curtains in my room. I look to my side and don't see Junior, but I hear murmuring and the sound of the TV in the living room.

I've grown used to waking up at the same time every day, thanks to Junior. Usually, he comes into my room and wakes me up to make him breakfast. Every now and then Brandon will come in and take care of that while I get some more sleep.

I get out of the bed and open the door, the talking becoming clearer. I see Brandon in the kitchen while Junior is on the couch, watching Paw Patrol as he lays on the floor. I lean against the door frame like I do every morning and watch Junior kick his feet in the air as he watches the show.

I found out I was pregnant about two months after the night that ruined my life. I was living with my mom at the time. I wasn't taking care of myself and the wound on my rib just made everything harder for me, so it was just better to live with my mom.

After all, I needed her.

I only ever felt comfortable breaking down in front of her.

I realized I hadn't gotten my period for a good month or so and I'd been throwing up every day for weeks. I thought it was because of what I went through but my mom made me take a pregnancy test.

When the test came back positive, I started crying in my mom's chest. I couldn't take care of myself and bringing a child into the world after that night felt impossible.

I went to the obstetrician and after they saw the wound, they asked questions. I told them a narrowed down version of what happened, and they asked me questions about me having sex. I told them I had sex around that time. They told me the embryo was not even formed at the time.

It was a high-risk pregnancy because of my diabetes and also because I wasn't taking care of myself. I had frequent doctor appointments, and my mom came to every single one.

There was not one day during the pregnancy or after

that, that I didn't cry. There wasn't one day for the nine months Junior was in my belly that I didn't stare at Hayden's phone number, feeling guilty that I didn't tell him about Junior. There was a time when I thought maybe Junior isn't even Hayden's because it could have been a fifty-fifty chance between him and the guys who ruined my life.

But then Junior was born with a head full of dark hair and light gray eyes, I knew Junior was Hayden's.

My mom and uncle asked me if I was going to contact Hayden, and I've thought about it so many times over the years, even came close to calling him but I saw him on TV beating a professional fighter to a pulp.

He was living the life all men wanted to live. In the spotlight with girls falling at their feet, with money overflowing out of their pocket.

Hayden was living the dream and me calling him would ruin his dream.

So, I left him alone and took care of myself and Junior.

After Junior started getting older and I finished my online college classes, I got offered a job to work at a press company in New York. I have been saving money and was ready to be a part of the world again.

Moving to New York was one of the best things to happen to me.

I've always heard the saying, "You can't heal in the

same place that broke you" and that was one of the truest things I've ever heard.

New York was a good decision and Junior likes the city.

"Hey," Brandon says, making me look at him standing in the kitchen in his usual blue dress shirt and black trousers.

He has two plates filled with bagels, eggs, and bacon. There is a smaller plate on the island that has a half-eaten bagel and then left over eggs with cheese on it.

"Morning." I smile before taking the plate from him and sitting on a high top chair at the island. "Were you here before he woke up?"

Brandon sits next to me at the island and starts digging in.

"Yea. Thought I'd let you get some sleep so I took care of breakfast this morning."

"You're literally a god," I say before taking a bite out of the bagel.

I met Brandon the first day I moved into this building. Brandon lives a couple doors down and he has been here ever since.

Brandon originally asked me out but I told him I couldn't get into a relationship of any sort because of Junior and because I wasn't ready. One time I got drunk while Junior was with my mom in California and

Brandon and I ended up hooking up. He saw the scar on my side and asked about it the next morning.

I told him everything and then cried in his arms right after. He understood why I needed to just be alone and not get into any relationship. I told him if he wanted to stop talking, that's fine because I didn't want to lead him on but he said he was here to stay, even as a friend.

Brandon and I never hooked up again after that. I don't like Brandon like that. That night I was just missing the feeling of being wanted and Brandon was there and I was drunk.

I hated myself afterwards because next thing I knew, I was feeling guilty.

"How'd you sleep last night?" Brandon asks.

"Better. Sleeping with Junior always helps," I say before looking at Junior.

He turns his head and smiles wide before getting up.

"Mama!" he yells while running towards me.

He knocks into my legs and I grab him and place him on my lap. I move his hair out of his face and kiss his cheek, making him laugh. A smile instantly pulls at my face.

"Hi, baby." I turn him to face me and hold him tight, making sure he doesn't fall off my lap. "Any crazy dreams last night?"

Every single morning, either during breakfast or on the way to school, Junior always tells me his dreams. He has the craziest dreams and that's only because he has such a creative mind.

"Well there was a dog and then there was a talking lion. They didn't like each other very much," he mumbles while playing with the ends of my hair.

"No?" I raise my eyebrows at him.

"No. They were fighting over who got to hang out with Spiderman that day."

"Spiderman was in the dream too?"

"Yea, he was swinging around and everything, mama. That's why the lion and the dog was fighting. They wanted to go on with him."

"Sounds like a crazy dream, bud," Brandon says with a mouth full of eggs.

"See, mama! Brandon agrees."

I can't stop smiling at my son because he is the only thing in this world that makes me happy now. He makes me smile in so many ways.

Yes, kids are a lot of work and there are times when he pisses me off, but I love him.

I can't even describe the type of love I have for Junior.

Every time I look at him, I can't help but smile.

"Well, we need to get you ready for school. We can't have Ms. Johnson mad at me again for you being late." Junior is in preschool. He started this year and he loves it. He is a very friendly kid, Ms. Johnson says. He talks to everyone in class and it makes me happy that he's so good with the other kids. "Did you take your medicine already?"

He nods his head. "Yup, and I ate breakfast too! I got eggs and bagels."

I laugh because of the little lisp he has when saying his 's's. It always puts a smile on my face.

"Great." I kiss his cheek twice and take him off my lap. "I'll be there in a little to pick out your outfit, okay."

Junior runs to his room and I'm about to follow but Brandon puts his hand on my shoulder making me look up at him. Brandon looks down at my food that I barely touched.

Oh right.

"You eat that and I'll get him ready. Don't forget to take your shot either." I nod my head even though I feel like doing anything but eating. Brandon gets up and takes his plate, putting it in the dishwasher after rinsing it. "I better see that plate empty when I come back."

I force a smile at Brandon. "Thank you."

"Anything for you."

Two

Jaclyn

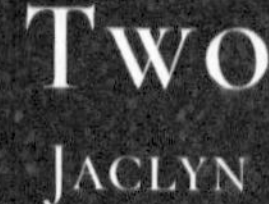

PRESENT

"How did therapy go the other day?" Brandon asks me as we walk into the office together.

Not only is Brandon my neighbor, a big coincidence is that he also just happens to work at the company that I work at. We see each other almost every single day.

Whenever he gets off work early he always helps me out by picking Junior up from daycare and then hanging out at the apartment until I come home. I sometimes get home late from work because Jules always has me working on new assignments everyday and she expects them done, on her desk the next morning.

Sometimes she'll give me a good week or two, depending on what the assignment is.

"It went well. She upped my medication for the nightmares."

"I don't want you getting used to those." Brandon gives me a scolding look.

"I'm not," I say, but I know that if someone were to take these pills from me I'd definitely make a fit about it. "They just help me."

"Have you ever taken antidepressants before? They can be addictive."

"I took them once when I was younger but I stopped because they weren't doing anything for me and I found other ways to make myself feel better."

I never told Patience about how I would use antidepressants in high school when I hated myself back them.

"Why can't you find ways to make yourself better now?" Brandon raises an eyebrow at me, making me feel like I'm getting lectured like a toddler.

I shrug. "They just help me, Brandon. It's not that serious," I say before walking away from him and going in the direction of my office.

I don't need to get scolded like a toddler who did something bad.

The pills help me.

Yes, they might be bad for me, but they have made the nightmares go away drastically in the past year or so. I still get some, but since I started the new dosage they haven't been as bad.

"Oh, Jaclyn, Jules said she wants you in her office to talk to you about a new, important project," Jules's assistant says as I walk past her.

"Sounds good, Diana. Thank you." I smile at her before going into my office.

It's small. I have a desk in the back of the room with a bookshelf to keep some of my books since I don't have a space at home. I also have a pretty good view of the city.

I've worked at Sports Calling Media for about three years. This was the job where I started my journalism career. It was hard juggling this job and taking care of Junior because I wanted to be with him constantly. I hated taking him to daycare and not seeing him all day. Sometimes Jules would let him stay in my office on days where he would have a hard time at daycare.

Jules said all of the remote positions were filled up, but she'd let me know as soon as one opened up.

I'm one of the head journalists here at Sports Calling Media. I go out and do interviews with sports stars and then write a column about them for our magazine or website.

I put my purse on my desk and grab my notebook and pen before walking out of my office to head to Jules'. I knock before opening the door. I smile at Jules as I walk in.

"Morning," I say as I sit in the chair in front of her.

"Morning, how's that little munchkin of mine at home doing?"

Jules loves Junior. Whenever he comes into the office, everyone always loves giving him attention. Jules loves it when Junior visits and she always spoils him with hugs and cookies she has in her drawers.

"He's good. He's been asking for cookies lately and I don't know how to get him to stop," I jokingly say.

"Well bring him in someday and he can get as many as he wants," Jules says before grabbing a paper from her desk and handing it to me. "This is your new assignment."

I look down at the paper and see a name that still haunts me to this day.

Hayden Night.

"What's this?" I ask, as my heart races.

"Your new assignment. We got offered seats to his fight this Friday, front row, and we're also able to have an interview with him after the fight in his dressing room. Media got in contact with his agent and we got an interview. We've been meaning to get one with him for months but Hayden Night is a hard person to get a hold of."

Whatever she says afterwards kind of fades into the background.

Hayden Night.

The boy who would appear in my dreams at night to try and save me before the black hooded man would arrive.

Hayden Night was my knight in shining armor; until he wasn't.

He's the boy who made me truly know what it felt like to be loved. He gave me the kind of love that girls would read in books and wish for.

The fact that I have a part of him with me every single day used to make my heart ache but now I just see Junior for who he is.

I look down at the paper and see all the information needed for this interview. Where his room is, the passes, the location, the time, everything.

This is happening.

But it can't.

I can't see him in person. It will ruin me.

Everything I've built back up will be brought down with just a single look from him.

"Jaclyn, what's wrong? I thought you would like this? You've always said you liked fighting."

"I can't interview him," I say, putting the paper on the desk.

She doesn't know the history between me and him. Only Patience, Brandon, mom, and Calvin know.

Jules doesn't know that this boy fucking ruined me.

Jules furrows her eyebrows and she now looks pissed and confused because I never turn down an assignment, ever.

For the past three years I have been at her beck and call

and that's why I am one of the lead journalists here. I've worked hard to earn my position by never saying no. But this interview is the one interview I can't do.

I would be forced to tell him about the son he never knew he had.

"You never turn down an assignment. Why this one?"

"I can't do this, Jules. I wish I could give you an answer as to why, but I can't."

Jules leans back in her chair and rests her hands on the arm rest. "You've been working here for three years, Jaclyn. You have never turned down any assignment. Why this one? If you can't tell me then you might as well not come back after today."

I furrow my eyebrows at her. She's never threatened my position, ever. But at the same time I've always been a good employee, saying yes to everything.

"I can't. This interview-"

Jules cuts me off. "If you can't tell me, then it must not be important," she says, making my heart crack a little. "This interview is so important for us, Jaclyn. It could get us so much publicity, you don't even understand."

"I do, it's just-"

"No, either you do it or you can just start packing your things up. I can have other journalists take this assignment. No one would pass it up." Jules sighs and she leans forwards, resting her arms on the desk. "I don't want to fire you, Jaclyn. You're a great asset to this company and

I know you need this job. But you can't let something like a cocky fighter stop you from something that could change your life." I nod my head and nip my lip. Jules is right, I can't let him control my life or emotions. I can be strong enough to do this. "I'm going to offer you something. I've been thinking about it for a while but if it will convince you to do this interview then so be it."

"What?"

"A pay raise. Say $115K a year instead of $98K?"

My eyebrows probably touch my forehead because that is such a huge pay raise.

I could use the extra money, especially since things are getting more expensive.

No one could say no to money.

Everyone has a price.

So I agree to the thing that will most definitely change everything in my now peaceful life. "Okay."

Three

Jaclyn

For Thanksgiving, I'm at the Night's with Hayden.

Last year I spent it with my mom but because I've been spending so much time with Hayden, he asked me to come with him. He told me his aunt, uncle, cousins, and grandparents are coming. When he was talking about them, he didn't seem too happy.

He told me that coming with him would make him feel better.

Right now, I am making the mac and cheese because last time I made it for Hayden at my house, he fell in love. He told Alex about it and she demanded that I make it.

I'm not much of a good cook but I can make a good-ass mac and cheese, that's for sure.

"I'm really happy you're here," Alex says from right

next to me. She's working on the yams. "Hayden has never brought someone home and you being here really makes him happy," Alex says with a sad smile on her face.

"I'm happy I'm here too. Hayden makes me feel special and that's all I could ask for."

"You changed him. In so many good ways, Jaclyn, and I can't help but be grateful for you."

I smile at her and shrug because I have no clue what to say to that. "I'm just showing him my love."

The past few months have been hard on us. Eric is following us around like a creep making me feel anxious and like there is someone constantly watching me in the shadows. I swear I sometimes see a man with a black hood following me. I don't tell Hayden anything because I don't want to worry him, especially since he started fighting again for Marco. He knows there is something wrong and how I feel anxious constantly but I don't tell him anything.

It's just a funk and it will go away.

"I just wanted to let you know. I appreciate you a lot and am very thankful to have you in Hayden's life. He needs someone like you." I smile at her before continuing the mac and cheese. Eventually we hear a door open and then the sound of a baby crying. "And there is my sister-in-law. Let me go get her so you can meet her and her family." I nod and Alex walks away. When she comes back she is holding a baby in her arms and a woman and man follow behind her with two boys.

"Woah," one of the boys says as he stares at me from across the room but next thing I know he is right next to me. "I'm John," the boy says before grabbing my hand and kissing the back of it.

I laugh looking down at him. "Nice to meet you."

"Jaclyn, this is Carter's brother Jake and his wife Via. These are their three boys. The one next to you is John. He is a little flirt with everyone."

"They're just saying that." John winks at me, still holding my hand.

"And then this little guy is Jax and that is Jared," Alex says while holding baby Jax and looking over at the older boy who is Jared.

"Nice to meet you guys." I smile from across the island. "I would shake your hand but it's currently being held onto by John."

"John, dude, let her go." I hear a familiar voice walk through the kitchen and my eyes connect with his gray ones. "She isn't into scrawny teenagers with acne." Hayden grabs John's shoulder and moves him away from me.

"Relax, Hayden. Don't worry, I won't steal your girl, yet." John winks at me. "I'll see you at dinner, *cheri*." John leaves the kitchen as he smirks at me.

"Little fucker," Hayden mutters making me look at him and glare.

"Be nice," I mouth to Hayden and he just rolls his eyes and winks at me.

I blush and look down at the mac and cheese bowl.

I was supposed to be mixing the cheese together.

Jake, Via, Alex, and Jax all leave the kitchen. Alex says she'll be back to finish up the yams after she catches up with Jake and Via and finds Carter.

"So you're Hayden's new girlfriend?" Jared sits on a stool in front of the island.

I furrow my eyebrows and look at Hayden who is now standing next to me. "New?"

"It's been a while since we have seen Hayden. Last time I saw him, he was dating this other girl."

"We weren't even dating." Hayden says before placing his hands on my hips and resting his chin on my shoulder.

"Then what do you call that kind of relationship?" Jared asks with a devious smile before looking at me.

"Fuck off," Hayden says, his grip on my hips tighten.

Jared chuckles. "I'll see you guys at dinner. Nice catching up Hayden." Jared gets off the stool and walks away.

Before I can turn around and ask Hayden what that was about he kisses my shoulder and moves away from me to the other side of the kitchen where the turkey is marinating.

Eventually the turkey gets put in the oven and is the only thing we are waiting for.

The doorbell rings and Alex says it's her parents.

I lick my lips and feel arms wrap around my torso. "Nervous?" Hayden asks in my ear.

I shrug. "Not really, I just want your grandparents to like me."

"They will. I mean my grandpa is kind of a dick. But, who wouldn't like you?" Hayden moves his lips to my ear. "Even that fucker John can't stop staring at you."

I turn my head to look at Hayden. "Are you jealous that your little cousin is going to steal me away from you?"

Hayden pushes me against the fridge. "No one is going to steal you away from me." He whispers in my ear.

I laugh and try to push him away from me but he keeps his hold on me and tries to pinch my waist. "Stop," I laugh, trying to push him away.

Hayden leans down and presses his lips to mine and I can't help but smile into the kiss.

I can't describe how much my heart is swelling up from him kissing me. He can do such simple things to make me happy.

"Okay guys! Let's sit down at the table," I hear Alex yell, making Hayden take his lips off mine with a soft groan that makes my legs feel weak. I hear footsteps and see Alex in the kitchen. She has a smile on her face while looking at Hayden and I, still against the fridge. "Can you check the turkey with your father, Hayden?" Hayden nods and then leans down to kiss my cheek. He lets go of me and walks towards the oven. I go to the dining room and sit down at one of the empty seats next to Natalia. There is another seat that's open for Hayden next to me. Carter, Hayden, and Jake start bringing the food out while Alex takes pictures of everything like a proud mom. "Looks amazing, guys."

When they're done Hayden sits down next to me and he pulls my chair closer to his, then rests his hand on my thigh making me blush.

Hayden smiles down at me. "It's so easy to make you blush," Hayden whispers before kissing my cheek.

"Shut up," I say, trying my best not to smile too much.

It's hard to explain how happy Hayden makes me. I don't think I've ever smiled so much in my life until I met him.

Carter stands from his seat. "Before we start eating I want to say how thankful I am to be sitting here, in this nice house with my family. I've always been one to dream big and I'm just grateful to have made it this far with the woman I fell in love with in high school," Carter says before placing his hand on Alex's cheek. I smile at the two because you can truly see how in love they are with one another. I look at Alex's parents and see them having a stink face looking at Carter. I haven't officially met them yet and I'm still nervous as hell. "Let's eat."

Carter sits down and everyone starts digging in.

"You look beautiful, princess," Hayden whispers, making me look at him.

"You're being so flirty tonight."

"I can't admire you?" Hayden smirks before looking down at my lips.

I laugh and shake my head lightly at him. I can't focus on eating when he is like this. I have a feeling I'm going to find out how much he admires me tonight.

"So, how did you meet Natalia and Hayden, Jaclyn?" Jared asks from across the table.

I have a feeling he likes starting trouble.

"I met Natalia in my journalism class and Hayden at a diner I work at."

Technically I met him when I was a teenager but he doesn't need to know that story.

"Is Hayden doing well in school?" his grandmother asks.

All eyes are on me but I don't know the answer to that. That's Hayden's business.

"I'm doing fine," Hayden answers before I can.

"You like business?" his grandfather asks.

"I'm not really interested in that class," Hayden states, while glaring at his grandfather.

"Well then, Hayden, what do you expect to be doing after college? You can't rely on Carter and Alex's money forever."

"Papa!" Natalia gasps with her eyes wide.

Jared has an amused smile while watching it all go down.

I hold Hayden's hand in my lap and he gives it three squeezes before saying. "I have told you and almost everyone I know that I don't need his money. I'm fine."

"You didn't answer the question."

"Dad, please," Alex says with pleading eyes at her father.

"Alexandra, I'm trying to figure out how Hayden is going to make a living. Natalia has her life figured out. She is dating Chris who will be a football player and she will make an okay amount of money from journalism. She can do better but at least it's something. What will Hayden do? He sure won't have a job or someone to help support him other than you and Carter. I doubt this girl is going to be around for long."

It's quiet in the room. You could hear a pin drop. Hayden grips my hand hard as he refrains from lashing out.

Before Hayden can utter a word, Carter says, "Leave."

Hayden's grandfather looks at Carter. "Excuse me?"

"I said leave. I won't let you disrespect Hayden like that or Jaclyn," Carter says.

Hayden's grandpa rolls his eyes. "Oh come on. I bet she is just one of those one-night-stands like you kids call it."

My eyes go wide because this has never happened to me before and I have no clue how to react.

"The fuck did you just call her?" Hayden asks while glaring at his grandpa. "She's far from that. What do you know? You don't know shit about our relationship. Who do you think you are?"

"I won't repeat myself Henry," Carter states.

Hayden's grandpa looks at Alex. "This is what your life has come to, Alexandra? An adoptive son and an asshole husband?"

"Dad, I think you should leave. What you said about Jaclyn isn't right and I don't agree," Alex says before looking at me. "She is one of the sweetest girls I have met, and I think she is good for Hayden. They are in love and if Hayden is happy, then I am too. I know Carter is also happy along with Natalia so if you don't agree with this relationship or if you disrespect Hayden like that again then you won't be welcomed into our home anymore."

"After everything he has done, you still forgive him?" Alex's father points at Hayden.

"Yes, because he is my son. Now leave," Alex demands.

"This is bullshit." Hayden's grandfather stands from the table and tosses his utensils down before leaving the dining room.

His wife stands up and mutters an apology before following him. We hear the door open and slam before silence erupts throughout the table.

"I am sorry, Jaclyn. My father is usually not this bad. He can be very judgmental sometimes," Alex apologizes with an embarrassed look on her face.

"Yeah, don't take what he says to heart. He is just a cranky old man," Carter's brother says.

I smile and nod my head at them. Hayden stands up from the table and leaves walking upstairs towards his room. My eyes follow him as leaves.

I want to go to him, but I don't want to be rude and leave the table.

"Go." I turn my head to Natalia. "Go. He needs you."

I don't waste another second before standing up and leaving the way Hayden left.

I walk upstairs towards his room and once I get closer and closer, I hear a lot of punching sounds making me run to his side of the hallway and open his door.

When I walk in, I don't see him but then I hear glass breaking from the bathroom.

I turn the corner and see glass everywhere on the floor. Along with blood.

"Hayden," I say, walking closer to him as he looks at himself in the mirror.

"Go away," he mutters.

"No," I wrap my arms around his waist and press my body against his back. "I am not leaving you."

"You should. You'll only get hurt."

"Then let me get hurt," I whisper before he turns around, towering over me.

I put my hand on his jaw, softly stroking his jawline. "I don't deserve you. After everything we've been through you're still here. It feels like a dream being with you and I never want to wake up," he admits, resting his forehead on mine. "I don't want you to leave. I can lose everything and anything but not you. God, not you Jaclyn." His lips go to my forehead, and he presses a soft kiss before letting out a shaky breath. "Please don't leave me, Jaclyn. I'm a fuck up in so many ways and you've only seen a glimpse but you make everything go away when I'm with you. You should leave, but don't. I need you to promise you won't. No matter what."

"No matter what, Hayden, I won't leave you," I promise, making it forever.

Four

Jaclyn

The Lego Movie is playing on the TV while Junior rests his head on my lap.

Brandon is sitting next to me, munching on popcorn. I still haven't told him about the assignment that Jules gave me. He was too busy worrying about my health to care what she wanted to talk to me about.

Junior is slowly falling asleep and I just don't want to talk to Brandon about it until he is for sure sleeping. He is slowly getting there as I rub his back.

"Are you still mad at me?" Brandon asks.

I look away from the TV and at him. "No, I just have to tell you something." I look down at Junior really quick and see that his eyes are slowly falling.

Brandon looks at Junior and then back at me. "You want me to put him in his room?" Brandon offers.

I shake my head and move hair out of Junior's face. His hair grows really fast. He got a cut two weeks away and it's already growing back so much. Junior's eyes finally close so I hold him closer to me and stand up with him in my arms.

I walk inside his room and put him on his bed. I cover him with his blankets and make sure to tuck him in. I rest his stuffed Simba next to him because he loves sleeping with it.

I lean down and press my lips to his forehead and then cheek. "Goodnight, baby," I whisper before kissing him once more and then standing up.

I walk out of his room and go to the living room where Brandon is waiting for me.

"What's wrong?" Brandon asks as I sit next to him.

I grab my laptop from the coffee table and rest it on my lap. I type in the words "Hayden Night" on Google and click the link where it shows his fight that's happening in a few days.

A fight I will be attending and where I'll be interviewing him.

I turn the laptop around to show Brandon and his eyes turn into slits as he glares at the picture of Hayden with the fight's information.

"Why are you showing me this douchebag?"

"Because I have to interview him this Friday."

"You're going to his fight?" Brandon sits up and his eyes turn wide. "Why?"

"Jules got in contact with his agent and she's making me go to the fight and interview him afterwards."

"She can't have someone else do it?"

I turn the laptop to me and look at the picture of Hayden.

For the past five years, he has changed so much. His hair is shorter, his face has matured more, and he also got bigger.

I try my best not to pay attention to ads that pop up with him shirtless on billboards and his name is big red letters. Seeing him always affects me because how can it not?

He was my world five years ago. He was someone I looked forward to seeing every day and he was someone I would spend all my time with.

Every now and then my heart and body wish I could just pick up the phone and call him but then the memories of that night haunt me and stop me from doing something stupid.

"No, she threatened to fire me and then also gave me a pay raise for doing this interview. She really wants me to do it and I can't say no when she was going to fire me and then also gave me a pay raise."

"Did you even explain to her what kind of person this guy is and how much he affects you?" Brandon raises an eyebrow at me and I just shake my head. "You need to tell her."

"What's done is done Brandon. I'm going to do the interview. I'll be okay." I put the laptop on the coffee table and bring my knees to my chest to hold them. "I'm just scared of telling him about Junior. I have to tell him."

"No you don't. Junior is your son, not his."

"Hayden is his biological father. He needs to know he has a mini him out in the world."

I'm just so scared of telling him. Hayden won't be happy if he were to find out. I don't want to tell Hayden because that would mean giving up my peaceful life with Junior away from him and the media.

Plus I've heard rumors about how Hayden is living his life as one of New York's most eligible bachelors though there is a possibility of marriage for him with this one rich model.

Knowing Hayden is possibly getting married breaks my heart, which is why I hate thinking about it.

It's a recent rumor that came up and I know rumors aren't always true but everyone seems to believe that this rumor isn't very much of a rumor.

Hayden comes with fame and fame can be ugly.

"So you're really doing this?" Brandon asks.

I nod my head. "Yea."

"How do you feel about it?"

"Scared and nervous. I haven't seen him in person in five years. We've both changed so much. I'm not the same girl he fell in love with and I'm sure he's changed just as much as me."

I have no clue how I'll react to seeing him in person. I wish I could know how he'd react.

Will he still be mad at how we left things? Will he ignore me and not even answer my questions? Will he be pissed and start yelling at me about why I left him?

Not knowing the unknown feels like the worst feeling in the world.

"You'll be okay. Are you ever going to tell Junior about Hayden?"

Junior sometimes asks me why he doesn't have a dad like all the other kids in school and he even asked me if Brandon was his dad.

I tell him that his dad is somewhere in the world, saving people like a hero in the movies. I told him that Brandon is just his best friend.

I can't use the hero excuse forever though, I know that.

I know that one day I have to tell him I kept him away from his dad in order to protect him. But I just hate how mad Junior will possibly be because if he's anything like his dad, he will be pissed.

But that's why I keep him away from Hayden before he is old enough to realize what I'm doing.

"I will. I just don't know when or how." I look at Brandon and give him a reassuring smile. "But it'll be okay. I got this."

Five

Jaclyn

Present

I wasn't able to sleep at all last night. I didn't bring Junior into my room to sleep with me either.

I just needed to be alone with my thoughts as I process what the hell I'm doing today. Junior even asked me to pay attention to him this morning when he was telling me about his dream. I laughed it off and said I was just daydreaming when in reality I was overthinking every scenario that could happen with Hayden today.

Brandon kept giving me worried looks but I ignored him. He was being a little bit pushy this morning and I always appreciate Brandon and his help but lately, ever since I told him about the new pill dosage, he has been up my ass more.

"Ready to go?" Diego, the cameraman says from the

driver's side of the car. I look at him and nod my head while I smile. I clench my hands in fists before releasing them and breathe out slowly. Diego is my partner when it comes to interviewing people on video. He records while I ask the questions. Sometimes he will ask follow up questions here and there but most of the time, it's me asking the questions. "Why do you look constipated?" Diego asks as we get out of the car.

I grip onto my notebook and hold it to my chest as we walk towards the arena.

"I don't look constipated," I argue.

"You kind of do," Diego says as he holds onto the camera and other equipment we need. "Are you nervous?"

I look away from Diego and instead look at the large posters that showcase Hayden with his name in big red letters across his waist.

I called up Patience the day after I found out I was going to interview Hayden. She told me that throughout the interview I just need to block everything out. I could think of Junior because he is my happy place but then thinking of Junior at the same time I am interviewing Hayden would make things worse because that would just remind me that Hayden has no clue he has a son.

Junior can't be my safe space today. I have to depend on myself and how strong I can be without him facing his father.

I wipe the sweat from my hands onto my dress as we walk inside the building, security holding the door for us.

For the fight, I'm wearing a red silky mini dress that has thin straps. It flows from the waist down which complements my shape.

I would have never worn this dress a few years ago. It took me a long time to bring my confidence back up after I had Junior. I gained so much weight and next thing I knew, I was back to hating myself.

I hated how whenever I looked in the mirror I would dread going outside because I felt so ugly. All of my clothes consisted of sweaters, leggings, or sweatpants. Even when it was hot outside I would wear large sweaters to hide what I really look like underneath.

"Have you ever been to a fighting match before?" Diego asks as we sit in our seats at the front.

The whole arena is filled with people. In the crowd I see a lot of red compared to green, which is the color that the other fighter reps.

Red is Hayden's color.

"Yea, something like that."

Only illegal ones.

The lights start to dim making everyone cheer. An announcer walks inside the ring and he taps the mic.

"Ladies and gentleman!" the announcer yells in the mic making the crowd go wild. "Welcome to the fight of a lifetime. Let's just get on with it and bring our fighters out!" the announcer says before turning to one area of the arena. "Let me introduce, Robert Chua!" I hear some people cheer but it's mostly booing. Robert walks inside the ring and starts to warm up and throw some small jabs while walking around the ring. "Now let's bring out our heavyweight champion, Hayden Night!"

"No Church In The Wild" by Kanye blasts on the sound system as lights showcase Hayden walking out from the hallway.

My heart aches as I see him walk towards the ring. I can't see him that well because he is far from us but on the big screen I see him clearly.

Just knowing that Hayden is only a few feet away from me makes the butterflies in my stomach swarm.

They shouldn't be swarming because once that happens you just end up getting hurt in the end.

The crowd goes wild for him as he walks towards the ring, not throwing punches or anything, simply just walking. He looks up at his fans who are cheering for him, but behind those eyes, there is nothing.

Whenever I would catch him on TV or a poster, I would see nothing in those eyes. It's like after everything that happened, he lost his light and what made him happy.

Hayden walks inside the ring with a familiar face behind him.

Freddie pats his shoulder and brings him towards his side of the ring.

Freddie is Hayden's lifetime coach. Freddie taught Hayden everything he knows when it comes to fighting. I've always seen Freddie as Hayden's guardian angel because he saved him from the streets.

Junior is the spitting image of his father, fortunately. Hayden is a good looking guy and I understand why all of the ladies, and some men too, love him.

In person, Hayden looks larger than life. I didn't realize how big he got until now. His biceps look like the size of Junior's head and I don't know if it's possible but he looks like he got taller.

He also has more tattoos. The same sleeve on his arm from college but now a new one on his other arm. He also has one on his back, a small crown right below his neck, at the top of his back.

And there is small writing right underneath but I can't tell what it says.

I immediately touch the tattoo on my ribs, or at least where the tattoo was before *they* ruined it.

Hayden stands up from his chair and my eyes go to his hands as he messes with a ring, on his ring finger. My heart stops as I watch him take it off and hand it to Freddie. Freddie puts it in his pocket and pats Hayden's shoulder again, whispering something in his ear before pushing him in the middle of the ring where Robert is.

There's no way he can be engaged already. How does he have a ring already?

Did him and that model get married already?

I've never seen that ring in pictures or anything.

That green, jealous side of me wants to come out and tell the world that I had him first and I'm the one who has his kid.

But I can't.

No one can know what I went through or how I left Hayden for that.

Hayden Night is the reason I can't ever move on, fully. He is literally a part of me forever, in my heart, my memories, and my life.

"And Hayden gives the first punch of the night!" the announcer yells, making me tune back into the fight.

I watch Hayden pummel Robert and push him against the ropes. Robert blocks his punches and tries to protect his face but Hayden's punches are too strong.

He has almost killed with those punches, I've seen it many times before.

"You good?" Diego asks, making me look at him and nod.

"Yea, I'm fine."

"You have that face again," Diego comments.

"What?" I furrow my eyebrows at him.

"That constipated face."

I roll my eyes at Diego and focus back on the fight.

Hayden and Robert are still going at each other, punching, and blocking as they pounce around the ring.

Robert goes to punch Hayden, but he misses as Hayden leans to the side and punches Robert across the face. Robert wobbles and Hayden walks forward and starts throwing punches at Robert repeatedly.

It still amazes me after all this time how powerful his punches are, but I can tell they are just as strong and deadly as they were five years ago. From one punch, Robert looks like he is going to faint.

I feel a weird sense of déjà vu as I watch Hayden fight.

I feel like I'm back in the club, watching Hayden become the beast he is while in the ring. Showing no mercy to anyone in his way.

He was always a great fighter. He was the best. I'm not surprised he is a champion today.

The bell rings and Hayden and Robert go to their sides of the ring. I watch Hayden sit down on his side of the ring as his team attends to him. Freddie talks to him while he pats his shoulder and checks his face.

Hayden nods and sometimes he just glares at Freddie while Freddie talks to him. I haven't seen him since Hayden and I broke up.

The bell finally rings and Freddie pats Hayden's shoulder making him get up and walk towards Robert.

But then Hayden does something that makes me feel like all my air is gone.

His eyes connect with mine from across the ring.

Six

Jaclyn

Present

I feel like everything in my body lights up when our eyes connect.

Time just stops for a moment as my mind replays every touch and every memory that contains Hayden Night.

It's been five years and Hayden Night still has the same effect on me as he did five years ago. My body still feels incredibly weak for him.

A bell rings in the arena breaking the moment and Hayden gets a punch to the face by Robert.

"And the first punch of the round goes to Robert! That's a first cause usually Night is on top of his game by handing out the first punch."

"Right, Gerald. It's a surprise to see Hayden not land

the first punch," the announcers discuss as Robert and Hayden start going at it again.

Hayden is going HAM on him, punching, not giving Robert a second to breathe. Right now, the beast is in place just like how it usually is whenever Hayden's in the ring.

"Wow, he's really good," Diego comments as he records the fight on his camera.

"Yea," I mumble, still staring at Hayden in awe because he's still got it when it comes to fighting.

His passion and strength for fighting is still there.

I know Hayden's good. I don't need anyone to tell me. Fighting is where Hayden thrives. Fighting gives him that escape he needs, he told me. He sees fighting as a release for everything he's feeling inside that he can't get out.

All the punches and hits he throws are for everything he has been through. All the pain and misery he talked to me about. That's what's being put in the punches that he throws.

Hayden throws one last punch at Robert making him land on the floor with a thud. The ref counts to ten and Robert's still on the floor.

I divert my eyes away from Robert who is on the floor, surrounded by his team. My eyes go to Hayden who is staring straight at me with a dark look in his eyes. I can tell from sitting down here while he has a crowd of people cheering his name.

One of the announcers walks towards Hayden and he raises his fist to the air. "You're the winner, Hayden Night!" the announcer yells as the crowd cheers for Hayden.

Hayden pays no mind to anyone except me as he stares down at me with those menacing eyes.

Freddie turns his head and his eyes connect with mine. Freddie nods in acknowledgment and I just smile softly at him. If possible, that seemed to make Hayden madder.

Eventually they have to pull Hayden away from the ring and to his dressing room where they hold interviews.

"Come on, let's go," Diego says as he grabs his stuff.

"Sports Calling?" a security rep comes up to us and asks.

"Yea, I heard we are first?" Diego asks.

"Correct. Can I just see some badges?" the rep asks, making Diego and I show him our badges with our names.

"Cool, you guys can follow me this way," he says before walking towards the hallway that Hayden came out of. We follow him down the hall and my hands seem to get even more sweaty than before. I take deep breaths, remembering Patience's words while wiping the sweat on my dress. "Over here. Good luck."

Diego smiles at him and opens the door that says "Hayden Night" in red letters.

"Hayden, interview one," one of his team members says as we walk inside the room.

Hayden is sitting on the couch, looking down at his hands while Freddie stands next to him and whispers something in his ear. Hayden looks up and we connect eyes once again.

"Hayden, this is Jaclyn King from Sports Calling Media. We spoke to Jules about setting up an interview for them, remember?" his manager, I'm assuming, says to Hayden.

I look at Freddie and he just smiles at me before patting Hayden's back and moving away from him.

"We'll be quick," I say as I walk closer to Hayden.

Hayden stands, towering over me. "It's fine, take your time," he mumbles, still not taking his eyes off me.

My skin feels like it's on fire just from the dark and lusting look he's giving me right now.

God those eyes.

Those eyes just make me weak, even after all these years. I look at his eyebrow where I see the eyebrow piercing. That eyebrow piercing always did things to me.

Blood is dripping from the piercing and his cheek where Robert punched him. He's also sweaty, everywhere. Sweat dripping down from his biceps and chest, rolling down.

God, even though he looks like a mess he is still as

beautiful as ever. God knew exactly what he was doing when he made Hayden.

Feeling his body heat right next to mine after five years feels like something I desperately need. It's like my body wants to go inside of him and stay with him forever. I all of a sudden want his arms around me where I can feel safe and protected from everything in the world.

Or at least for a little while until someone ruins it like five years ago.

A team member gives Hayden a mic. "Ready?" I ask before licking my lips. Hayden looks down at my lips, licking his own before meeting my eyes. He tilts his head slightly and I blush and look away from him before he can see how much he affects me. "Go," I tell Diego.

"Rolling," he says before counting down with his fingers.

"Jaclyn King here with Sports Calling Media," I say with a smile. "Tonight, I'm here with Hayden Night, Heavyweight Boxing Champion." I look at Hayden and he is just smirking down at me with amusement in his eyes. "Tonight was a big match for you. Robert Chua was once an undefeated Heavyweight Boxing Champion. How did you feel when first going into the ring?"

"My fans and family know I'm never nervous about fights. I'm confident and I think that's why I'm where I am today. Confidence gets you places."

Oh yes it does.

"Is there anything you do to prepare for a fight? Some routine or ritual that you do the night or day before?"

"Well cardio is a big one for me. I also try to build up my testosterone for fights."

"And how do you do that?" I ask, tilting my head up to look at him.

A smile cracks on his face.

He looks at the camera before looking down at me with a wide smirk on his face. "Eating healthy, working out regularly and training. No sex either, which is unfortunate."

Oh I bet it is, considering how he's probably having sex with every women in the fucking state.

"You took a strong hit to your face in the second round, was there any particular reason for that?" I ask, probably with a little attitude.

Hayden's smirk softens. "Let's just say I didn't expect to see someone in the crowd. I got distracted, it happens to the best of us."

I blush and bite the inside of my cheek.

How dare he make me feel this way in front of a camera? It's like he knows the effect he still has on me and I hate that he knows.

I bite the inside of my cheek and want to glare at him so badly, but when the whole world is probably watching me interview him, it isn't the brightest idea.

"Is there anyone you want to thank tonight for your win?"

Hayden looks behind him. "I'd like to thank my team for always being there and being great. I'd like to thank my trainer and long time family friend, Freddie." Freddie smiles at Hayden and then Hayden turns his head and looks at me. "And then I'd like to thank someone else in the crowd that helped me in ways they couldn't imagine throughout this fight," he says as my heart feels like it's going to burst out of my chest.

"And what are you going to do tonight to celebrate the win?"

"Hopefully have a good dinner and rest," he says but it sounds like he is trying to insinuate something, but then again, it could just be my overthinking.

I force my thoughts away and look at the camera. "Well there you have it, viewers, Hayden Night, the Heavyweight Boxing Champion." I say before relaxing as Diego puts the camera down. "We can go now. Thank you guys," I say, as Diego packs the camera. I start walking away, trying to hurry out of the room but I feel a hand, warm and familiar, catch mine. I turn around and see Hayden's hand holding mine. It's been five years since I was last touched by Hayden Night and this time around his touch feels more powerful, like a simple touch from Hayden can just break down my walls like it's slowly starting to do. "Yes?"

"Get out of here with that yes bullshit. I want to talk," Hayden says and he pulls me closer to him, his hand still holding onto mine.

I see Freddie move from behind Hayden. He raises an eyebrow and I just shake my head and look at Hayden.

"I can't. But it was nice seeing you, Hayden. You look really good," I say before looking at his arms that I want to just lick.

"Yea, I can say the same about you," Hayden says, as he looks up and down my body.

Yeah my breasts got bigger from Junior but I'm a fucking stick now from how much I starve myself.

Can he see the insecurities radiating off of me?

He always knew whenever I felt uncomfortable in my own skin.

Now I realize this is the first time I've thought about Junior since the fight, which is unlike me because he's on my mind twenty-four seven.

And Hayden has no fucking clue.

"Hayden-"

"Please, it's been five years. I want to talk to you."

I lick my bottom lip making Hayden look at it before meeting my eyes. "About what?"

Hayden gives me a knowing look and raises his eyebrow that's pierced. "You know what." A memory of me in that dark room with the black hooded man comes to mind and I shiver. Hayden furrows his eyebrows. "What was that?"

"What?" I raise an eyebrow at him and take my hand out of his.

"That shiver right there?" He tilts his head while looking at me intensely.

"It was nothing. Like I said, it was nice seeing you Hayden, but I have to go." I turn around again but he grabs my hand. I take it out immediately, forcing the tears away that all of a sudden want to fall. "Please, Hayden."

"So after five fucking years, we finally see each other again and you pretend nothing ever happened? Bullshit. Remember the last thing I said to you?" he says, walking up closer to me. I just glare up at him, holding my ground. My heart wants him, craves him, but I know that I shouldn't. My mind is telling me to leave, go back to the peaceful life with Junior and never let another man touch me again. "Please, I'm literally begging you."

I shake my head and back away from him. "I can't, I'm sorry." I turn around and go to Diego who is waiting near the door.

I force myself not to look at Hayden one last time before I leave through the door following Diego out.

Seven

Jaclyn

I watch Junior as he cuddles into his pillow.

Brandon told me he was good today while I was work-ing. I got home maybe around thirty minutes ago and since then I've been in Junior's room watching him sleep.

I haven't taken my Lantus or my nighttime meds.

As if they will do anything to calm my racing thoughts down.

I also have been pointing out every small detail about him that is similar to Hayden.

His eyes are the most similar thing. I have seen a few baby pictures of Hayden and when Junior was a baby, he looked a lot like him. I wish I could have the two pictures side by side to see how much they actually look alike.

Today was a lot.

Seeing Hayden, after five years of healing my broken heart and building those walls back up, all I wanted to do was fall into his arms and pretend that what happened back then was just a bad dream.

But it was reality and I still think about it to this day.

I press a small kiss to Junior's forehead. I pull the blanket over his shoulders and stand up to leave his room.

Brandon is sitting down in the living room on the couch, watching Hayden's fight.

He recorded it, plus my interview that was live on another channel. I place my heels on the floor next to the couch and sit down next to Brandon.

We watch Hayden start the second round with a punch to the face. Everyone screams his name and the crowd goes crazy.

"He looked at you when that happened, right?"

"Yea," I say, my eyes still on the TV as I watch Hayden pummel Robert against the ropes.

"I watched the interview," Brandon says before he changes the recording to where it shows me and Hayden on the TV.

Seeing us both together, standing next to one another makes my heart ache. Our height difference, the way he looks down at me. I look up at him like he is my world and vice versa.

"Did Junior see?"

"No. I put him down before I watched it." I nod my

head and reach for the blanket next to me to cover my legs. I still haven't changed my dress. "You see the way you look at each other, right?" Brandon asks as I just stare at the screen ahead. Of course I see the way we look at each other. The way Hayden's lips would lift in a smile every now and then and the way I would blush simply by his words. "I mean, the way he looks at you makes me think he still loves you the same. Maybe even more."

"No, he has a fiancé, remember?"

Brandon rolls his eyes. "That's a rumor and you know it."

"He had a ring. I saw him give it to his trainer, so I know it's not a rumor."

Brandon nods his head at that before asking. "What happened after the interview?"

I lick my bottom lip. "He wanted to talk and I said no."

"So you didn't tell him about Junior?"

I look at Brandon and see that he's giving me a disappointed look.

"No. I didn't because Junior's life is at peace with just me. Adding Hayden, who is possibly getting married and is a famous fighter who comes with fame, is not a good idea for him or me. My history with Hayden also just happens to be something that I can't deal with either."

"I know you went through a lot that night, I do. But

that's Hayden's kid. You have to tell him somehow. What happens if he were to find out?"

"He won't find out, Brandon." I roll my eyes and get off the couch.

I don't want to talk about Hayden anymore. He is someone from my past and I want him to stay there because I'm so scared of getting hurt again by him.

Do I miss Hayden?

After seeing him today, hell yes. But I won't make the same mistake twice and that's why I ran. I know I promised him I would stay but I couldn't.

That night ruined me.

The girl he fell in love with is gone and replaced with something that's empty and void.

I only ever feel light with Junior and I'm okay with just sticking with him for the rest of my life if it means not getting hurt like I did all those years ago.

"What if he does? What if he goes on your Instagram one of these days and digs too deep?" Brandon asks as I go into the kitchen and grab the pitcher of water from the fridge.

I don't post Junior on social media because I want him to stay away from that place but my mom posts about him on her private Instagram. Hayden wouldn't follow her because he was never close with my mom like I was with his parents.

"He won't. I'm not worried, Brandon."

Brandon gets off the couch and he walks towards me. "You need to stop being selfish for once and think about him. What if Junior wants to meet his dad someday? Are you going to refuse him?"

I glare at Brandon. "I thought you didn't like Hayden so why are you trying to stick up for him?"

"Because if I had a son out there, I would do everything in my power to see him and make an effort to show him I want to be a part of his life. You don't get to choose whether Hayden gets to see his son or not," Brandon argues, getting frustrated because I'm not listening to him. Brandon has a point but I don't want to face Hayden. Life is okay without him and without acknowledging him. I place the pitcher on the island counter. "Hayden loves you, too. He would want to be a part of your and Junior's life. Yes, he'll be mad if you never tell him but he will still be there."

"How do you know? I was so destroyed that night Brandon, you have no clue," I say as tears start to form in my eyes.

I already cried on the way home and Diego even asked me if I was okay.

"He took a mad punch to the face, simply because he saw you in the crowd. He was smiling the entire interview while you were talking to him. I would sometimes watch interviews of him and this is the first time I've ever seen him smile that wide on television. He's never looked so happy in an interview."

I shake my head and a tear finally falls from my eyes. "I can't, Brandon. I can't risk it." Brandon sighs and he walks around the island. I feel him wrap his arms around me making me turn around and hug him back. I press my face into his chest and just cry. "I'm sorry. I'm scared and I just can't go through that again," I say, trying to calm down my breathing as I cry into his chest.

Seeing Hayden again, just changed everything for me. I feel like I'm back to where I started.

EIGHT

Jaclyn

I asked Patience if I could come see her first thing Monday morning. I've had the weekend to think and reminisce even though I wish I didn't.

It's like when I saw Hayden, all the memories just came back. I never thought much about him in the past five years. Yes, I thought about him here and there but never this much.

At night I found myself searching up his Instagram and looking through his profile. I looked through his following list and his story highlights. Most of the story highlights on his page are fights, training videos, traveling photos, etc. He doesn't post much about his family, I noticed. In the comments, girls are just commenting thirsty things for him which made me jealous so I closed my phone before going to bed.

"Okay, tell me everything that happened. Let's start from the beginning of everything between you and Hayden." Patience sits back in her chair and she puts her notebook on the side table.

"Why? Why go back to the beginning when it's been years of just constantly talking about it?"

"Because obviously this relationship affected you a lot. It gave you severe trauma and instead of clinging onto Junior to make it go away or trying to ignore it all, we should talk about it. Sometimes that's the best thing we can do," she explains.

I lean into my chair and lift my knees to my chest. "I was around 15 or 16 when I first met Hayden. It was in an alleyway. My parents were fighting so I got out of the car and ran to the alleyway where I found him."

"You look pathetic when you cry." I hear someone say making me turn my head to the side. A boy enters the alley, looking mean and cruel. He looks young like me and I hate how he is so attractive yet rude because I would like him if he was nicer. "Are you going to say something or are you going to ignore me and continue crying like a child?"

I wipe the tears from my face and try to calm down my breathing and rapid heartbeat. I just need to relax.

"Nobody asked you to stare at me like a weirdo, so just

leave," I say in a nasty tone, not in the mood to deal with anyone.

I just wanna go home and pretend everything is okay by reading because reading and writing my thoughts down are the only things that seem to make me happy anymore.

Everything in fictional worlds are better than reality.

Nothing could compare.

"It wasn't the best way to meet someone. My dad made me sad and I ran into Hayden who probably was having a bad day." It's funny how Hayden and I never really talked much about that day even though it was the day we first met. "After that day I didn't see Hayden again until I was 19 and moved to Arizona for college. I became friends with his sister and somehow I grew closer to her and the rest of the group. But Hayden and I always had tension when we were together. I don't know what it was but it was like, every time we were around each other something sparked."

"After a while, Hayden and I got involved and we started seeing each other as more than friends. We dated for a good year. When we started dating I knew he was in illegal fighting and worked with bad people but I didn't care because I was blinded by the way he loved me and the way I loved him. During the year we were dating, I felt someone watching me, constantly. Sure, we were harassed and followed by Eric but this was something different."

My skin breaks out in goosebumps as I feel someone behind me. I turn around and see a black hooded man. I recently started seeing him in my dreams and seeing him in real life feels dangerous.

I haven't told Hayden about these dreams because I don't want to worry him but I started having them after seeing my dad the other day. He has still been calling non-stop, not leaving me alone. I don't know how he always manages to ruin things for me.

The black hooded man is standing still, just watching me. I can't see his face clearly but I don't need to, to know to be scared of him.

"What's wrong?" I look up at Hayden who is staring down at me with a worried look on his face. He looks in the direction I was just looking at but then looks back down at me. I turn my head to look at the black hooded man, but he's gone. "Was it Eric?"

I look up at Hayden and pull myself closer to him. "No, I just thought I saw something," I say as he wraps a protective arm over me and kisses my forehead.

"I found out that it was Marco all along. Eric is the one who kidnapped me that day though."

"Stop!" I scream and try to get out of his hold. He holds a long needle and before I could knock it out of his hand he stabs me in the neck and I feel cold liquid run in my veins. "No!" I scream, still trying to get out of his hold but he holds me against the seat.

Natalia, she's still out there waiting for me.

"I was going to school with Natalia that morning because I slept over at her and Hayden's apartment. I left my stuff in her car so I told her to go to class while I get my stuff. I didn't know that I would be taken away," I say, as chills run down my spine. It's like I still feel that stuff the black hooded man injected me with. "I woke up in a dark room with only a bed and a sink. First person to come in was Marco. He came in and started to..." I stop, memories starting to run through my head.

The way he would touch me and erase everything Hayden did to me. The way he held a knife to my neck while doing it all.

"You feel so good. Now I know why Hayden was so possessive over you."

"Please stop, please!" I scream, clawing his arms to get him off of me.

"Don't make me bring in Eric to help out, Jaclyn," he threatens, still moving inside me as I cry and beg for it all to end.

A tear falls from my eyes and Patience notices because she asks, "Do you want to take a break?"

I shake my head. "After that, it was Eric's turn. He would use me and after he got bored, a few days later he carved out the tattoo I got for Hayden. Eric was the only person to touch me and go into the room other than Marco. I never saw Marco again after the first day," I say, wiping a tear away. "I know it could never be Hayden's fault for me getting kidnapped. I can never blame it on him. I know he thinks it's his fault because I made it seem like that but it wasn't, it never will be."

"So why did you end the relationship if it wasn't his fault?"

"Because of all the memories that came with him. It was because of the possibilities of that happening again. I was scared to be with Hayden. I wish I wasn't but what they did to me in that room is something I will never forget and every time I think or thought of Hayden, those memories would come back. It's weird though because the only times I've ever felt safe were with him."

"How did you feel when you saw him at the fight? Be completely honest with me on this too. I want to know the honest truth."

"I missed him. I felt safe knowing he was there. And the way we were talking to each other during the interview and how we were looking at each other felt like nothing between us changed. There was still something there even after all the trauma and history," I say honestly.

"Have you ever felt something like you did with Hayden, with anyone else?"

"No." I shake my head. "And to be honest, I don't think I ever will."

"A part of you will always love Hayden. He was your first love. You gave him your virginity, your trauma with your father, your secrets, everything. No one ever forgets their first. You also went through a lot during that period of time. It's only been a few years. It's still going to affect you," Patience explains.

"Yeah, I guess. I was just doing so good this year though. I haven't felt like this in a while and it kind of scares me," I explain, but the pills help calm my thoughts down. I wish they were enough right now. "I'm just scared of what's to come. Especially since I have someone else to look after now."

"Why?"

"Because I am afraid of something like that happening again."

"Let me ask you one more question and I want you to answer truthfully. As much as you can." I nod my head. "If Hayden asked you for another chance would you give it to him?"

Would I?

I would and at the same time, I wouldn't.

My head is telling me to stay away from Hayden while my heart and body want him. It's like a war that is going on between my head and heart. They are constantly screaming at each other and I don't know who to listen to.

My heart could get me hurt again and my head could play it safe, but it wouldn't make me happy like I was before.

Hayden made me so happy but is that kind of happiness worth it?

I don't even know the kind of person Hayden is right now.

"I don't know."

Nine

"What's going on with you? You've had almost an entire week to complete this column Jaclyn, and I haven't seen anything," Jules says while rubbing her temples. "I don't understand what's going on with you and this interview. It shouldn't be hard to write a column about some cocky fighter."

But what Jules doesn't know is that I've replayed that moment Hayden looked down at me with a familiar softness in his eyes.

She has no clue that he is all I've thought about this entire week. I've been stalking his socials, going to therapy every other day, closing my eyes, and pretending that he is holding me when in reality I'm just alone in my room.

It's so hard to try and focus on this column when I'm too busy focusing on how to get Hayden out of my mind. I feel so pathetic, crying in the shower about him when he is probably not thinking about me at all. My mind is yelling at me for being stupid thinking he still thinks about me the way I think about him.

"I'm sorry. Things have just been rough for the past few weeks. It's not an excuse, I know but things have just been hard."

"Is everything okay?" Jules asks, with concern filling her face.

I nod my head and force a smile on my face. "Yea, things with Junior have just been hard. He isn't making this month easy on me. But it's fine. I'll finish it right now," I assure her but she still gives me a concerned look.

Jules worries about Junior because of his VSD and because we still haven't gotten the chance to do surgery for him yet because our health insurance doesn't cover it.

Problems after problems after problems.

But the meds help him.

But for how long?

Jules nods her head. "Okay. If you can't finish it today, that's fine but I need to send this column to our editors by the middle of next week. If you can't handle writing it, tell me before then."

I shake my head at her. "I'll finish it right now, Jules. Don't worry." I smile before standing up.

I leave her office and make my way back to mine.

Patience said to keep my mind off Hayden and I should be keeping myself busy. But it's hard when all I do is take care of Junior, who is Hayden's son, and then go to work, where I have to write a column on Hayden.

Everything in my life seems to revolve around him. It's fucking PATHETIC.

I feel so stupid for thinking of him and it's stressing me out constantly. The nightmares are still there but Hayden is in them, saving me from the black hooded man and then telling me to promise him to not leave.

I wipe a tear that has fallen from my eye. I didn't even realize I was crying or even overthinking so much until now.

I sit on my chair and rest my head on the desk.

I just need a break.

From work, from him, from everything.

I raise my head and wipe my eyes before shaking my hands to get the nerves out. I place my hands on the keyboard and stare at the screen in front of me.

"Hayden Night..."

That's all I've been able to start. The rest of the sentence would just go on talking about our history. Kind of like my own little story about him which I never thought of doing until now.

The sound of my office door opening makes me flinch before looking at the door. "Hey," Brandon says as he walks in and closes the door behind him. He sits on the chair in front of my desk. "What are you doing?"

"You couldn't have knocked?" I raise an eyebrow at him.

"Oh, come on, you love me," Brandon says before winking at me. I give him a small smile and look at the word document, thinking about what to start writing. "You look stressed."

"I am." I look away from the document and at Brandon. "I still haven't finished the column on Hayden and Jules is getting pissed."

"Wasn't that assignment supposed to be done at the beginning of the week?"

"Maybe?" I give him a guilty smile. "I just can't think of the right words to write about him."

Brandon nods his head in understanding. He gets it because he knows the history between Hayden and I. Maybe not the intimate moments but he knows the significant ones.

"Well, the reason why I came up here was to tell you that someone is downstairs asking for you," Brandon says.

I furrow my eyebrows at him. "Who?"

"Someone with the name Natalia. She asked to come up, but they weren't letting people upstairs, so the receptionist asked for me to come and get you."

I stand up from my desk. "Alright. Do you know what she wants?"

"She just said that she was an old friend and she needed to talk to you."

An old friend?

Someone from college?

Especially after the fight with Hayden.

Natalia from college?

Hayden's sister?

I mean who else could it be?

"Okay. I'll go now." I'll just start writing after lunch. Maybe I just need some food in my stomach. "My lunch starts now anyways."

I stand up but Brandon stands as well, coming close to me. "Are you sure you're okay? I need to make sure you aren't going to fuck yourself up again over this guy. I hated seeing how you got when I first met you."

I put on a fake smile and nod my head. "Yea. He's just some guy. It'll go away and I'll be okay again. I just need to focus on myself right now." I hug Brandon before leaving my office. I walk towards the receptionist desk when I get out of the elevator. "Hey, Brandon said that there was someone here to see me? Someone with the name Natalia."

The receptionist points to the person behind me. "She is sitting right there."

I turn around and see a familiar blonde haired girl.

Someone who I thought I would never see again.

She lifts her head and a smile spreads on her face.

She stands up and walks towards me. "Jaclyn? Jaclyn King?"

Ten

Jaclyn

PRESENT

I never expected to be faced with someone from my past. College is a time where I would like to forget everything because remembering all the good memories hurts.

The good memories hurt to remember more than the bad ones because I know what I lost. I lost my happiness and the person I used to be. I lost the love I had for so many people and it makes my heart ache.

Just thinking about everyone I left behind and all the memories makes me want to cry again. But I can't allow myself to cry because I have Junior watching me. I can't have him know that his mother is broken beyond repair, despite all the therapy and talking.

"You look great." Natalia smiles, radiance glowing from her.

Right now, we are at a small coffee shop having lunch. I decided to take my lunch early because she wanted to catch up and she recommended this coffee shop down the street from my office.

Natalia looks happy and healthy.

I remember in college she would look drained despite the smile on her face that she would give everyone. She still has an amazing jawline but her face looks more filled out. She has the same beautiful smile that people wish they had. Her hair is a gorgeous golden blonde color which makes me assume she dyed it because she used to have dirty blonde hair.

She looks stunning as usual and it's nice to see her so healthy and glowing.

I smile. "Me? Look at you. You look so healthy and beautiful. Not that you didn't before but something has changed about you."

Natalia blushes. "Well, having a baby gives you a different kind of happiness."

My eyes widen in response.

That's something I didn't expect her to say.

I trail my eyes down to her breasts and they definitely look bigger. She always had small boobs.

Fuck, I hope I don't look different to the point where she notices.

I didn't know Natalia had a baby. I never looked at her

Instagram or anything and Hayden doesn't ever post his family on social media so I was never curious.

"A baby? How old?"

"Around 4."

Natalia pulls out her phone and turns it to me.

I see a girl with bright blonde hair and blue eyes smiling at the camera. She's wearing a pink dress and hugging a stuffed frog.

I smile. "She's beautiful Natalia, what's her name?"

"Lilah. She's amazing, Jaclyn. I never knew a kid could make me so happy. Chris is great with her and she's just a little ball of happiness. I wish I could take her everywhere with me."

I get what she means. Right now, all I want to do is go home to Junior and sit on the couch to watch TV with him.

"You're still with Chris?"

Natalia nods. "Yes. We're married now. We got married right after graduation. He proposed right when I told him I was pregnant. He told me at the time he's been wanting to propose for a while but with Lilah, he just thought it was the perfect time. But we're still together. He's playing for the Giants."

"Nice. Does he like it?"

"Yea, he loves his teammates a lot. He fits in and is great with the other players. They work well together."

"Is that why you moved out here?"

"Yea. He needed to be close to the training center and since Hayden lives out here we thought it'd be good."

"Nice. Do you like it out here?"

"Yea. It's very different from Utah and Arizona. It's a bit loud and chaotic but I love it," she says, still with a small smile on her face. "But things are really good for me. I'm really happy. And I saw your interview with Hayden and just had to see you."

I nod my head lightly. "Yea, I'm happy you came. It's great to see you and that you're doing good. I wish I stayed in contact."

Natalia's smile changes into a sad one. "Yea I know. You just needed time." I stay quiet because I have no clue what to say to her. "How have you been lately? Are you doing good? You look a lot skinnier. I wish I could look like you."

I smile shyly while rubbing my palms against my dress pants.

It's because every time I feel like eating I think I'm going to gain back all the weight I lost. That's why I sometimes overdose on meds so that I make sure not to eat that much.

But I don't say that and in everyone else's head and eyes I'm doing good. I'm happy and healthy and it's all because I want to do better for Junior.

"Yea, I've just been busy with work mostly."

Technically I'm not lying. I'm just not giving her all the information she should know.

Because if I tell her I'm hiding her brother's baby she's going to tell him and then I'll be dragged back down and all the progress I've somewhat made will be gone.

"That's good. I've wanted to reach out after the whole situation happened but I know you needed time."

"Thank you, I appreciate it a lot, seriously. Time does heal wounds." *Sometimes.*

Natalia smiles while she gives me a once over, probably to make sure that I look okay, which I should. I take vitamins to make my face glow and I drink energy drinks once or twice everyday to make sure I look like I'm awake and not a character from *The Walking Dead.*

"I know you probably have to go soon but why don't you come to my house this weekend for lunch? Chris will be home and he would be happy to see you." I really want to but I can't help but think that might be a bad idea because the outcome is unknown. Will Hayden be there? Will I start talking to Hayden again after I become close with his sister again? Will I have to face him and tell him the truth? "If you're worried about seeing Hayden, he won't be at the house. He is always having weekend lunches with his agents."

I lick my bottom lip, relief rushing through my body.

One lunch at Natalia's house doesn't mean I'll start talking to Hayden again.

It's just two friends catching up.

"Okay. Lunch sounds great."

Eleven

Jaclyn

I pull up to a tall house with a bunch of windows in front and trees on the sidewalk. I close the car door and walk closer to the house.

Natalia lives in Brooklyn Heights, a richer part of Brooklyn where there are a bunch of expensive houses and a private school down the street.

As I look at her house, it looks like Chris and her are very well off and they are making enough money to live very comfortably.

I walk up to the front door and knock twice. I fidget with my purse trying to calm my nerves but that feels impossible.

When Natalia invited me over, all I could think about was my involvement with Hayden and what would happen if she were to find out he has a kid he doesn't know about.

Today, Junior is with Brandon. Brandon said he would take Junior to the park today and then get some ice cream even though it's cold today. Junior likes to use his cuteness to get what he wants all the time. He watched Shrek a couple months ago and saw Puss the cat make that face with the big pouty eyes and since then Junior has been using that to get his way, which works most of the time.

The door opens revealing a familiar blonde guy.

Chris looks exactly the same, if anything a little bigger because of the training he probably does. His hair is shorter and he has a light scruff on his jaw.

Chris smiles. "If it isn't the girl who ran away." I smile lightly, trying not to feel uncomfortable with the comment. "Jaclyn King, how are you? Natalia told me you were coming over." Chris pulls me in for a hug and I hug him back.

"Yea, I'm doing good." I pull away from him and put my hands in the pockets of my coat. "Natalia told me to come over for lunch and I couldn't say no." I walk inside as Chris holds open the door for me.

Chris opens a door that reveals a closet full of coats. I take off mine and give him it.

"Yea, when Natalia told me you were coming I was shocked because we haven't seen you since college," Chris says, and I know he probably isn't thinking about the reason why I left like I am. "Lilah and Natalia are in the living room." Chris closes the closet door and I follow him through the hallway. If the house outside looks big, being inside it looks even bigger. Their house looks so luxurious and beautiful, I'm jealous they have so much room. I wish I could give Junior this instead of just a small apartment with a small room where he can barely fit all his toys. We walk inside the living room where Natalia is with Lilah on the floor taking pictures of her playing with her toys. "Babe, Jaclyn's here."

Natalia turns her head and her smile widens. She stands up and runs over to me before pulling me into a hug. "Ahhh, I'm so happy you made it." I hug her back and smile because I have always loved her hugs.

I remember one time crying in her arms because I was worried about Hayden fighting and she hugged me and reassured me that night that everything would be okay. Natalia is the only real friend I think I've ever had.

"I'm happy I made it too. I'm ready for food." I chuckle and let her go. "You guys have such a nice home."

"Thank you. Chris and I tried really hard to make this feel super welcoming and homey." Natalia smiles.

"I'm going to go finish up in the kitchen," Chris says before kissing Natalia on the forehead which makes me smile.

Natalia grabs my hand and pulls me towards Lilah

who is on the floor. "Lilah, baby. I want you to meet someone," Natalia says as she makes me sit down. I rest my bag on the couch and scoot towards Natalia and Lilah. Lilah is playing with two Barbies and it looks like they are having a conversation. Junior sometimes does that with his animal figurines. He always makes the lion and tiger fight. Lilah looks up at me and smiles. Her smile is just like her mother's and she has bright blue eyes just like her father. She is a perfect combination of Chris and Natalia. "Lilah, this is Jaclyn. I went to college with her. She was my best friend."

Lilah smiles at me and she wraps her arms around me. "I love new friends!" she cheers and lets go of me. She admires the features on my face. "You're so pretty like mommy."

I smile down at her. "Thank you. You're pretty just like your mama."

Lilah blushes and then gets off my lap to go back to playing with her dolls.

"So you barely told me about what's going on with you. Talk to me." Natalia pulls her knees to her chest and rests against the side of the couch.

I smile nervously. "Well like I said I've just been busy with work."

"How have you been after the whole thing happened?"

Time freezes, as I think about that answer.

I don't want anyone knowing what a mess I was. Crying to my mom every night until I moved out. Waking up to horrible nightmares. Looking in the mirror and hating what I saw. Tracing the scars with my nails, wishing it would just go away.

My mom said she never saw me like that and she hopes never to see me like that ever again. My mom worries about me a lot and after that whole situation it just made her worry more.

I had a seizure from how low my blood sugar was one time because I was so stressed out about everything else and it didn't help that I had Junior in my belly.

"Things were rough in the beginning but I'm doing better now," I say.

It's not really a lie because I am doing better than before. I'm just trying to continue to work on myself.

Yea but taking pills every goddamn day.

"Hayden told me everything," Natalia says, tears threatening to appear in her eyes. "I'm so sorry you had to go through that. He told me that you guys broke up the night he saved you. He didn't come home that night and didn't answer anyone's calls for two days. I thought he was with you but then when he wasn't answering anyone I knew something was wrong. He came home two days later with a busted lip and a bruised eye. His knuckles were bruised and cut and when I looked in his eyes I couldn't see anything there. I was so scared for my brother but I also couldn't help but wonder what happened to you. Hayden has never been like this with anyone so I was worried as hell."

I never knew how Hayden was after I broke up with him. I knew he was mad but I didn't know to what extent. "So you know why I had to leave?" She nods her head. "I'm sorry, Nat. I just had to leave. I wasn't myself. I felt horrible but I couldn't love Hayden and deal with everything at the time. I wanted to be alone."

Natalia gives me a sad smile. "I know, but you look better and are hopefully doing better so that's all that matters."

I nod my head. "What do you mean by 'there was nothing there'? When you mentioned how Hayden looked when he came back?"

Natalia sighs and licks her bottom lip. "When he came back, I looked in his eyes and they looked dead. It looked like his soul left his body and there was nothing behind his eyes. He looked like that for a few months. Coming in and out of the apartment with bruises and cuts everywhere. Sometimes he wouldn't even come home. He barely talked to anyone. But then he met his brother and things changed."

I furrow my eyebrows.

Brother?

"Brother?"

Natalia was about to answer but then the doorbell

rings. Natalia gets up. "I'll be back. Chris, I'm getting the door," she yells as she walks out of the living room.

I look at Lilah, playing with her dolls, furrowing her eyebrows every few seconds when one doll does something to the other doll.

My mind goes back to Hayden and his brother.

Hayden never mentioned a brother to me.

All he told me about his biological parents is that his mom died from drugs and then his dad died from a gunshot. He never met either of them but he never wanted to either.

He never mentioned a brother.

Natalia walks back into the living room with a girl, she has blue eyes and dark brown hair. She looks like a mean version of Megan Fox. She is wearing a black workout set that compliments her curves that I'm jealous of and I can't help but want to look like her.

She looks so familiar but I can't pinpoint it.

Natalia looks annoyed as she walks her to the living room. "Jaclyn, this is Nicole Earnings. Nicole, this is Jaclyn King."

Nicole Earnings.

I knew that name was familiar.

I look down at her hand and she has a big diamond on her ring finger.

This is the girl Hayden proposed to.

Twelve

PRESENT

Nicole looks me up and down, making me feel uncomfortable with her gaze on me like that. She definitely doesn't hide her dislike.

She looks away from me and looks back at Natalia who heads to the kitchen. "So where is he? I asked Killian and Rowan but none of them want to tell me what he's doing. Pretty sure he is with both of them."

"Jaclyn, come and have some wine," Natalia says. "I don't know Nicole, you know how he is. When he wants to be alone he'll be alone," Natalia answers as I get off the floor and walk to the kitchen.

Chris has his back facing us while he stirs something in a mixing bowl.

Nicole crosses her arms over her chest. "I need to

know where he is because we leave for Italy soon and I need to make sure that he and my dad have everything set. He hasn't even decided on what to wear for the wedding or reception."

My heart drops.

Just a little.

But it's fine.

He's not mine anymore so I can't act sad or butt hurt. I'm the one who left him.

I can't be sad that I'm not the one getting married to him in Italy.

I remember telling Hayden one night that my dream wedding would be held at Lake Como at the Villa Balbiano. Hayden asked if we were to ever get married where I would want it. When I asked him he said that he wouldn't care as long as I was happy.

I bite the inside of my cheek to stop myself from crying or tearing up.

It's pathetic I still feel this way after this long. I'm not allowed to think of those memories and miss them.

Nicole continues to complain about Hayden while Natalia just looks at me and gives me a sympathetic look. I give her a reassuring smile and just listen to Nicole.

Lilah is still playing with her dolls in the living room and Chris is barely even paying attention to Nicole.

Nicole turns her head to me. "Where did you say that you and Natalia met again?"

"College. I met her in our journalism class."

It's like realization sparks on Nicole's face. She widens her eyes lightly, making it noticeable that she knows exactly who I am. "So you're *that* Jaclyn?"

"What do you mean by that?" I raise an eyebrow at her.

Nicole smirks. "You're the one who dated Hayden in college right? You weren't just a part of Natalia's friend group?"

Natalia rolls her eyes at Nicole. "You don't have to answer her, Jaclyn. She's just mad that Hayden doesn't care about her."

"Eat shit, Natalia." Nicole shakes her head lightly before focusing back on me. "Well?" She raises an eyebrow waiting for me to answer.

Someone needs to knock some manners into this bitch. "Yea, we dated. But we broke up so there's nothing really to talk about," I say, before sitting down on the stool next to the island.

Natalia pours wine into two glasses. She takes a sip of hers and pushes another towards me.

A little wine won't hurt, especially with Nicole asking about my history with the group.

"So you know the boys well?"

I nod my head and take a sip of the wine. "Yea. We all hung out pretty much everyday."

"They all mentioned you. Hayden never said a thing

about you to me but I would overhear conversations that he would have with his brother. And then Max never stops mentioning you. Don't get me started on this one here." Nicole looks at Natalia but Natalia just glares at her.

"We were all pretty close." I shrug. "How did you meet Hayden?"

"Family acquaintance introduced us. We were at a business party when my dad met Hayden through a family acquaintance," Nicole says, like it's nothing. Usually people who are engaged would smile and talk about how happy they are with that person but Nicole looks so nonchalant. "How did you end up becoming close with Natalia and the boys?"

"No clue. We just grew closer as time went by. Natalia and I got along instantly."

Can't say the same about Hayden though.

"Has Hayden always been bad at answering the phone?"

Not with me.

Natalia rolls her eyes again. "Nicole, stop being stupid and just leave Jaclyn alone. She's here to have lunch with me, not to get intimidated by you."

I furrow my eyebrows. "I'm not intimidated by her. I just think it's funny with all the questions she's asking," I say, a smile slowly growing on my face. This girl seriously sounds desperate with how much she is asking about

Hayden and my past with the group. "Hayden does what Hayden does, Nicole. No one can really control him or keep him in check."

"Let's hope he fixes his fucking attitude once we're married. I thought this was going to be easy."

"No one's forcing you to marry him," Natalia mumbles as she sips her wine.

Nicole glares at her before looking at me. "Have you ever been to Italy?" I shake my head 'no'. "You want to come to Italy for a wedding?"

Did she just ask if I wanted to come to her wedding?

Is this bitch high or something?

She wants her fiancé's ex to go to her wedding? What's wrong with this girl?

Before I can say no, Natalia speaks up with a smile returning to her face. "Oh my God, Jaclyn, yes! You have to come. Nicole's dad is setting us up in the nicest hotel near Spiaggia della Gaiola! Super nice."

I shake my head. "I don't think that's a good idea."

For the first time since we have been in the kitchen, Chris turns his head. "You should come. It'll be fun and you'll get to see everyone again," Chris suggests.

Going to Hayden Night's wedding where I'll be face to face with Hayden, the boy whose heart I broke while breaking mine in the process? The father of my son?

How is that a good idea?

Yes, I'll be able to see everyone but I'll also have to see Hayden and see him kiss the girl he is marrying.

Why the fuck would I want to do that?

"See? You should come? We'll be going to clubs, parties, nice bars, the beach, everything. You'll have fun." Nicole smiles but I can tell it's fake.

"I have work." I smile back. "I won't be able to."

Not to mention I won't be with Junior.

And the thought of that alone scares the shit out of me.

Since I had Junior, I've been with him every single day. There hasn't been one day where I was without him.

"Tell your boss that you are going on a business trip. It will be for research purposes. You can tell her that you are going to Hayden Night's wedding, the famous world champion boxer, and you will get an interview with him and details about everything. Your boss won't say no to that and I'm sure my brother will happily accept." Natalia gives me a mischievous smile that I know means bad news.

Jules has been pissed off with me lately and if I tell her about this opportunity she will without a doubt let me go.

One big con is just seeing Hayden.

Why the hell would I want to say 'yes' to go and see him?

That's screaming for trouble.

But my heart can't help but say yes.

So like a fool, falling I say, "Yes."

Thirteen

Jaclyn

Hayden's friends from high school invited us over to the club that Hayden used to fight at.

Thanksgiving dinner was tense. When I found Hayden standing in front of a broken mirror with glass on the floor, I wrapped my arms around him and rested my head on his back while he begged me not to leave. He told me if I stayed with him any longer I'll get hurt, and with Hayden I know I will.

But I don't care.

I love him.

I can't express how in love with Hayden I am. It almost scares me how much I love him. He told me that he knows he will mess up and there will be ups and downs but as long as he has me, he'll be okay.

It's like I'm his armor, the only thing to protect him, when in reality he is the one who is protecting me.

He was vulnerable with me that night. He's never been vulnerable or expressed his feelings or concerns to me. It meant a lot that he did that.

Today when we were at the mall he saw his friend as we were walking out of the store and he invited us to the club that Hayden used to fight at.

Lately, Hayden hasn't been fighting much. He is hiding something from me though. I know he is because sometimes when I ask to hangout he says he is busy and doesn't explain. I can't help but think it has to do with Marco, even though Hayden assured me that everything is fine.

I know when Hayden is hiding things and I can't help but worry. My overthinking has been going into overdrive because of everything he isn't telling me. I can't help the thoughts of cheating running through my mind even though I know he would never do that.

"Stay close," Hayden whispers in my ear, bringing me back to the present. He holds onto my hand tightly as we manage to pass through a crowd of dancing people in the club. The song "I Wanna Be Yours" by The Arctic Monkeys is blasting throughout the club. This club looks similar to the one in Arizona. A bar on the side, a fighting cage in the middle, tables, and a dance floor off to the other side. "If you need to use the restroom, tell me so I can go with you."

"Why?" I ask loudly.

"Because I don't want to leave you alone. Understand?"

I squeeze his hand twice and he kisses my forehead before looking ahead. Hayden brings us to the bar where we see the guy, Adam, from earlier today who invited us.

Natalia and Chris are grabbing us tables to sit at. Even though Hayden's friends invited him, he said he'd rather stay with me, Natalia, and Chris.

"Hayden! Glad you could make it," Adam says before standing up from the bar and giving Hayden a small hand-shake. Hayden still keeps his arm around me and holds me close to his side. Adam smiles down at me. "Glad you could make it too, Jaclyn. It'll be a fun fight to watch. Definitely different from Arizona." I smile and nod my head. "Let's go to the table that Alexa reserved."

"Alexa's here?" Hayden raises an eyebrow at Adam and he squeezes my hand in his.

Who's Alexa?

"Uh yea? I told you yesterday, remember?" Adam says before he walks away from the bar.

"Not really," Hayden mutters while he follows Adam.

I look up at him and see his jaw clenched.

I bring his jaw down so he can look at me. "Are you okay?" I ask.

Hayden lets out a deep breath before nodding his head. "Yea, let's just go," Hayden says before pulling my hand to follow him. We all scoot into the table. "Where are the others?"

"I invited Luke, Ross, Maddie, and Alexa. They are all here now. They are just getting drinks." Adam looks behind us before standing up. "There they are."

I turn my head and see two boys walk up to the table.

Hayden stands up with Adam and turns to the group.

"Is that Hayden Night?" one of the guys says before giving Hayden a bro hug. "Man, I haven't seen you in ages. When was the last time I saw you?"

"Probably last Thanksgiving." Hayden shrugs before sitting back down next to me.

"Last time you were in Arizona, I heard you beat up some guy at a party? Trent was it?" The guy asks, looking at Adam and Adam nods his head.

"Dude's fucking crazy. Always trying to start shit." The guy shakes his head lightly.

Hayden turns his head to the other guy. "Luke, haven't seen you in a minute. How are you?" Hayden asks Luke as he sits in the booth.

"Good. Still fighting. How about you?" Luke responds.

"I'm good." Hayden turns his attention to me, his eyes lighting up as he smiles down at me. "This is my girl-friend, Jaclyn. Jaclyn, that's Luke and Ross."

"Nice to meet you." They both say with a small smile.

I smile. "Nice to meet you guys too. How long have you known Hayden for?"

"Since we were all in middle school. This guy got into a fucking fist fight with a kid who was a grade above us. Beat the shit out of him and it was on his first day too. So we took him in." Adam says with a proud smile. "So what have you been up to? Still getting into petty little fights?" Adam asks Hayden.

Hayden leans back against the booth and wraps his arm around my shoulders, pulling me closer to him. "Nothing, just busy with school."

"Are you still fighting?"

Hayden shrugs. "Here and there."

I know he's lying because I'm here.

I know he still goes to fights but he doesn't bring me or tell me about them because he is scared that Marco won't keep his end of the deal.

"You know there is one opening tonight for a fight. If you want I can get you in. Give the people a good show for old time's sake?" Ross offers.

"Who's fighting tonight?"

"Some new guy who is from out of state and then Ben, too."

"Is this new guy good?" Hayden furrows his eyebrows.

"Yea, he's pretty good. You might know him. He is

from Arizona and it's his first time fighting here," Adam explains.

Hayden tenses. "What's his name?"

"Eric Thompson."

This time, I tense.

Since Marco let Hayden and I go that night of the fight between them, Eric has not left us alone. He stalks us on the daily, to the point where it's concerning.

One night, Eric cornered me in the diner when Hayden wasn't there. Luckily Franky was there and dealt with him. When Hayden found out what Eric did, Eric almost ended up in the hospital. Eric still manages to follow us around like a creep but he learned his lesson about getting near me.

Doesn't stop him from trying to talk to me here and there though.

"You know him, Hayden?" Ross asks.

"Unfortunately," Hayden mutters. "I'll take the fight if he is the one I'm going to fight."

I glare at Hayden.

Is he stupid?

"You don't even have your gloves and you're not dressed properly," I say, making his friends look at me.

"I have an extra pair in my car. Pretty sure you're the same size as me and I have some shorts you can use?" Ross offers.

Hayden nods his head. "Okay. I'll do it. When's the fight?"

"Maybe like thirty minutes?" Luke says before looking at Ross. "Where did the girls go by the way?"

"No clue. Maybe the restroom? You know how they are." Ross gets out of the booth. "I'll go get the stuff for you. They're in my car and then I'll get you a room and set up the fight."

Hayden nods his head and looks at Adam. "Well this will be interesting. I remember fight nights with you. Parties afterwards were crazy. Alexa will love this. She always loves watching you, remember-"

"No," Hayden cuts off Adam and he takes a deep inhale.

"You didn't even let me finish," Adam chuckles.

Hayden looks away from Adam and avoids eye contact with me by looking at the cage in the middle of the club.

I want to pull him out of the booth and talk to him. I want to ask him what's up with this Alexa and why he took the fight with Eric.

He's pissing me off.

"Alright, I'm here, Luke. You can stop texting me." I turn my head and see two girls walking towards the booth.

One of the girls has bright blonde hair with hazel eyes. She is wearing a white denim skirt with a blue halter top that showcases her stomach. How can she wear something like that when it's freezing cold outside?

The other girl has long brunette hair. She is wearing a black Harley Davidson tank top and black denim jeans. She has a black leather jacket resting on her shoulders.

"Well, Maddie said she wanted to look good for when Ben fights. She is still trying to get his attention," the brunette says while rolling her eyes. "Scoot, Luke."

Luke scoots down and the two girls sit down next to him.

Adam chuckles. "Of course you want to get his attention. Sweetheart, he doesn't date anyone, get the hint!"

The brunette chuckles before looking at Hayden. "Hayden Night. The one who got away."

Hayden doesn't say anything. He stays quiet and just stares at her.

I scoot away from Hayden making his arm fall from my shoulders. Hayden looks down at me with furrowed brows.

I can't help but feel annoyed and jealous.

Why would he act like this in front of a girl? She has to be an ex.

Does he love her? What kind of relationship did they have?

He has to still like her if he's acting like this right?

"Haven't seen you in a bit. Last I heard of you was at that party where you punched Trent. Heard it was wild. But I'm not surprised. Any party with you involved is always a show. I would know." Alexa smirks and she turns her attention to me. She smiles widely. "Who's this? New fling?" Alexa gives me a fake fucking smile that I want to punch off her face. "Look love, this won't last long. These flings of his never really do-"

"Enough, Alexa," Hayden says, cutting her off.

So this is Alexa?

"Why? Because it's true? I mean you did that with me but then again you always came back."

Hayden snickers. "You're embarrassing yourself. In high school, you would always come back to me and I would just push you away. You acted like lice. The irritating kind that don't get out of your fucking hair. Trust me when I say this, she isn't like you at all." Hayden looks at Luke. "Where is the dressing room I'm going to?"

"I'll show you." Luke makes his way out of the table.

"Cool." Hayden stands up and grabs my hand.

I take my hand out of his and go to follow Luke.

Hayden pulls me against him, his lips touch my ear. "What did I fucking say about staying close?"

"Screw you." I roll my eyes and continue to follow Luke while Hayden grips onto my wrist.

We go to the dressing room and Hayden closes the door behind us. There are already gloves, wraps, and shorts on the table.

"Go ahead and argue. I know you want to." He says after I cross my arms over my chest and glare at him.

"Well you can't expect me to be happy. You think I

want to meet your ex and see you fight the guy who's been stalking us?'

"First of all, Alexa isn't an ex. She was just someone I would hook up with. She wanted more from me but I didn't see her like that. All we did was argue and she would always be rude to Natalia. I never liked her."

"Why didn't you tell me about her?"

"Because I didn't feel like telling my girlfriend, who I love to death, about a girl I couldn't give two shits for."

Hayden takes off his shirt and starts to take off his pants leaving him in his boxers. My eyes go down to his v-line because I love his v-line, even though I'm mad at him. It's a weakness of mine. I meet his eyes and see him smirking.

"It's not funny, stop laughing."

Hayden walks towards me. "But I love it when you get all mad. Remember what I said about you?" Hayden leans down, his lips grazing my ear making me shiver. "Seeing you mad turns me on, princess."

I force him away. "No, you're not distracting me. What's up with the fight with Eric?"

Hayden's eyes darken. "You know why I want to fight him."

"I just don't think you should try fighting Eric anymore. What's it going to do? You're wasting your energy on him."

"It gives me satisfaction to hurt him knowing all he

wants to do is hurt you. What he deserves is for me to put him six feet under after spending hours taking my time killing him." Hayden turns around and grabs the shorts, putting them on.

I sigh while looking at him. He sits down on the couch and grabs the wraps, starting to put them on. I walk towards him and kneel in front of him. His eyes fill with lust. I grab his hand and a wrap.

"Well, make sure not to get hit in the face too much. It's your only good feature," I tease.

Hayden grabs my chin with his other hand. "Don't be a brat."

I smile, teasingly. "Or what?"

Hayden lowers his head and his lips meet mine. He pulls me up so I can sit in his lap. I can feel the evidence of how hard he is underneath me, pressing against the zipper of my jeans.

It makes me want to rock against him

"Or I'll spend all night making you come until you're writhing and begging me to stop. But I won't. I'll keep going until my back is bloody from how much you scratch me. So keep teasing me, Jaclyn."

His hands, that aren't finished being wrapped, go under my shirt. He touches my stomach and goes up to my breast. I moan against his mouth as he tugs one of my nipples.

A knock sounds on the door. "Night, you're up."

Hayden bites my bottom lip before pulling away with a grunt. "Fuck, I wish we were home." He rests his head on my shoulder. He looks up at me. "Where will you be?"

Sounding out of breath from his confession and kiss, I say "with Natalia and Chris."

Hayden licks his bottom lip that is a little plump from the kiss. "Okay, good. Stay next to them at all times. People here are fucking sick and you are fucking beautiful. I don't want anyone to take you away from me." I nod my head. "What's your blood sugar?" I pull my phone out of my pocket and turn it on. 199 is what it says on my phone. Hayden looks down and he looks pleased with the number. "Okay good." He pecks my lips one more time before moving me to the side. "Didn't even get to finish wrapping my hands because you distracted me."

I laugh and roll my eyes at him. "I'm going to go then."

"Okay. I love you." I kiss him on the lips.

"Love you, too," I mumble against his lips.

I leave Hayden in the dressing room and easily find Natalia at one of the booths. "Hey," Natalia says as I sit down next to her.

"Hey," I say back.

"Nervous for Hayden?"

"No. Hayden is good at what he does. I'm not worried," I say, with a reassuring smile.

I'm more worried for Eric.

The lights dim and we see an announcer walk on the stage.

"I'm going to go watch him closer."

"I'll come," Natalia says.

We walk towards the cage and hold onto the gate separating us from them.

"Hello everyone! Who is ready for a showstopper tonight?!" Everyone cheers, yelling 'yes' and 'get on it with'. "Great, then let's announce the fighters. First, we have Eric Thompson. He is originally from Arizona. 6 '2 weighing in about 195 pounds of pure muscle." Some people cheer for Eric and some people boo him, one of them being Natalia.

"Eric's here? How in the hell is he here?" Natalia asks.

I shrug. "I don't know. Hayden is fighting because of Eric."

"That makes so much more sense," Natalia says, diverting her attention back to the announcer.

"Last but most certainly not least, Hayden Night."

Everyone was going crazy for him. They cheer and yell his name over and over.

Some people yell, saying they missed him and are happy he's back.

"Hayden Night is and always will be our champion in the fighting club. He was one of the best fighters here and never lost a match. He is 6'3 and weighs about 200 pounds!" Everyone cheers for Hayden again. "Now from what we have seen tonight, Eric Thompson is definitely not a newbie to this whole fighting thing. Can he handle and take on Hayden Night tonight?! Let's find out and bring out our fighters!" the announcer says.

Hayden and Eric both come into the ring from opposite sides.

"Touch gloves?" The ref asks but they don't do anything making the ref step back. "On the count of three. One, two, three!" The bell rings and Hayden lunges at Eric, full speed punching him in the jaw.

Everyone in the crowd winces and cheers as they watch Hayden strike at Eric. Eric doesn't tumble down but he holds his jaw. Hayden goes to strike at Eric again, but he moves out of the way and thrusts his fist into Hayden's torso.

After that, punches start flying to the head and chest. They both go at it, not stopping. The boys are spitting out blood as they punch each other.

"He's gotten better," I turn my head and see Alexa watching Hayden fight.

"He's good at what he does." I say.

Alexa turns her head to look at me up and down before meeting my eyes. "I don't see why he would choose you. You don't seem like his type at all. You're too good."

"I don't either, but I guess he likes what he likes right? Or loves?" I give her a fake smile but she just returns it back.

Alexa raises her eyebrow. "He said he loved you. That's such a lie. Hayden Night doesn't love anything or anyone. He only cares about himself."

I turn my body to face her. "See that's where you're wrong. You may have known him throughout high school, but you have no idea what he has been through or what he's like. You don't know Hayden."

"I wouldn't be surprised if the next time I see him, you aren't wrapped around his arm. Enjoy the fight."

Alexa flips her hair like a fucking diva she thinks she is before walking away from me.

I roll my eyes and focus back on the fight.

I hear a bell ring and Hayden throws Eric on the floor. Hayden holds him down as the countdown starts.

1...2...3...4...5...6...7...8...9...10.

The crowd goes crazy and the ref pulls Hayden off of Eric.

A medic attends to Eric as the ref holds Hayden's fist in the air.

"Your winner! Hayden Night!"

Fourteen

Jaclyn

"Okay, baby. I love you so much." I kneel down to be at eye level with Junior. I pull Junior in my arms and he lays his head against my chest as I hold him tightly. I promised myself I wasn't going to cry when saying goodbye to him. "You promise you'll be good for Brandon?" Junior nods his head against me and sniffles.

When I told Junior I was leaving and won't be back for almost a month, he started to cry and ask me why I was leaving and if I would ever come back.

I explained to him that I was going on a work trip and that I'll be back. I told him that we will FaceTime every night before he goes to bed, even if that means I have to wake up early to see him and say I love him.

Brandon said that he will mostly be sleeping over at

my apartment since Junior's room is there but if anything, he can always go to his apartment too.

My mom said that she will fly to New York to stay with Junior for a week to make sure he's okay. She doesn't fully trust her only grandchild with my friendly neighbor yet.

"Please don't leave," Junior mumbles against my shoulder.

I look up at Brandon and see him giving me a sympathetic look.

When I told Brandon my plans, the real ones, he almost lost his shit. He never thought I'd be the type of person to go to Hayden's wedding, especially after all the shit that happened.

But I just can't help myself.

The dreams I've had lately almost always focus on him and in each dream he always tells me how much he misses me and then he kisses me, stealing away my breath.

Brandon told me he supports whatever I'm doing and that's what friends are for. I appreciate Brandon and everything he is doing for me.

I pull away from Junior and he has some tears falling from his eyes. "Don't cry baby. It's okay. You're going to have so much fun with Brandon and you'll be such a good boy for me, won't you?" I smile at him, wiping away the tear stains on his cheeks.

He nods. "I'll miss you."

I kiss his cheek and hug him one more time. This time I put my nose in his neck and smell him, wishing I could just take him with me.

But with Hayden and the rest of his family there, it will just cause trouble.

I'm still trying to figure out how to tell Hayden about Junior. I know I should.

I know I'm in the wrong about not letting Hayden meet him but I'm just scared as hell. Just thinking about it makes my mind go into overdrive.

"I'll miss you, Junior," I say softly.

"I love you, mommy."

"I love you more," I whisper in his ear. I kiss his cheek one more time before standing up. I wipe a tear that fell and then smile down at Junior. I look up at Brandon. "Please call me or text me if anything happens." I go to hug Brandon.

"Anything. Everything will be okay. Him and I will have fun." Brandon hugs me back. "You just figure out your shit with Hayden," he whispers in my ear before letting go of me. Brandon looks down at Junior. "We're gonna get into some trouble together right little dude?"

Junior smirks, looking just like his father, before nodding his head.

"Not too much trouble," I scold Junior, which makes him laugh. I grab my luggage and, because I can't help it, I kiss Junior one more time. "I love you, bub." I stand up and leave Brandon and Junior.

After I get all checked in with security and baggage, I go to the front desk to check in. "Hi, I'm here to check in."

"Perfect. What's your name and phone number?"

I give them my name and phone number and then say "I should have a premium economy seat."

She types on her computer and furrows her eyebrows. "You're mistaken, you have a first class ticket, Ms. King."

Natalia already got me a ticket for Emirates.

I was already guilty about her getting me a ticket with this airline because I know how expensive these tickets are.

"That has to be a mistake. I was booked for premium economy with you guys, not first class," I say, furrowing my eyebrows.

She shakes her head with a small smile. "No, Ms. King, you have a first class ticket with us today."

"Is there a way I can refund that and just get a regular economy seat?"

She shakes her head again. "I'm afraid not. We are all booked for this flight. The only way to get to Gaeta would be to stick with your seat."

What the fuck?

That ticket has to cost more than ten grand.

That's too fucking much for a ticket.

"There's no way I can change it? I wasn't booked for first class."

This lady probably thinks I'm crazy for refusing a first class ticket.

"No miss, I'm sorry. I wish there was more I could do," she says, giving me a sympathetic look.

I nod my head. "Okay, thank you."

"You still want to keep your seat?"

I don't want to but then Natalia's money would be a waste and she really wants me in Italy. "Yea, it's fine."

She smiles again. "Perfect. Take a seat and we'll be calling passengers in shortly."

I take my carry on and sit down in one of the chairs in the waiting area. I pull out my phone and text Natalia, asking her if she changed my ticket and why I'm getting first class.

About fifteen minutes pass until they start telling people to line up.

The bunk they have me in, in first class, is luxurious, almost to the point where I feel like I don't belong.

There is a huge screen and a soft seat I get to sit in. The window next to me is large, giving me a perfect view of the sky. Don't even get me started on the drinks menu or the small touches they have in the bunk.

As I get situated I feel my phone buzz in my pocket. I take it out and read the text.

Um, I didn't get you first class. I booked you for premium economy.

———

I slept for a good five hours on the flight before I got bored of sleeping and just decided to work. I finished up a lot of small projects for Jules which she was pleased with.

Currently I'm in an Uber, on my way to the hotel.

Natalia sent me the address so that I could give it to the Uber driver. Natalia said that Hayden is busy running errands and Nicole is with her family, preparing stuff for the wedding. She told me just to stay in my room since she knows I don't know my way around Italy.

What errands could Hayden possibly be running?

Those are the questions that always stay stuck in my head.

Maybe he is getting ready for the wedding? He must be so excited to marry his fiancé so he is trying to make sure everything is perfect.

Natalia said that Max and Kayden should be here tonight, which I'm excited for because I haven't seen them in such a long time.

"Thank you," I say to the driver after he helps me get my bags out of the car.

He gives me a small smile before getting back in the

car. He drives off while I walk towards the entrance of the hotel.

The hotel is definitely luxurious. There is a long driveway and a valet offered at the front where I see people getting in and out of fancy cars like Ferraris, Lamborghinis, Rolls Royce's, and many others.

I even saw a fucking G-Power BMW which I definitely took a picture of. It reminded me of Kayden since he loves BMW's or from what I remember he does.

"Need help with any bags?" a guy asks. He has light brown hair and a soft smile on his face.

I smile back and hand them to him. "That'd be amazing, thank you."

"Of course. What's your name so I can go put these in baggage so they can get sent to your room."

"Jaclyn King."

He nods his head before walking away with my bags. I walk up to the front desk and a woman looks up and smiles at me.

"Ciao. Welcome to the Grand Hotel Mazzaro. What can I help you with today?"

"Hi, I am here for check-in."

She looks down at her computer and types a few things before asking, "Name?"

"Jaclyn King."

"Are you here for the wedding of Hayden Night and

Nicole Earnings?" she asks me and I can't stop my stomach from churning because I hate that reason.

I can't help but feel like a green monster, jealous that Nicole gets to marry him and that I'm just here to watch.

"Yea," I say, putting a fake smile on.

"Can I have some ID?" I pull out my ID and show her. She gives me the room card and tells me the directions of where to go. "Enjoy."

"Thank you," I say before walking away and going towards the elevator.

As I wait in the elevator, I look down at my phone to see my notifications. I see a text from Brandon, so I text him back quickly.

He sent me a picture of Junior eating and laughing. Junior has marinara sauce all over his face, making me laugh.

> I didn't think you watching over Junior would mean he would get all messy. Better not burn down my kitchen!

> We'll be fine! Enjoy Italy.

> Don't forget to give him his meds!

I sent that last text because I just can't help it.

I exit the elevator and as I'm walking, a hand, warm, strong, and almost familiar, grips my waist and pulls me inside a room.

Just from the heat and his familiar scent I already know who it is.

And the butterflies in my stomach can't stop swarming.

My heart beats so hard against my chest I feel like it's going to burst.

He locks the door and turns around, his grayish eyes turn to me, heat filling them.

It's been five years and he still manages to make me feel like the world stops and it's just us two.

"Hayden," I whisper.

Fifteen

Jaclyn

My body feels like it's on fire.

The windows in the room are open and I'm only wearing shorts and a tank top. It's not even that hot outside but I feel like I'm burning up.

It has nothing to do with the weather outside but the way that Hayden stares down at me like I'm the only thing he wants.

The way his eyes pierce through mine makes me think that he knows everything about me even though we haven't seen one another in years.

His eyes are just like Junior's which makes my heart clench.

Hayden has no clue he has a mini him in the world.

It makes me feel so fucking shitty but how else am I supposed to protect myself let alone Junior?

"Hayden-"

Hayden walks closer to me while looking down at me with those intense eyes of his. His eyes travel all over my face, admiring every tiny detail before he goes down to my body. I feel insecure as he looks at me like that, his eyebrows furrowing just a little before hiding his confusion.

Why is he confused?

His eyes then go to my arm where I have my Dexcom.

I know we stopped talking but I still wonder if he ever kept the Dexcom follow app on his phone.

I always had to squash that tiny little piece of hope, wondering if he still cares about me like that or just hates me.

While he admires me I take a good look at him.

He is wearing a suit, black dress shirt, black pants, and a black coat. I have never seen him wear a suit I don't think.

And he looks damn good in one. To the point where I would want to see those clothes on my bedroom floor.

I look at the chain necklace around his neck and it looks like the same one he would always wear in college. His eyebrow piercing still gets to me because he always looked good with that damn piercing.

My eyes go down to his hands that are by his side. He

has one single ring on his finger, more specifically his ring finger.

My stomach churns again for the millionth time this week.

That must be his wedding band. But don't they do the bands at the ceremony?

I feel his hand on my cheek and he tilts my head up making me look at him. His hand feels warm on my cheek and I want to close my eyes and get lost in the feeling.

This is the first time in five years that Hayden has touched me like this. His hand on my cheek, his chest almost brushing against mine, and his breath so close to hitting my cheek.

I wish I could fall in his arms and be absorbed by him.

It would be so easy to drown in him.

But that little voice in the back of my head always ruins it.

Yea, you'll drown in him but then eventually you'll just become suffocated and won't be able to breathe.

You want that to happen again?

"Hi," Hayden whispers before looking down at my lips and meeting my eyes again.

"Hi," I whisper back, not knowing what else to even say or do.

"You're here," he says before his lips turn into a small smile, so small you can barely notice it.

"I'm here."

"I've been wanting to talk to you. I missed you."

I missed you too.

More than you'll ever know.

"Hayden-"

"Don't ruin it," he says, almost begging. "Seeing you at the fight fucked me up. I wanted to do and say so much to you but you looked fucking terrified."

Because I didn't expect to actually see you.

I thought the world was tricking me when I saw him in the ring in person that day. I felt like it was all just a dream because it happened so quickly.

But this?

The slow caress on my cheek, the soft breathing coming from both of us, the way he's looking at me like he is starstruck by me.

"It's just, I wasn't prepared to see you," I say softly. I force myself to back away, remembering why I'm here. He's getting married. He can't touch me like that. It looks like I fucking shot him when I back away from him. "You can't do that, you know. Touch me whenever you want. You're getting married."

Hayden licks his bottom lip before biting the inside of his cheek, like he's forcing himself to not admit something. "Don't."

I furrow my eyebrows at him. "Don't what? Don't mention your fiancé that you're marrying in less than a month?"

"You don't even know." Hayden chuckles softly but he definitely doesn't think it's funny. "How was that first class ticket?"

My eyes widened. "You changed my seat?" I ask, and he nods his head. "Why would you do that? I was fine with the tickets that Natalia got me. Those first class tickets must have been expensive."

"13K is pocket change," Hayden shrugs.

"Bet your fiancé wouldn't like that you did that," I raise an eyebrow at him and cross my arms over my chest.

His eyes go to my boobs before meeting my eyes. "What I do is none of her business and never will be her business. I'm not hers."

Then who do you belong to, Hayden Night?

Hayden takes a step closer to me and I take a step back.

We do this little dance until my back hits the wall. "What are you doing, Hayden?"

"Something I'll probably get in a lot of trouble for."

Hayden grabs my face in his large hands and pulls me against him.

My lips touch his.

I haven't kissed Hayden in five years and after so long I thought I would never feel this anymore.

But he's kissing me, his tongue instantly gliding against mine making me close my eyes and get lost in him.

The world finally pauses as he kisses me.

It's just me and him and he's stealing my breath away. His fingers caress my jaw as he kisses me like he needs me to live longer. Like I'm some potion and he's in need.

His lips are still the same after so many years. Soft, plumped, and almost feel like they are mine.

I sigh into his mouth before pulling away. "Hayden."

He rests his forehead on mine and closes his eyes, breathing heavily. "You're different."

"What do you mean?"

"You've changed." He lifts his head from mine and looks down at me with almost hurt in his eyes. "You're more guarded. I don't know how to get to you anymore."

I feel like my heart's been hit. Of course he would notice I've changed.

Everyone fucking changes.

"People change. That's life isn't it?"

Hayden shakes his head. "It's different. You're colder."

I push him away from me lightly and walk away from between him and the wall. "Like I told you that night Hayden, the girl you knew from college died."

Hurt flashes in his eyes and his jaw clenches. I look down at his hands and they are formed in a fist. "Then fucking tell me what happened instead of pushing me away. Let me help you."

"I'm fine," I lie.

That lie has been in my mouth since that night.

Pretty sure Brandon knows I'm lying. And my mom.

"Bullshit. You're skinnier, to the point where it's not fucking healthy. You have this dead look in your eyes like there is nothing there. And don't even get me started on the bags under your eyes. It looks like you're not even getting sleep. This isn't the Jaclyn I know."

"She's fucking dead!" I yell, getting frustrated. Tears are threatening to spill from my eyes but I don't let them. It feels like my heart is being squeezed so hard that it will crush and I'm just barely holding on. He doesn't even know. He has no right to judge. He has no clue what I went through in that room and how I had to get some part of myself back. I went through hell and he doesn't even know. "Don't stand there and judge me. You have no clue what I went through in the past five years. You don't know so don't fucking stand there judging me and how I look. I'll never let anyone ever do that to me again."

Last time someone did that was my dad and I promised myself I wouldn't let anyone judge me or how I look after that.

I know I'm fucking skinner but that's none of his business. I know I look dead but that's because I feel like it almost everyday.

But that's none of his business.

As if Hayden realizes what he did was wrong, his face changes to sympathy. "I'm sorry. I didn't mean it like that or mean for it to come out like that. I'm fucking worried about you. I know your past with your eating and your diabetes. I'm fucking worried about you."

"You have no right to be. That's not your job anymore." Hayden's jaw clenches again and he puts his hand in his pockets. "You can't kiss me again. You have a fiancé. You're being disrespectful to her and me because I won't ever come between a marriage and be the other women. Figure out your shit." I grab my bag that fell on the floor at some point. I bend down and grab it. When I stand back up, Hayden is standing closer to me again. "Hayden-"

"I just wish things ended up differently," he whispers. "I wish I could have saved you and been there for you. It's been five years and somehow I can't fucking get you out of my head." He rests his forehead on mine.

I can't help but let a tear fall down my cheek.

Because no matter how hard I try to push him away and pretend I'm okay, I'm not.

All I want to do is cry in his arms as he holds me and tells me that everything will be okay.

That I'm safe and that the black hooded man isn't out to get me still.

Only Hayden can save me but he is also the one who ruined me.

Hayden presses his lips against my forehead. "Go," he whispers.

I force myself away from him and leave the room.

Sixteen

Past

Jaclyn

"I've been having a hard time on these terms," I say while looking over the worksheet that my professor provided for me and the rest of the class.

We have a test in the next few days so Kayden is helping me out with studying since I suck at it.

I was never the best at studying so I was put into special education where they basically helped me and took more time to work with me and my academics.

"It's really easy. This test will basically have the answers in it, all tests usually do."

"We had to watch this documentary about these triplets who didn't even know one another existed. We have to write an essay about them for the test as well. I swear my professor loves to torture us," I explain.

"I've seen that," Kayden answers over the phone. "It's interesting. The background story is fucked up though."

I'm about to agree with Kayden but then I hear loud knocking on my door making me pause. "I'll call you tomorrow, Kayden. Someone is at my door."

Kayden says goodnight and lets me go.

I get out of bed and leave my room. More knocks sound on the door as I hurry and open it.

When I open it, my jaw drops. Hayden stands in the walkway with a bloody eyebrow where his piercing is and a bruised cheek.

"Hayden," I whisper as he walks in and closes the door. He leans against the wall near the door and closes his eyes. He's only wearing a black jacket where the zipper is open and black shorts. I walk closer to him and grab his hands. His knuckles have deep cuts on them and they already look like they are forming a bruise. "What did you do?" I look up at him, worry filling my eyes.

Hayden and I haven't talked in a while because we got in a fight. I know he's been hiding things from me and I know it has to do with Marco but every time I would ask, he would brush me off.

One day, after work, Eric came and threatened me. Hayden beat the crap out of him and then he and I got into a fight.

I asked him what's going on with him and why we barely hang out. He made some stupid excuse and I told him if he couldn't tell me the truth then we should take a small break until he figures his shit out.

He got pissed and I left him alone in the parking lot.

It's been a week since then.

"I'm sorry." He looks up at me, hurt flashing in his eyes. I know Hayden has demons and I know that fighting gives him a way to release those demons. I just hate all the problems that come with the fighting. I don't have peace anymore but at least I have Hayden. "I'm fucking sorry. I wish I told you."

I grab his hand and swing his arm around my shoulder. "Let's go to my room."

Hayden and I go to my room. Calvin is upstairs sleeping so I don't want to wake him up.

I bring Hayden to my bathroom and make him sit on the toilet. I grab the first aid kit underneath the cabinet. I take out the alcohol pads and small band aids before standing between Hayden's legs. He immediately rests his hands on my hips and I let him as I work on the wounds on his face.

"After that date we had that one night. I got a message from Marco saying he needed me to start fighting again," Hayden starts saying as I clean his cuts. "Since then I've been fighting at the club again. Marco's just been making me come in and out of fights, not giving me a break."

I remember the date. He was being weird during dinner, looking at his phone. Because of that I just told him to drop me off at home and he did. Since that date, things have been different. I hate how far Marco and Eric have been pushing us.

"Why couldn't you just say no?"

"Because they threatened you again. I'll go through fucking hell before I let them have you."

It's been a few months since Hayden's fight with Eric and since then, things are just tense. Marco said he wouldn't come after me but it seems like he changed his mind. Hayden told me once that Marco is never a man of his word.

He is a bad man with fucked up morals.

Hayden thinks he is a psychopath and I wouldn't be surprised with the kind of tendencies he has.

"I thought we were done with this? I thought Marco was over this fixation."

"I don't know what it is about him wanting you. He's never wanted someone this much and I know it's not for him to fucking have sex with you. It's something else, something more," Hayden says, looking like he is in deep thought.

"Then we need to do something." I throw the alcohol pads in the trash.

"You aren't doing shit," Hayden demands, roughly might I add.

I turn my head to look at him as he stands up and

walks towards me next to the sink. "Yes I am. This isn't just about you."

"It's fucking dangerous. Marco is a damn psycho. I don't want you in his vicinity," Hayden says, leaning down close to me.

I put my hands on my hips and stare up at him. "Don't care. We need to figure out a way to get him off your back and mine. We need to figure out what his goal is."

Hayden shakes his head lightly and a smile threatens to spill on his lips. "You're fucking crazy."

"Maybe I am." Next thing I know I feel Hayden's lips on mine. A full body tremor goes through me as he caresses my lips with his and thrusts his tongue inside my mouth. Hayden devours my lips as if he is obsessed. He pushes me against the wall and one of his hands goes to my jaw and the other goes to my thigh, resting his hand on the side. "Hayden," I moan against his mouth as he grunts and pushes against me.

I feel his hardness against my core making me squirm against him.

Fuck I haven't kissed him in so long.

I missed him and his touch.

His pretty words that make me melt against his body.

Hayden grabs onto both of my thighs and wraps them around his hips. "Fuck, I've missed this. The way your body melts into mine," he mumbles as he carries us out of my bathroom and into my room. He rests me against the bed and starts kissing his way down my neck. I lean my head to the side to give him more access. I spread my legs, giving him more room to move against me. "God, you're a fucking dream, princess."

"Hayden," I pant, feeling like I can't breathe from the simple kisses he's giving me.

Hayden takes my tank top off and throws it behind him as he starts to go lower. I suck in my stomach which Hayden gives me a glare for.

I love how much he knows me and because of that he always reassures me not to be insecure around him.

"I wish I could do this to you forever. Kissing you is equivalent to owning the world," he mumbles against my stomach. While kissing my stomach he slowly slides my sleeping shorts down my legs along with my underwear revealing my bare pussy. "You drive me fucking insane, princess," he says before leaning in and devouring me. His lips make contact with my pussy as he kisses me and licks me. I swear I see stars as I arch my back and moan his name. His hand presses against my stomach hard making it impossible to stay still. Hayden holds my thigh with another hand as he traces my clit with his tongue. "Look at me, princess. Look at what I'm doing to you."

I force my eyes open and look down at him. He keeps eye contact with me, making my stomach fill with butterflies. I try to close my legs around him but he forces one of my thighs against the bed.

"Hayden," I moan, slowly starting to close my eyes. He nips my clit making me scream and lift my hips. He pushes me down as ecstasy floods throughout my blood. "Hayden, oh-oh my God!" I cry out his name as my orgasm seeps out of me.

Hayden kisses my thighs before standing up, cleaning me up while I calm down my breathing. Once he's done, he stands up and I watch as he takes off his belt, slowly. Once his pants and briefs are gone he puts his hand on his cock, stroking it slowly a few times.

I love it when he touches himself while looking at me like I'm his world. It makes me feel so special and like I'm the only girl in the world.

Hayden comes down on me and forces my legs apart. He leans down and presses his lips against mine as he pushes inside me in one go.

I choke on a moan and wrap my arms around him, my nails scraping his back.

It's been more than a week since he was last inside me and I swear every time we have sex, it feels like the first time.

I'm always burning with need and heat. My legs and pussy become sore as he fucks me slowly and roughly.

"Fuck," he grunts, thrusting inside me once before resting his head on my shoulder. "Look at you. Taking me so well. Welcoming me into your pussy like it's home, baby," he says, lust coating his voice. "God, I never want to leave. I wish I could stay here forever."

He pulls out before pushing back in rough.

There's no barrier between Hayden and I and I can't get enough.

Hayden's hand goes to my nipple, playing and twisting the bud making me cry out against his mouth.

"Hayden, oh God, please."

Hayden takes his hand off my nipple and rests his hand on my throat. "Shhh, can't have your uncle knowing that I'm fucking his niece in the middle of the night," he says against my lips.

I melt into him and his dominance, getting lost in his touch.

The roll of his hips against me becomes harder and faster, making me know he's going to finish soon just like me.

"Hayden, I'm-"

"I know, princess. Tell me you're mine."

"I'm yours," I say, kissing him from his lips down to his neck. "I'm always going to be yours."

"You're mine. Your pussy, your body, and your fucking heart. All of it's mine."

"Yes," I moan.

Hayden leans down and nips my nipple making me cry out his name and clench my thighs around him. My mouth forms into an 'O' as I clench around him. Pleasure bursts throughout my body.

My back arches against him as he keeps going in and out of me roughly, not taking a second to stop.

"Fuck," he grunts, still holding my throat as he pushes inside me one last time, staying buried to the hilt. I feel his warm cum spurt inside me as I tremble against him. His lips move to mine as he says, "I love you. There's nothing I wouldn't do for you."

I kiss him back and say, "I love you."

Seventeen

Jaclyn

"Can I get the Pasta alla Norma and the kid's pizza please?" Natalia asks before giving the menu to the waiter.

"I'll just get the tomato soup." I set down the menu and he takes it.

"Can I get you guys anything else? Maybe drinks from our specialty menu?"

Natalia raises an eyebrow at me. "I'm good. Thank you. The water is fine."

"I'll get a glass of your best wine. White, please," Natalia says.

The waiter nods his head and then leaves our table.

It's the next day.

I couldn't sleep all night because all I could think about was Hayden and the feel of him.

The way his lips caressed mine and how his warm, rough hands held my face, making me feel like I was special and delicate.

I'm not going to sit and lie and say that I don't miss him because god, after yesterday I miss him. I miss how he would hold me and touch me.

But then the memories of that night come back into my mind and I'm back to wanting to protect myself and my peace.

I may not be happy but at least I'm at peace.

But at what cost?

"So who's coming?" I ask Natalia while sipping on my water.

Lilah is sitting next to her, watching something on her tablet instead of paying attention to our conversation.

She is kind of like Junior.

He is always wanting to watch TV or a video on his tablet or my phone. I sometimes don't let him because I hate how focused he is on that. Sometimes I let him watch TV while we eat but only on rare occasions. Most of the time I want to talk to Junior about his day at school, what he learned, what he did, or how he got along with his friends and classmates.

Natalia arrived in Italy this morning and immediately wanted to have lunch. She also said a few people will be joining us which makes me assume it's my old friends from college.

"Chris is coming with Max, Max's boyfriend, and Kayden."

I widen my eyes because how in the hell does Max have a boyfriend? "I didn't know Max had a boyfriend."

"They started dating like two or three years ago. After you left, he kind of hit a dry spell I guess, saying no one attracted him and he was just bored. But one night at a club he met Martin, his boyfriend, and they both got drunk before hooking up."

"I would have never guessed he would run that way. He always seemed so cocky with girls." I chuckle lightly and Natalia nods her head.

She looks behind me and her smile widens. "Speak of the devil."

"Well if it isn't Jaclyn Marie fucking King." I turn my head and see Max. My smile widens and I stand up before bringing him into a hug. "Knew you couldn't stay away from me forever, diner girl."

I laugh and let go of him. I take a good look at Max and notice a major difference with him. He has short, platinum blonde hair instead of dark brown hair. He looks good with this hair color. I would never expect him to rock light colored hair but it looks charming on him. It fits him really well.

"You look great, Max. I love the new hair."

Max smirks. "Me? You look just as beautiful as I remember."

I force a smile on my face at the comment.

He's fucking lying.

I mean look at you.

I look behind Max and see Kayden standing next to a guy I don't know. "Hi, Kayden." I walk towards him and hug him. He hugs me back. I have missed Kayden. He is the kind of friend that everyone needs in their life. Kayden listens and won't judge, no matter how bad or crazy you are or sound. I let go of him. "How are you?"

Kayden still looks the same. Brown hair, light eyes, and the same brooding look on his face.

"I'm good. Have been busy with work mostly but I had to come out and see if you weren't just a ghost and if Max was being serious about you being in Italy," Kayden says. "How are you?"

"I'm good," I say and smile, making sure he doesn't see the facade.

But Kayden knows.

He is observant just like Hayden. "Okay," Kayden says before nodding his head.

He knows I'm full of bullshit.

Max introduces me to his boyfriend Martin before we all sit down. Chris is sitting next to Lilah with Natalia next to her. I am sitting next to Max and Kayden with Martin on the other side of Max.

"Hayden couldn't make it. He has to do some things with Rowan and Killian."

Kayden rolls his eyes. "Better not be doing stupid shit."

"He always does stupid shit," Max chuckles.

"Killian is a horrible influence on Hayden. Rowan is the only one who keeps him in check," Kayden mutters.

"Who are Killian and Rowan?" I ask.

"Killian is Hayden's boss slash friend and Rowan is Hayden's older brother."

My eyes widen. Natalia had mentioned this but never explained. "Brother?"

Kayden looks at me and nods. "It's a long story."

One that I would like to know.

I can't believe I wasn't there for Hayden when he met his biological brother. It makes me feel like shit that I left him alone and wasn't there for him when he found his brother.

"Anyways. Let's change the subject," Max says before turning his attention to Kayden. "This motherfucker won't take pictures of me and Martin."

"Because I don't feel like taking pictures of you two having sex. Sorry."

Max's jaw drops and he looks like he wants to jump across the table and bitch slap Kayden. Martin chuckles and rests his hand on Max's shoulder. "I'm going to kill you one day."

"You keep saying that." Kayden rolls his eyes before

looking at me. "We have a lot to catch up on. Can you believe that Max was gay this whole time?"

"Shut up, dickhead. I am not gay, I'm bisexual. I like boys and girls," Max says while glaring at Kayden.

"Do your parents know?" I ask.

I know Max's parents are super strict and prejudiced.

Max nods his head. "I told them a month or two after I started dating Martin. When I told them they didn't feel comfortable or happy with me swinging the other way. My father thought I was less of a man or whatever bullshit he makes up in his brain. My mother was more accepting. It just took her some time. She convinced my dad and they both had a talk with me and met Martin. Everything's all good now."

I smile while saying, "That's great, Max. I'm happy for you. You look happy with Martin," I say before looking at Martin as well.

Martin is looking at Max with love in his eyes and for a second I just wish I could have that.

When can I have that? Love seems so impossible now and all I want to do is give up sometimes.

But I know someone is out there for me who won't leave.

There was and then you fucking ruined it.

God, I need to take my meds and possibly talk to Patience about these thoughts.

"Thank you. Martin makes me happy," Max says, smiling at his boyfriend.

I look away from them when Max pecks Martin's lips. I look at Kayden and his face looks similar to how I feel.

Longing, wanting, waiting.

But for the moment I fake the smile and pretend everything is fine because it is.

I need to focus on bettering myself.

I can't focus on a guy, or Hayden, to be more specific.

Eighteen

Hayden

"Jaclyn King? I don't understand what's so special about her," my brother says, as he sits across from me in his office.

We are at his house in Lombardy. It's about an hour or two flight from here to Gaeta, where everyone else is staying.

Rowan can't come back and forth too much because of the academy and his family. So I came here since I needed to talk to him.

Seeing Jaclyn, touching her, having her in my arms after more than four years fucked me up.

More than seeing her at the fight did.

And then when she mentioned Nicole and how she doesn't want to help me cheat, I almost punched the fucking wall because she literally couldn't be more wrong. But it's not like I can tell her because that will fuck things up for Killian.

I just have to wait for him to finish finalizing this deal before I can rid myself of Nicole and her family. They have been a goddamn headache since I met them a year ago.

"I don't know either." I lean into the chair and rub my jaw. "She frustrates the fuck out of me even after this many years."

"She's the girl who ran away five years ago?" Rowan asks and I nod my head.

Rowan has dark brown hair like mine but his eyes are different. He has hazel eyes, dark blue mixed in with brown making them unique. He's taller than me by a few inches although I have more muscle on me. Other than the small differences we look similar.

He is what I imagined my biological brother would look like.

I knew exactly who he was when I first saw him. Kayden took me to a fight about an hour or two outside of town. We ended up at a high end club where people with tuxedos and gowns were watching grown men almost kill each other in a cage. They would bet a lot of money and sometimes even buy the fighter for some shady business they were involved in.

That night I met Rowan.

He came into my dressing room after my fight and

explained how I'm his brother and I'm not the only one. I have more siblings. A few sisters and a lot of brothers.

I've met them all in the last four years but I'm the closest with Rowan because we share the same parents.

He told me my dad was a piece of shit who would rape anything with two legs. I know he killed him because one day when I was eighteen I got a call from him saying our father died from a gunshot wound.

He didn't know our mother much. He just knew that our mom was a druggie who couldn't stand the thought of not getting high off some fucked up shit daily.

I haven't told him about my past with her because I don't like reliving those memories.

The ones where I had to hide in the cabinets so she wouldn't find me and ask for me to try some of her new *candy* with her.

Jaclyn does though.

She knows everything because I ripped my heart out of my chest and laid it in front of her for the taking.

And what did she do?

She fucking left it on the floor like it was nothing.

Like my love wasn't enough.

"I always knew we were going to face each other again. There's just something about her that I will never be able to forget. If it's not her Rowan, it's no one."

Rowan licks his bottom lip before saying. "I understand that. She was a big part of your life and you both went through hell together. You will always be in love with her. There is no way to stop that."

I stand up from the chair and pace. "I just fucking wish I could do something about it."

"You did. You kissed her."

I did.

And it felt fucking amazing.

I swear I saw stars when I was kissing her. It felt like everything was okay for just those few seconds and like the world wasn't falling apart anymore.

Everything was quiet.

When I told Rowan, he wasn't happy and I knew that Killian wouldn't be happy either if I told him.

But I couldn't help it.

I swear I'm not someone who "cheats" but with Nicole, we aren't even together. It's all for show and Jaclyn just doesn't know that.

"She's different but not in a good way."

Rowan furrows his eyebrows and tilts his head to the side. "How so?"

"She lost a lot of weight and I don't think she did that by being healthy. She's colder, more guarded."

"She went through a lot, Hayden. You have no clue what happened to her in that room."

"I know. Fuck, I know. I wish I did so I could help her," I say, my voice growing louder as I get more frustrated.

"What are you going to do about Killian?"

Killian is not just a friend but he's also my boss. He is one of the most powerful people in the world. His father used to take the crown but Killian is more ruthless and cold.

He cares for no one. If someone is in his way they will get burned by him. If you're in Killian's way, you may as well be dead.

Killian wanted to meet me because he knew about my fighting history. He hired me as his personal fighter. Taking care of his dirty work but also earning money in underground clubs. Killian doesn't have a second in command but he has men.

I don't know what that makes me to him but he trusts me a lot to involve me in his business and not just the fights.

But if I fucked with his business, for example, messing up this arrangement with Nicole, I'm considered dead.

"I have no clue. But he won't find out."

Rowan shakes his head lightly. "You're playing with fire. Literally."

"It's okay if I get burned, as long as I have her."

Rowan was about to say something but the door of his office opens.

Apollo and Mateo, Rowan's two sons, come running in. "Papa, papa! We made pictures!" Mateo says with a lisp.

He is about four, I think.

I never really paid attention to their ages. But I know Apollo is seven or eight.

He has a daughter, Rosalie, but she is with her mother somewhere in the house. Mateo and Apollo are always getting into trouble, causing Rowan and his wife headaches.

But Rowan and his wife love a busy and loud house.

Rowan stands from his chair and grabs Mateo, holding him on his hip as he looks at the picture. Apollo stares at his father with a big smile on his face.

"Looks amazing, Mateo. Let me see yours, Apollo."

Apollo gives his father the paper and Rowan smiles as he looks down at the picture. He loves his family, that much I'm sure of.

Anytime I see him with his kids or his wife I always wish that was me. Yes, being alone is peaceful and calm but I can't help but want someone, a specific someone, to have a family with me.

I had that but then it all fucking burned down.

"Mama said mine was better," Apollo says with a smirk, looking just like his father.

"Liar!" Mateo says before looking at me. "Uncle, look at my picture and say it's better!"

I laugh at Mateo. I walk towards them and look at the pictures. Rowan eyes me probably thinking, 'you better not break their little hearts you little shit.'

"Both look amazing." I smile at them, but that's not the answer either of them were hoping for.

"Where's your mother and sister?"

"In the kitchen," Apollo says before running out of the office.

We all leave Rowan's office. Rowan is still holding Mateo as we walk inside the kitchen and see Rowan's wife, Jane, and his daughter baking while laughing. Rowan's daughter is around nine years old but she still looks so tiny and young still.

Rowan puts Mateo down and he walks behind his wife, placing his lips on her neck while she squeals and blushes. She turns around and kisses him back passionately.

"Ew! Papa, that's gross," Apollo yells while grimacing.

"Shut up, you idiot. They are cute," Rosalie says with a smile as she watches her parents just fall in love.

Rowan stops kissing Jane and he wraps his arms around her.

"Hi, Hayden. I didn't know you were here today. How are you?" Jane asks.

I can see why Rowan is so obsessed with her. Jane has beautiful brown curly hair and dark brown eyes. She is wearing a blue summer dress that compliments her skin well. But her smile is what makes me understand why Rowan loves her so much.

I love seeing Jaclyn smile.

It's one of my favorite things on this fucking planet.

He was her bodyguard for a good few months before they started dating. She used to have selective mutism but then after a while she started talking with Rowan and they became closer before dating.

"It's going good. Been busy. You know how it is with Killian and my brother."

Jane's best friend happens to be Killian's sister, Thalia. I only have met her a couple of times during family dinners that Killian has invited me to.

Jane glares at her husband. "I hope you aren't giving him a rough time."

"Little shit is fine. Always causing me and Killian trouble."

If by trouble you mean trying to get the girl who ran away back, then yeah.

Jaclyn King has no clue what's coming.

Nineteen

Jaclyn

From what Natalia showed me yesterday, Gaeta is absolutely beautiful.

We walked along the beach after lunch and caught up some more. I learned that Martin is a clothing designer. He showed me some of his cool designs. He told me he loves street style and he is always having an idea spark whenever he is out and about. Max is his number one supporter but also his main model which I love for them.

Max looks so incredibly happy with Martin. He looks like he's in his element.

Kayden has been traveling to London a lot, visiting one of his friends out there. He is living in his hometown in California. I didn't know he lived there because he never mentioned it.

He told me he doesn't like to think too much about his time there.

After we finished catching up, we all went back to our rooms. When I got into my room I watched some TV and worked for a little while until I got a call from Brandon.

Junior was getting ready for school when they called me. Junior told me he was having fun hanging out with Brandon and that he misses and loves me.

I was asking Brandon to make sure that Junior took his meds and ate a good breakfast. Brandon got annoyed with me and hung up so that they could leave, but not before Brandon asked me if I've been taking my meds.

The only thing I feel like could help me and my confidence is just seeing Junior in person.

I wish I could just grab Junior through the phone and squeeze him in my arms.

I turn the water off and grab my towel from the rack. I wrap myself in the white towel before opening the bathroom door.

I scream and flinch when I see a familiar tall figure standing in front of the window. Hayden turns around, a soft expression on his face when he looks at me.

I hold onto the towel for dear life as I stare at him. "What the hell are you doing here?"

Hayden walks away from the window and towards me. "Enjoying the view." His eyes rake over my body and I swear I see his pupils dilate. He turns his head to the window. "You have a nice view of the beach."

I narrow my eyes at him when he looks back at me.

Today Hayden is wearing a cream colored collared shirt and black trousers. The shoes are Loro Piana which are a very expensive brand.

He dresses so differently from how he dressed in college. His style is more mature and clean. On his Instagram, I would sometimes see him in his usual street style whenever he's out and about in New York.

My eyes go to the ring on his ring finger.

Why would he kiss me with that stupid ring on his finger?

"How did you even get in?" Hayden ignores the question and walks closer to me. I back up once but he doesn't stop until he has his hand on my waist and pulls me closer to him. "Hayden-"

"Shh," he says quietly before leaning down. I can't help but shiver as he leans down and puts his face in my neck. I suddenly remember that I am wearing just a towel with absolutely nothing underneath. Hayden's soft hair grazes my jaw as he presses his nose against the side of my neck. "God, you have no clue how much restraint I have," he whispers, huskily. "The only reason I haven't claimed what's mine yet is because I am giving you time to adjust to the fact that this is happening," Hayden says in my ear before leaning away from me and looking down at my eyes.

God.

I always knew that Hayden was intense and had a way with his words, but Jesus, I didn't know that he somehow became more smooth.

Even the way he looks down at me like he wants to grab me by the neck and show me that I'm his makes me feel weak in my knees.

But you're not his.

You never will be, remember? He's getting married.

I push myself away from him and glare. "Stop doing that."

Hayden smirks down at me. "Doing what, princess?"

My face softens at the pet name he would always call me.

I was his princess and he was my knight who would always fight for me.

But then that one night happened and ruined everything.

Hearing that nickname after so many years does something to me. It makes me want to run into his arms and forget about the past.

Pretend like nothing ever happened but it did.

I wish sometimes I could just forget everything and not remember what it felt like to finally fall after flying.

"You need to stop flirting with me when you have a fiancé. You're practically cheating on her."

Hayden's smirk vanishes and instead he has on a mask. It's like the ones he puts on in fights so that no one knows what his next move is.

"You need to stop assuming things."

I raise my eyebrows. "Assuming things? You are literally having a wedding in Italy."

Hayden shakes his head lightly. "How was your shower?"

"Fine," I say, while gripping onto my towel together as if it will fall right off. "Can you leave so I can change?" Hayden chuckles lightly as a knock sounds on the door. I leave Hayden standing in the middle of the room as I go to the door. I open it a little and see two familiar faces. "Alex! Carter! How are you guys?" I ask while bringing Alex into a hug. Carter was never the type of person to hug people.

"It's so good to see you sweetheart," Alex says before I let her go. "How have you been? We've missed you so much."

She has a wide smile on her face while Carter just has his regular straight face on.

Even though he isn't Hayden's biological father, Hayden and him are so similar it's almost creepy.

I smile while saying, "I'm doing great. Just busy with work mostly."

"That's good. What are you doing right now?" Carter

asks before his eyes move to Hayden who comes up from behind me. "I didn't know you were in here."

Hayden pulls me behind him and it's only now that I realize I'm in just a towel.

I need to change asap.

"I came to check on her. She loves sleeping in and well we are in Italy. We can't be sleeping in when we have such little time here, yes?" Hayden says and Carter just glares at Hayden.

So they still don't have the best relationship.

Alex smiles, looking up at Carter. "Isn't that sweet? It's great that both of you are here actually." Alex looks back at Hayden and I. "I need you guys to go to the store for me and grab a couple of things if that's alright?"

"Of course, Alex," Hayden smiles down at her before looking at me. "You aren't doing anything anyways right?"

I look away from Hayden and look at Alex who has a smile on her face.

I nip my bottom lip and curse at Hayden in my head.

"Sure. I'd be happy to." I smile at them. "I just need to change."

"Of course. We'll let you get to it." Alex says before leaving with Carter.

Carter takes Hayden out of the room so I can change.

While changing I think about what a horrible idea this is.

Twenty

Jaclyn

We walk outside the hotel doors and a beautiful red Ferrari Spider is parked right in the front.

A valet guy hands the keys to Hayden as he walks around to the passenger side of the car and opens the door.

What the hell?

I knew Hayden has always had a lot of money. I mean in college he did have a Porsche but that was mostly Carter's doing, not Hayden.

I'm sure now with all of his success, Hayden has his own money to buy any kind of car he wants.

"This is yours?" I ask, walking closer to the car.

"Yea. I leave it here because I sometimes come out here for work so it's just easier. Get in."

When I sit down in the passenger seat, Hayden closes the door and comes around to the drivers side of the car and gets in.

The car roars to life, sounding absolutely beautiful.

He drives off as I admire the inside of the car. I've never been inside a Ferrari before so I'm a little starstruck. Ferraris are one of my favorite cars right behind BMW.

I don't know what it is about BMWs but they have my heart.

"What do you do for work other than fighting?"

"It's all mostly fighting. I just have to do other stuff that involves fighting which earns me a lot of money."

"Is it like back in Arizona?" I ask, hesitantly.

Neither of us have spoken about Arizona, mostly because I don't want to speak about Arizona. I just hope that what Hayden's doing is smart and he isn't being stupid and ruining his life by doing dirty fighting again.

Hayden slows down the car so that a mother and her child can cross the street. He takes the time to look at me, guilt appearing on his face.

"Not exactly," Hayden mutters before laying on the gas.

What could he possibly be doing if he isn't exactly doing what he did in Arizona?

For some reason I feel like what he is doing now other than professional fighting isn't a good thing.

My phone buzzes, making me look down. I see a text

from Brandon so I turn my body slightly away from Hayden so he doesn't see the text. Hayden looks over at me and furrows his eyebrows. His hands on the wheel tighten but he doesn't say anything.

> Junior had a good day at school. He is currently coloring a page that his teacher gave him for homework.

Brandon then sends a picture where Junior is posing with the picture he colored.

I can't help but smile down at the photo of him. I have always loved his smile. I can't help but feel like everything is okay when he smiles.

It's just so ironic how much he looks like Hayden. He is a mini version of Hayden and if anyone were to see Junior and Hayden side by side they would think so as well.

"Who's that you're texting? Boyfriend?" Hayden says, making me look up at him.

I turn off my phone and put it in my pocket. I'll text Brandon later, I just can't risk Hayden looking at the photo and seeing Junior.

I need to wait a little before I tell Hayden the truth.

I first need to figure out our shit and how this co-parenting would work before I tell him about Junior.

"No. It's just my friend."

"The smile on your face says otherwise." Hayden mutters.

I roll my eyes and can't help but smile at Hayden. I can't believe he is jealous of his own son and doesn't know it. "I'm not allowed to smile?"

"You're only allowed to smile at my texts."

"I don't even have your number. Get over yourself, Hayden," I chuckle.

Hayden's hands clench around the wheel but he continues driving.

He eventually parks in the parking lot of a mall. Hayden quickly gets out and before I can open my own door, Hayden is already on it. I get out and he closes the door. Before I can walk away from him he grabs my wrist and pushes me against his car.

I try to ignore the fact that I can smell his cologne that makes me want to put my head in his neck and smell him forever.

"Your phone. Give it to me," Hayden demands.

I raise an eyebrow at him and almost laugh.

He thinks he has the right to boss me around?

"Excuse me?"

"Your phone. Give me it."

"Why?"

"You said that I don't have your number, well give me your phone so we can fix that."

I roll my eyes.

There is no way I'll give him my phone. He could probably snoop and see pictures of Junior.

"Give me yours, I'll put mine." Hayden takes out his phone and hands it to me. I type in my number and hand it back to him. "Let's go, we don't have all day." I walk out from between Hayden and the car. Hayden follows me after locking his car. "What do we need to get for your mom?"

"Just some stuff for the beach and some melatonin pills for her since she has insomnia."

"She has trouble sleeping?" I ask, feeling bad for Alex because I never knew that about her.

"Yea. It's not bad or anything. She just can't sleep unless she has melatonin. She would take the drugs her doctor prescribed but she doesn't like the effect it has on her."

I wish I could take melatonin instead of the drugs that Patience prescribed for me. I am almost running out and I just hope I have enough to last me this trip but since I'm taking one every single day, I'm not sure.

Hayden and I walk inside the convenience store and head to the medical section. "How's your diabetes? I never asked."

"It's okay." I lie.

I mean I'm doing better than I was before I had Junior. But it's sometimes hard to manage it, especially if I'm having one of those days.

"Is it seriously okay or are you just trying to make sure I don't worry?" Hayden asks, giving me a side eye probably knowing that I am lying.

"It's better. Despite what you might think, I am doing a lot better than I was five years ago."

"I believe you. I just can't help but think something else is wrong or there's something you're hiding from me."

This should be the time where I tell him, "Oh you have a four year old son, whose name is Hayden Junior Night and he looks exactly like you. I lied because I was protecting myself. I wish I could have told you sooner but you just reminded me of all the bad memories, so I had to hide from you to make sure I don't have those memories again. Sorry."

But in the middle of the day in a convenience store is not the time. Especially since he is getting married soon.

It's just not the right time.

But will it ever be?

Instead, I don't say anything to Hayden. I just walk past him and go to the vitamins. Hayden looks at all of the containers and grabs two that he thinks are the best.

Hayden pays for the melatonin and we leave the store. We walk around the mall, not really saying much to one another. Hayden would ask questions and I would answer but that's it.

He asks about my career, me living in New York, how my mom and uncle are, etc.

I try not to ask him much because I don't want to build that relationship we had. I don't want to be interested in him. I want to forget about him and pretend that what we had doesn't affect me everyday.

Hayden and I walk inside another store that has a beach vibe. They have bikinis on one side and then stuff for the pool and beach on the other. Hayden goes to where the sunscreen is and he grabs a couple of bottles of it. Probably for everyone to use since there are a lot of people that might need it. Hayden then walks towards where the clothes are.

Hayden looks at the bikini section and a smirk appears on his face. He looks down at me and says, "Wanna try some bikinis on for me?"

My face can't help but turn red.

Memories of Hayden and I at Victoria Secret come to mind.

One time when we were in Utah visiting his family we went to the mall and Hayden took me to Victoria Secret because he wanted to buy me some stuff there. He ended up fingering me in one of the dressing rooms. After that he bought me all the lingerie I tried on and it came out to almost $700.

Hayden's smirk widens as he sees my face turning even more red probably. My face feels so hot I think I might explode or something and then the butterflies in my stomach decide to make an appearance as well.

"No," I say before walking away.

I need to get away from him. This flirting between us has to stop.

He is getting married!

I can't be doing this.

I feel horrible for letting Hayden kiss me already when he has a fiancé.

And the fact that I can't stop these feelings from arising again makes me feel even more shitty.

Hayden and I don't talk when we pay for the stuff. We walk back to his car in peace and I help him put all of the stuff we bought in his trunk.

I shiver while putting the stuff away. I wish I brought a jacket instead of just wearing this dress.

Today I decided to wear a blue summer dress with small flowers on it with white tennis shoes. I felt cute today and my hair looks good so I wanted to dress nice for my first day out and about in Italy.

Hayden grabs his jacket from the trunk and he puts it around my shoulders. I turn my head to look at him and see him looking down at me with that same soft expression he's been giving me lately.

I feel myself getting lost in his eyes constantly now. It's impossible to just look away from him and forget the feelings I have for him.

I always knew that Junior's eyes looked familiar and now I know why. His father has the same intense gaze as him but it's completely different.

Junior looks up at me with adoration and love while his father looks down at me like he wants me for himself and never wants the world to look at me.

Hayden looks at me like every girl wishes to be looked at.

"Thank you," I mutter and he just nods his head and closes the trunk.

Hayden opens the door for me and I get in. He gets in afterwards and starts the car.

"What's wrong?" Hayden asks as he drives off.

"Nothing," I mutter and look out the window.

The car stops in the middle of the street and I feel Hayden's hand grip my chin forcing me to look at him. "When I'm talking to you I want you to look at me. Understand?" I glare at him and take my face out of his hand. When I don't answer him he grips the steering wheel. "Do you understand, Jaclyn?"

"Yea, whatever," I say, rolling my eyes at him.

Hayden's jaw clenches. "Why are you mad?"

"I'm not."

"Really? I think you keep forgetting that I know you, even after five years. I know when you're lying, when you're low, when you're sad, mad, tired, or when you need help with something. I even know when you're about to fucking orgasm. I know it all, princess."

My jaw drops and I look at him with wide eyes. "You can't just say things like that, Hayden."

Hayden rolls his eyes.

God we're all just rolling our eyes a bunch today, aren't we?

"Why not? It's true."

"Because you have a damn fiancé!" I argue.

"Will you stop assuming shit like that? You have no fucking clue." Hayden chuckles lightly but he for sure doesn't think I'm funny.

Hayden parks the car in front of the hotel after the rest of the drive being silent.

"I hate you so much," I mutter, as I get out of the car and grab my bag.

"What'd you just say?" Hayden asks but I ignore him and close the door. I hear another door open and close making me assume that Hayden got out of the car. I feel his hand grip my wrist and turn me around to make me look at him. "Why? Why do you keep lying?" Hayden holds my face in his hand and his face is just a few inches away from mine. "Why do you keep telling me lies from these pretty little lips that were once mine?"

I look up at him and try not to cry because every time I try to hate him I always feel so frustrated because it's hard to hate Hayden after everything.

Especially after the last thing he told me that night.

"Whenever you're ready, I'll be here. I'll be waiting for you," he mumbles before letting go of me and leaving without looking back.

"Because you were the one person who I truly felt loved by. I can't help but feel horrible for missing these moments and wishing everything could go back to normal when we both know they can't. And the fact that I have to be here and watch you get married hurts, Hayden. It hurts, right here," I say, while pressing a finger to where my heart is. "I know I told you we needed to go our separate ways but I just wish it was easier to do that. I sometimes wish I didn't meet you so that I didn't have to know what love felt like." Hayden's face softens as he looks down with sympathy. "You are the one who truly cared enough to love me enough to go to the extreme for me and now I have to live with the fact that you are marrying someone else after you made love to me and cared for me the way no one else has."

In reality I don't hate him.

I can never hate Hayden. I just hate the fact that I ruined everything.

I walk away from Hayden and his hand disappears from my cheek.

Twenty-One

Jaclyn

The sound of my phone rings, waking me up. I turn in my bed and grab my phone. The time on my phone reads 5:06.

A picture of Hayden pops up on my phone as he calls. I answer and bring the phone to my ear, laying back down in my bed. "Hi," I say before yawning.

"Hi, princess. Sorry for waking you," Hayden says from the other side of the phone.

"It's okay. What's up? Is everything okay?"

"Yea. Everything's fine. Get dressed and make sure to wear something comfortable like leggings and a sweater," Hayden suggests.

"Why? It's five in the morning and it's still dark

outside," I say before sitting up in my bed and rubbing my eyes.

"I know. But I told you we would be doing something today, right?"

I take my phone away from my ear and see the date. March 22nd.

Yesterday was Hayden's birthday. For his dinner, the group went to the diner and then after that Hayden dropped me off home.

He said that I had to go home if I wanted to get some sleep tonight and now I remember why.

Today is our one year anniversary.

Hayden and I have been dating for a year now and somehow it feels like we just met yesterday.

"You don't just want to come to my bed and sleep?" I offer but Hayden just chuckles.

"No. I'd rather take you somewhere and we can just chill there. I'll be there soon okay?"

"Okay."

Hayden and I end the call so I get out of bed slowly and get ready.

I change into a pair of black leggings and a black zip up jacket with a tank top underneath. I brush out my hair and throw it in a ponytail.

My phone buzzes on my bed so I walk over and see a text from Hayden.

Come out, princess.

I stuff my phone in my pocket and grab my bag before leaving the house. I go down the driveway and see Hayden's black Porsche parked in the front. Hayden is leaning against the door and as I walk closer he opens the passenger door.

I see a big bouquet of pink and white peonies. There is a red box labeled Cartier next to the bouquet.

My jaw drops and I look at Hayden who has a small smile on his face. Hayden almost looks shy as he watches me in complete awe of the flowers and gift.

I still have the tiara necklace from him since last Christmas. I don't ever take it off and sometimes I see Hayden looking down at the necklace with a proud smile.

I mean, I got him a gift too but it wasn't this extravagant.

Kind of.

"Hayden, you didn't have to get me all this." I smile up at him and he just grabs my hand and pulls me closer to him.

"I wanted to. Plus, you love it when I give you flowers."

God I do.

I have a box full of small notes and flowers that he has given me over the past year. Sometimes he plucks random flowers from the grass and he gives me them. I think those flowers are the best.

"I know but you didn't have to get me anything expensive."

"I wanted to. Now get in. You can put the flowers in the back." I put the flowers in the back seat with a big smile on my face and he grabs the box from me and stuffs it in his pocket.

I already have a feeling I know what's inside the box but I don't say anything. Hayden gets inside the car and closes his door. Before he puts the car in drive I lean over to his side of the car and kiss him.

"Thank you, Hayden," I mumble against his lips before he kisses me back passionately.

"Happy Anniversary," he mumbles before he leans away and kisses my cheek. "I have to stop kissing you now or else I'll start kissing you between your legs."

"Hayden!" I squeal, my cheeks turning red.

"It's true," Hayden says, before he starts driving and pulls out of my driveway.

Hayden drives for a good twenty to thirty minutes before he pulls over to the side of the road.

We go to the abandoned building all the time. Hayden says it's our spot and whenever we need a break from the group or to hide away from Eric and all of the Marco bullshit, this is where we come.

I love this spot because this is where we can just be vulnerable with one another.

Hayden and I get to the building and he lays down the long blanket he always brings for us. I rest the other blankets and pillows on top of the blanket and then sit down.

Hayden sits next to me and he pulls me closer to him before turning my head to face his. He captures my lips, in a demanding and passionate way that steals my breath and makes me feel needy for him.

It stays romantic and sweet, our feelings seeping through the contact between him and me. His body heat is radiating onto mine making me feel much warmer than I was a few seconds ago. His touch is gentle but firm, drawing me closer to him.

His rough and demanding kisses always make me want to melt because I love the way he makes me think about nothing other than him.

I lean away from him a little. "I have something for you."

"Me first," Hayden says before bringing out the Cartier box. He gives it to me and I smile, taking it. I open the box and see a ring with a heart covered in diamonds.

"Hayden," I whisper while staring at the ring in awe. This ring probably costs so much money and I hate how much money he always spends on me. He doesn't always give me expensive gifts like this but when he does, he always goes all out. "You really-"

"I got this ring for you because I am going to marry you one day." Hayden takes the box from me and grabs the ring from the box. "I don't want to marry anyone else other than you. If I'm not marrying you, I'm not marrying anyone." Hayden slides the ring on the ring finger of my right hand. "This is a promise ring if you can't tell," Hayden jokes and I smile at him completely and utterly in love and awe.

I look down at the ring and smile. "I love it so much." I lean forward and kiss him on the lips lightly. "Thank you."

"Anything," Hayden mumbles against my lips, trying to deepen it but I move away from him to stop him.

"My turn." I back away from him and take off my jacket. I lift up the side of my shirt and reveal the tattoo to him.

Hayden's eyes darken with lust and he leans closer and places his hand on my ribs, lightly touching the tattoo. I flinch and suck in a breath, loving his touch on me.

"Jaclyn," he says, not looking away from the tattoo. "Why did you get it?"

The tattoo is a small outline of boxing gloves with Hayden's initials underneath.

"Because no matter what happens, I won't ever forget you or be able to forget you. Whether we stay together, fight, or break up, I never want to forget you or how you made me feel," I say with complete honesty. "Do you not like it?" I ask, worried about his reaction because he isn't saying anything.

Hayden furrows his eyebrows and looks up at me. "God, no. I love it." Hayden leans towards the tattoo and kisses the spot. "I wish I could have gotten one before you."

"You want to get a tattoo for me?" I ask, pulling my shirt down.

"Yea. I've been wanting to get one." Hayden nods his head and then he pulls me closer to him so that we are touching one another again.

"Of what?" I ask, smiling up at him.

"Maybe a crown or peonies. They just remind me of you."

I can't stop smiling or looking at him with love in my eyes because I genuinely am so in love with this boy that I know my heart is in so much trouble.

"I love you."

Hayden leans down and presses his lips against mine. "I love you."

Twenty-Two

Jaclyn

"You look so pretty, mommy," Junior says, thrusting his face into the phone as Brandon holds it.

"Thank you baby. Did you do all your homework today?" I ask.

"No. I wanted to see you. I miss you," Junior says with a guilty smile.

I can't help but smile at him. "I know baby, I miss you too. So much. Brandon has been telling me that you've been such a good boy. I'm so proud of you, baby." I say, making Junior's cheeks turn red.

God I love it when he is shy. He looks so cute, especially when he hides his face into Brandon's chest while blushing.

Tonight I'm going to dinner with the group, Alex,

Carter, Nicole's parents, and Nicole's friends. It will definitely be interesting since I've never been with Hayden and Nicole in the same room and I'll be meeting Nicole's parents as well.

I'm nervous as hell but Natalia said I shouldn't be.

I'm wearing a long black, silky dress with a slit in the right thigh. It's not too revealing but it's also not too modest which I think makes this dress perfect. I've had this dress sitting in my closet for a while but never got the chance to use it. My hair is straightened and I did my makeup too.

"Well, I have to go Junior and you need to do your homework. But I love you so much and I miss you a million."

"I love you too." Junior smiles widely.

We end the call after I say bye to Brandon.

I grab my bag and leave the hotel. The restaurant is not too far so I decided to walk.

Natalia asked if I wanted to go with her and the boys but I had to FaceTime Junior, so I told them I'd just meet them there.

The walk isn't long to the restaurant. About ten minutes.

A gentleman opens the door for me and welcomes me in. I walk up to the hostess stand and she smiles at me and asks me what I need.

"I'm Jaclyn. I'm here for a reservation for Nicole Earnings."

The host nods her head and grabs a menu. She tells me to follow her which I do. She brings me to the table and Natalia stands when she sees me but Nicole is the one who walks up to me with a smile on her face.

Oh my God, does she know I kissed her future husband?

"Jaclyn! So happy you made it!" Nicole says before wrapping her arms around me and hugging me.

I tense as she hugs me but I hug her back and force a smile on my face. "Sorry I'm late. I decided to walk," I say before looking behind her.

My eyes immediately go to Hayden who is staring at me. He doesn't look that happy.

We haven't talked since the day we went to the mall for Alex. It's been two days since then and I've mostly just been hanging out with Natalia and the boys. I don't know where Hayden has been and when I asked Kayden, he said that Hayden was in Lombardy with his brother.

Nicole pulls me towards an older man and woman, making me look away from Hayden. "These are my parents, Jonah and Maria." Jonah and Maria stand up and shake my hand but I notice the fake smiles appearing on their faces. "This is Jaclyn."

"You're that reporter that interviewed Hayden a few weeks ago?" Maria asks.

"Yes," I say with a small smile.

"How do you know them?"

How does she know that I know them?

"I met Natalia and the boys in college. We all just happened to grow closer. But your daughter invited me to the wedding which I was happy to attend."

"Strange," Maria says with furrowed eyebrows. She looks at her daughter and then back at me. "Well I hope you enjoy dinner."

I smile and nod my head. Nicole smiles at me, a little too wide might I add, and then she sits with her parents.

"Jaclyn, here," Natalia says, making me turn around to look at her sitting on the other side of the table. I walk towards her. She is sitting next to Lilah while Chris is sitting on the other side of her. "You look so beautiful," Natalia compliments me before leaning closer. "Sorry, the only seat was the one next to Hayden," Natalia whispers. I look behind her and see Hayden talking to Kayden who is sitting across from him.

"That's fine." I smile down at her but I'm really cursing her out.

I know what she's doing.

She's been talking to me about Hayden non-stop in the past two days. She told me that Alex and Carter told her that they caught us together in my room with only a towel. I explained to her that it was a misunderstanding and Hayden and I weren't hooking up.

I'm not the type of person who helps someone else cheat.

I walk to the chair next to Hayden's. I place my purse around the chair and sit down next to him. "Hi, Kayden," I say with a small smile.

"Hi. You look nice," Kayden says with a smile that would probably make a girl's underwear melt off her.

Kayden has always been attractive to me but Hayden is the one who stole my heart.

"Thank you. So do you. How are you liking Italy?"

"It's nice. I'm loving the beach and getting a small break from the city."

Everyone at the table gets into their own conversation. Alex and Carter are talking to Nicole's parents. They are just talking about how Hayden and Nicole were as kids. Carter is barely talking, it's mostly Alex who has a sweet smile on her face.

"Why are you avoiding me?" Hayden says in my ear, his lips bumping against my lobe.

Goosebumps break out on my skin but I try to ignore the way my stomach fills with butterflies.

"It's only been two days. How can I avoid you when I've barely had the chance to see you. You've also been in Lombardy."

"Asking about me?" Hayden says and I can practically see the smirk on his face.

I turn my head to face him. "No."

"Natalia said you have to do an interview with me for your work?"

"And?" I raise an eyebrow at him.

"Tomorrow on the beach."

I chuckle lightly. "Not happening. Kayden and I are hanging out tomorrow on the beach. Sorry." I say with a fake smile before looking away from him. But when I try to talk to Kayden again, I feel a warm hand on my thigh where the slit is. "Hayden, get your hand off my thigh. People will see," I say, glaring at him from the corner of my eye.

I remove his hand but he just puts it back on. Before I can tell him again the lights in the restaurant dim.

"Shh, the show's about to start," Hayden says in my ear.

"Ladies and gentlemen, we have a special performance tonight by Leo De Palma. He will be singing the Italian Version of "I Wanna Be Yours" for a special lady in the audience tonight. Enjoy." The announcer says before leaving the stage.

A man comes on stage and he starts singing.

"I'm going to ask you something and I need you to give me a straight answer, understand?" he asks as he trails his hand up my thigh. "Why do you hate me?"

I look down at his hand and see that fucking golden ring on his ring finger. God I hate this fucking hand right now. I want to cut off his finger so that he won't have that stupid ring anymore.

The feeling of Hayden's hand on the inside of my thigh makes me widen my eyes but I don't look at him. "Hayden, you can't do that with people around," I whisper to him.

"Are you okay?" Kayden asks me, making me focus on him. I smile and nod my head, afraid to speak out loud.

Kayden looks away from Hayden and I and focuses back on the stage.

"Tell me why you hate me," Hayden demands as I feel his finger press against my underwear. "Fuck, princess, you're soaked for me," he whispers in my ear before moving my underwear to the side.

Holy fuck.

I can't believe this is happening.

And I can't believe I'm about to let it happen.

His finger touches my bare pussy and he rubs my clit slowly. "Hayden," I whisper and close my eyes.

"Tell me why you hate me," he whispers in my ear before pushing one finger in.

I grab my water and force myself to drink it instead of letting out a moan.

I can't.

I can't do this.

I can't believe he is doing this.

Oh my God.

"Look at you, princess. Wetting my fingers while we are sitting with other people at the table," he says, getting more aroused by his words. "If you don't tell me, I'll take my hand away and you'll just go back to your hotel room aching and needy." Hayden leans closer and I feel his lips next to my ear. His finger is still moving inside me making me feel weak and sensitive. I'm close. I know it and he knows it too because of the way his finger presses against my clit. I move my hips slightly and let out a soft moan that I try to cover with a cough. "Tell me why you hate me. Tell me why you hate me while you ride my fingers, desperate to get off like my good girl, princess."

I turn my head to him, my face close to his but I try not to lean too close to him.

"Because you belong to someone else. I'm not allowed to touch you, kiss you, or anything. Me and you can never happen again and I hate that," I whisper and close my eyes. "Please, Hayden."

"We'll see about that," he says before he applies more pressure to my clit and forces two fingers in going at a rapid pace.

I come all over his hand and purposely drop something on the floor. I pick it up as I cover my mouth from letting a moan escape and close my eyes while coming on his hand.

Holy shit.

I can't believe I did that.

This is not like me.

Oh my god, I just helped him cheat too.

Jesus Christ I'm such a bad person.

I can't believe that just happened.

That didn't happen.

Holy shit.

That felt so good. I want it to happen again.

I haven't felt that good in so long.

I grab the napkin I threw on the floor and sit back up in my chair.

Hayden removes his hand from my dress and I watch him with my jaw dropped as he licks his fingers discreetly.

Fucking prick.

Twenty-Three

Jaclyn

Present

A big black blanket is laid out on the sand for Hayden and I to sit on.

The nerves in my body are erupting and I can't stop fidgeting with my pen.

Every time I'm near Hayden I always feel like something is about to happen, good or bad, I don't know.

Let's not forget about the butterflies in my stomach either because they just won't leave whenever Hayden is around.

I plan on using my phone to record the conversation so that I can focus on the questions I'm asking him. After I'm done with the questions I'm going to try and get this project done as soon as I can so that Jules doesn't bug me about it.

Most of the questions are things that fans want to know.

His love life, his fighting, his routine, what he eats, etc.

All very basic and simple questions he can answer easily.

Yelling from behind me makes me turn around. I see a group of girls swarming Hayden while yelling for a picture.

Hayden is wearing black shorts and a white button up that is unbuttoned and showing off his beautiful chest and abs.

He looks like every girl's wet dream, I swear to God.

Why does he have to look so perfect?

All I want to do is trace the muscles on his stomach and then watch them clench.

I swear, I feel the spot between my legs pulse as I think about it.

Every time I would give Hayden a massage it would always end up with me screaming his name and asking him to stop but he just went even rougher and faster.

Oh my God.

Married man, Jaclyn.

Married man.

He is getting married.

You already let him kiss you and finger fuck you at a table in front of his future wife.

God I'm so horrible.

Hayden walks up to the blanket after he is done taking pictures with his fans. He gives me a soft smile as he sits down on the blanket. "Sorry, I'm late. I hope you weren't waiting too long."

"It's fine. I was just enjoying the sun," I say, making Hayden nod his head lightly and look down at my body.

I'm wearing a white bikini but I have a tank top covering the waist up.

I just don't want Hayden to see the mark on my side and I know if he sees it, he will make a big deal out of it and demand the story from that night.

The night he only saw blood, but he thought it was from something else, not the tattoo.

Hayden is looking at me like he wants to rip my clothes off and own my world.

I put my phone on record. "Okay, first question," I say, clearing my throat. "Are there any upcoming fights you are excited about?"

"No," Hayden states and I cross off the question.

"The media is going crazy over your engagement to Nicole Earnings. Why did you decide to marry her in the first place?" I read off my notes.

"Because the girl I wanted wasn't there," Hayden states as he stares at me with a straight face.

"Hayden, you can't say things like that in an interview." I narrow my eyes at him.

Hayden looks away from me and stares down at the beach instead. "Wanna go for a swim?"

I raise any eyebrow at him, wondering what kind of drug he is on.

"What?" I say, making Hayden look back at me.

Hayden stands up. "Sorry, let me rephrase. We are going to go for a swim."

I put my notes and pen to the side. "Hayden, you wanted this interview. I am here with a recorder, pen, and paper. I'm not here to go swimming with you."

Hayden leans down so that he is at eye level with me. Him being this close to me awakens my nerves and makes me feel like fire is spreading throughout my body.

Fuck how does he do that?

"Just for a little." He holds out his hand to me and like the fool I am, I take it. He helps me up and I take off my tank top.

Hayden keeps his eyes on me, his eyes burning holes into my chest. I swear I see them darken as he admires me. It feels good that even after so much time has gone by, he still stares at me like I'm the only thing he wants.

But I also can't help but wonder if he is also thinking about everything that could possibly be wrong with my body.

Am I too skinny now for him?

Are my boobs too big from gaining weight from having Junior?

What's wrong with me?

When I turn slightly his eyes go to where the tattoo I got for him used to be. It's now ruined by a scar that Eric created when he dug a knife in my side. It hurt like a bitch and every time I stared at the scar, I would always cry because I felt so weak remembering that moment.

But I'm better now.

I don't cry when I look at the scar, instead I don't look at it at all.

Junior sees the scar sometimes and he always worries about it and wonders why it's there.

I ignore Hayden's eyes and instead walk past him to go in the water.

The water isn't that cold. Hayden and I go deep enough to where the water is over our chests but we still have our feet touching the bottom.

"Do you like your job?" Hayden asks me, making me focus on him.

"Yes," I answer. "Do you like yours?"

"It's fighting. Of course I do," he says with a small smirk.

Hayden and I are close enough to one another to the point where he could just grab me and hold me in his arms while I wrap my legs around his waist but we aren't going to do that.

"How did you start? Most people start professional fighting when they're in their late twenties."

"Are we having our interview in the water?" he teases.

I look around. "I don't see a pen and paper anywhere," I joke.

Hayden smiles at me, swimming closer. The smile on his face reminds me of how he used to smile in college.

His genuine smile lit up my world.

"That can be a story for another time," he says, looking down at my lips before meeting my eyes.

"Will there be another time?" I ask before thinking.

"I want there to be."

I lick my bottom lip before saying, "You know we can't be friends Hayden. We can never be just friends."

Especially since you and I have a kid together that you don't know about yet.

Suddenly, I feel Hayden's warm hands slide on to my waist and pull me closer. I don't push him away, instead I wrap my legs around his waist and hold onto his chest.

God, I'm going to hell.

But I don't care.

Right now, my mind feels quiet and there is no pushy voice in my head telling me what to do.

"I don't want to be just friends with you. I never have." Hayden leans his head against mine. "The day I saw you in that fucking alley, I knew you were going to come knocking on my heart. You dug yourself so deep that I can't fucking get you out, no matter how hard I try to, princess."

I shake my head lightly. "You have to stop saying things like that."

Hayden leans his forehead off my mine and furrows his eyebrows at me. "I can't tell you something that is true?"

"You can't say stuff like that to a girl you aren't marrying," I whisper before looking down at his lips, because I can't help it. I meet his eyes again.

"I just wish that life had better timing for you and I," Hayden says before putting his hand on my cheek. He strokes the skin softly and my eyes flutter closed. And for just a second I pretend that Hayden is mine and I am his. We didn't lose the last five years of our life together and everything is okay. I pretend that I'm happy. "Do you remember what I said to you that night we broke up?" he whispers in my ear.

Hayden turns around to look at me. A tear falls from his eyes and I can't help but let out a sob as I look at him.

"Please don't make this harder. I just need to be alone for a while, Hayden. Trust me, it's not you. It will never be you. I just can't feel anything other than emptiness and numbness."

Hayden walks towards me slowly and he wraps his arms around me and rests his forehead on mine.

We stay like this for what seems like forever until he kisses my forehead. I feel his tear on my forehead and that just makes me cry harder.

"Whenever you're ready, I'll be here. I'll be waiting for you," he mumbles before letting go of me and leaving without looking back.

"Yes," I whisper as a small tear falls from my eye.

Hayden leans forward and presses his lips against my forehead. "Good."

Twenty-Four

Jaclyn

Natalia and I are on our way to school right now. We decided to drive together because I slept over at Hayden's last night.

This morning, he wouldn't let me leave the bed. I had to fight my way out of his bed because he wouldn't let me go. And before I left, I kissed him goodbye. He tried to deepen the kiss and make me stay but Natalia dragged me out of the room.

Natalia right now is talking to me about how Chris is thinking about moving out and playing for the Giants in New York. She and Chris have been talking about plans for what happens after school. I know for a fact that Chris might get drafted for the Giants because he is an amazing player and they have already been talking to him about the opportunity.

Natalia doesn't mind moving to New York. She says that there are a lot of opportunities out there.

Them talking about their future makes me think about what Hayden and I are doing after school. We haven't talked about it but with the promise ring he gave me not too long ago, he made it sound like I was here to stay.

He doesn't want me going anywhere.

I just have no clue what his plan is and he is graduating next year while I have one more year of college.

Will he stay in Arizona with me or move out when he is done with school?

The thought of him leaving me makes me so anxious and scared.

I don't even want to think about it.

I know for a fact I want to become a sports journalist. I love interacting with people and being a sports journalist can make you some good money.

I would want to live in either New York or California. I love everything about New York, the city, the lights, how loud it is, etc. It just feels so alive but it's so expensive to live out there. California has the beach which I love. It has perfect weather all around.

Once we get to school, I park the car and cut the

engine. Natalia and I get out of the car and I lock the doors.

"Your birthday is coming up. What are you planning on doing?" Natalia asks as we walk towards our building.

My birthday is next week and I have no clue what I'm doing. I haven't had the time to think about it with all the issues with Hayden and his fights.

Eric has laid low for a while which makes me think something is wrong. The feeling in the pit of my stomach makes me want to throw up sometimes.

"No clue. Maybe hangout with you guys and have dinner?"

"Hayden doesn't have anything planned?" Natalia asks and I shake my head. He hasn't mentioned anything and neither have I because I'm sure we will do something small. "Do you have the key card?" Natalia asks as we walk towards the elevator.

I remember I didn't take it with me. It's still in the car. I usually keep it in the center console.

"Shit, no. It's okay, I'll go get it."

Natalia shakes her head. "It's fine, we can just take the stairs."

"You go ahead and I'll catch up. I have to get the key card because I need it for the library later."

She nods her head and I turn around and leave the building. I get to my car and unlock the doors before getting in. I look through the center console, trying to find the card when the passenger door opens.

Fear floods through my body as I see Eric sit in the passenger seat and lock the doors. "Get the hell out, Eric," I say, pushing my back against the door.

Anytime he is around me, it never ends well and the way my stomach keeps making flips makes me nervous as hell.

"Relax, Jaclyn. I'm not going to hurt you. Just wanna talk."

"Talk to someone else and get out," I demand.

"Nah, I wanna know how Hayden doing? Are the ribs healing?" Eric asks.

Hayden had to fight three people in one night and it ended up with him having his ribs fractured. He is healing pretty fast but he has pain sometimes.

"Of course you would know he has fractured ribs, you stalker." I put my hand on the button to unlock the door. "I wanna say it was nice talking but I would just be lying."

"Now, now, now, Jaclyn. You can't just leave right now," he says while holding onto the lock button. "We still have so much catching up to do," he says with a menacing tone that sends chills down my spine.

I don't like this.

I need to get out.

I need to leave.

"Fuck off," I say before pulling on the door but it won't open because he is holding the lock button. No matter how much I try to unlock it, it won't fucking unlock.

"Wish this would have been easier to do." I hear Eric say before a needle pricks my neck. I try to move away from him as my neck starts to sting from whatever he did. Eric holds me against the chair. "Just relax. You'll like this, trust me," Eric says in my ear as I plead for help in my head.

I can't move or talk but I can feel everything. My head starts to get heavy, like it weighs tons until I see nothing but darkness.

———

"Hey!" Someone yells in my ear. "Hey! Time to wake up!"

I jolt awake and open my eyes. I lift my head but don't see anything.

Everything is dark.

"Tell Marco she's awake," a familiar voice says.

Oh no.

Fuck.

Oh my God, please let this be a dream.

"No," I whisper to myself as anxiety fills my veins. Blood rushes through my body at a rapid pace and my breathing starts to get heavier.

I can't breathe.

Why can't I breathe?

"Jaclyn." The cloth gets ripped off my face and I see Eric staring down at me with a smile. "Finally you're awake. You've been asleep for a good day now." Eric grabs my jaw and moves my face to the side. "Yikes, that's going to bruise," he says, eyeing my neck. He presses his finger to the spot on my neck and I hiss, flinching away from him. "Yea that'll hurt for a bit." Eric lets go of me and he squats down to be at eye level with me. "Morning."

I look around me and see I'm in a room. There is a bed at the corner but nothing else.

It looks depressing and almost scary in here.

"Let me go, Eric. Please," I beg.

I'll do anything at this point for him not to touch me or go near me.

Eric shakes his head side to side. "That's not how this works. I wish things could have ended up differently but Hayden had to push." Eric stands up and turns to a guy behind him. "Did you tell Marco?" Eric asks and the guy nods.

A tear falls from my eye as I connect the dots.

They took me because of Hayden.

But Hayden won the fight. After everything Hayden has done and dealt with Marco, he can't just go back to his world.

The door opens and I see him walk in.

I have met Marco a total of maybe two or three times. He has always made me feel like something bad was about to happen. He holds darkness inside him that I've never seen anyone have. It's scary.

I have met Marco a total of maybe two or three times. He has always made me feel like something bad was about to happen. He holds darkness inside him that I've never seen anyone have. It's scary.

"Jaclyn, nice to see you again." Marco closes the door behind him and walks up to me. "How are you?"

"What do you want from me? Hayden won. You should have left us alone," I say as another tear falls.

It's like my body always knows what is going to happen, it's just preparing itself.

"Straight to the point. Definitely Hayden's girl, eh?" Marco smirks down at me.

"Let me go," I beg.

This can't be happening.

This is a dream that I'll wake up from or Hayden will come in and save me.

He always does.

Hayden is always there to save me.

Is this what I'm going to deal with while being with Hayden?

After being with him for a year I thought this would stop eventually but it's just gotten me here.

"Hayden is a talented guy. He is strong and fast. He

uses his head too," Marco states while looking down at me. "He has so much potential Jaclyn and you should know that out of all people," he explains. "I offered Hayden the deal of a lifetime. Endless years of money and he declined because he didn't want to be in that kind of environment."

"It's probably because of your gang bullshit," I say, getting frustrated.

My heart is beating so fast I think it will burst through my chest.

"So, he did tell you?" Marco raises an eyebrow at me. "Well, you know far too much it seems. We have to fix that." Marco looks at Eric. "Give us some privacy, would you?" Marco asks before moving his eyes to me.

Eric smirks, looking like Satan himself, and he leaves the room.

"No," I say while backing away from Marco who is walking towards me. "No! No! No! Please! Please, Marco. Please." I say as my eyes water and tears stream down.

"They all beg. It does nothing for me," Marco says as he grabs my wrists and throws me against the floor. I bang my head against the floor making me scream in pain. My forehead throbs as I cry. Marco gets behind me, his hips pressed against my butt. I widen my eyes and thrash away from him.

"No! No! Please, no! Don't Marco, please, please," I say, sobbing against the floor.

"Shhh. You're okay." Marco takes a knife out of his pocket and he cuts open my jeans.

And all of a sudden, everything stops.

Everything pauses.

My mind is blank and I can't feel a single thing.

For a second, I honestly think that I'm dead.

Twenty-Five

Jaclyn

Hayden and I get out of the elevator and walk in the direction of my room. He decided to walk me to my room even after I told him I was fine and I could walk by myself.

I need to be by myself because after spending time with Hayden at the beach, I need a minute to just clear my head.

We spent most of our time in the water. We didn't kiss or anything but he held me against him in the water. The entire time I was worried about someone seeing us since a lot of people know he is in Italy and if someone were to take a picture of us we'd both be in deep shit.

And I'm afraid he would somehow find out about Junior if more of the public knew about me.

Although I was overthinking about everything, being

with him with his arms around me, I felt safe and happy. I missed his touch and assurance.

I missed him in general.

No matter what my mind says, my heart will always long for him.

But this can't happen between him and I.

Hayden is getting married and I have morals and self respect which I can't just break. One kiss and him touching me is enough damage.

I still am cursing at myself and overthinking about letting him hold me in the water.

But for some reason, being with him doesn't remind me of the bad memories. When I'm with him, all I feel is longing for more and maybe even love.

But did my love for him ever go away?

I remember when I saw him at the fight, I was terrified because I haven't seen him in years, but being in Italy, away from our jobs and the public, everything feels somewhat more relaxed then over there.

Hayden opens my door and we both walk inside.

I put my bag on the bed and turn to the side slightly. I feel Hayden's eyes burning holes where the scar is, again. When we got out of the water he looked pissed when he saw my side.

That night, he didn't know they cut me because the wound wasn't bleeding anymore because the blood dried.

I had blood on my shirt but Hayden didn't know where it came from.

"Who did that?" Hayden asks, still looking at my ribs.

I grab a shirt and throw it over my head so that he can't see the scar anymore.

Am I still ashamed of it when people ask about it? Of course.

I try not to think about that night at all.

Hayden walks closer to me and grabs my wrist as I try to turn around. I don't want to look at him because I can't help but feel like I'm going to cry if he brings up this situation.

"Jaclyn." He turns me around to look at him and I feel my eyes start to water a little. "Tell me."

I push him away from me. "Don't worry about it. It's done." I walk past him and go to open the door but Hayden stops me and instead he pushes my back against the door. "You need to leave." I glare up at him.

"I'm going to ask one more time," Hayden whispers and leans down. "Who did that to you?" he asks. "Marco? Eric?"

I try to force him back but he doesn't budge. "Don't worry about it. It's in the past and doesn't matter anymore."

"It does if they fucking did what I think they did. I swear to god-"

"What are you going to do? They are both in jail. It won't make any difference. You knew they touched me."

"I didn't fucking know they carved out the tattoo you got for me," Hayden says, his jaw clenched and his hands near my head.

"Well they did. It's too late to do anything. They are in jail where they should be."

"I'm going to fucking kill-"

"Kill him?" I raise an eyebrow at him.

I always knew that Hayden had this darkness inside him that he never showed other than out in the ring.

"Yea. I'm going to fucking kill him and then Marco next."

I roll my eyes at him. "You're unbelievable."

"I'm unbelievable! You're the one who got fucking carved and God knows what else but didn't say shit to me that night."

"Because we broke up!" I yell, getting frustrated with him. He isn't making this any easier.

"That was because of you," Hayden says, pointing a finger at me. "Because you didn't want to stay with me. Because you were fucking afraid."

"Why does it matter anyways? You're getting married," I say as tears fall from my eyes, finally.

I can't fucking do this with him.

It hurts too much to talk about the past with him,

especially because I sometimes regret breaking up with him.

Junior would have a dad.

I'd probably be happy and healed.

"I don't fucking want her. I want you but you decided to fucking leave."

I push him off of me and walk past him. "You need to leave. I won't ask you again; go to your future wife-" I get cut off by the feeling of Hayden's lips on mine. I wish I could just resist the fight and feel him move against me again but this is wrong. It's all wrong. I press my hands against his chest and push him back. I look up at him with pleading eyes. "Please stop. Just being near you is hard. Every time, I have to hold my breath because whenever I think of you it's a painful reminder that you're not mine."

Him doing all of this just makes me feel like a horrible person for wanting to be with him again.

But I can't.

He isn't mine anymore.

Hayden closes his eyes and rests his forehead against mine. His hands hold onto my jaw. "Five years ago, I promised you that I would do anything to bring us back together. I told you that I don't break my promises." Hayden sighs. "You know how fucking vulnerable you make me? I never begged anyone for anything yet here you are making me beg without even doing anything."

"Why did you propose to Nicole if you weren't ready?"

"Because it had to be done. I didn't want to, God I didn't because I knew there was still you in the world. But it had to be done."

I shake my head against his and lean back to stare at him. "Then why are you with her if she doesn't make you happy?"

"Because you weren't here. I keep telling you over and over but you aren't understanding."

"Because you can't just marry someone for the sake of marrying them," I say but Hayden shakes his head and lets go of my face.

"You don't get it."

"Then explain it to me!" I yell, getting frustrated.

He is hiding so much from me and that's what started this whole issue in college.

But I'm hiding way worse.

Junior, the pills, that night . . .

"Will you tell me what happened in that fucking room? Will you tell me what fucking killed you that night?"

Another tear falls from my eyes as I shake my head.

Telling him would kill him.

He will be furious and I'm sure he will find Eric and Marco and kill both of them.

"Then there you go. I won't tell you anything until

you come forward with what I want to hear. It won't make a difference in Eric or Marco's life because they going to be dead either way," Hayden says before letting go of my jaw and turning around.

"You know, Hayden. There are two things I'll never forget," I start saying before he turns his head lightly with his hand on the door knob. "It's the way you first looked at me in the alleyway and then the last time you looked at me that night."

Hayden stays there, absorbing my words before he twists the knob and leaves the room.

Twenty-Six
Jaclyn

"We are going to have so much fun." Natalia exclaims as she straightens her hair in front of the bathroom mirror.

I can't help but smile at her as I work on my makeup.

I decided to straighten my hair as well. I love it when my hair is pin straight. I feel like I don't look good with curly hair so that's why I never curl it.

Plus straight hair looks good with the black mini dress I'm wearing. I bought this dress before I got pregnant with Junior and since I gained weight during the pregnancy, I was never able to wear it, at least until now.

Tonight Nicole is hosting a party at the hotel for their wedding. It's mostly for all the friends of Nicole and

Hayden to hangout and drink. Nicole's dad is making the bar empty for us.

"It's cool that Nicole's dad is having the bar emptied out so no one will come in."

Natalia shrugs. "Yea, it's pretty cool I guess." She turns her head to look at me. "So I heard from someone that you were seen with Hayden at the beach the other day."

Who the hell could have seen us in the water?

I mean no pictures came out from the paparazzi or anything so I thought we were good.

I furrow my eyebrows at her. "Who told you that?"

"Kayden."

Little shit.

Of course he saw us. I thought he was going to the beach to take pictures or something, not spy.

"What about it?"

"You two have been talking a lot. What's with that?" Natalia asks with a small smirk starting to appear on her lips.

"Natalia, just because we're talking to one another, doesn't mean we are fucking. He is getting married and I'm not that type of person."

Even though I already kissed him and came around his fingers at a dinner that his fiancé's parents hosted.

"I know, but you guys are talking again," Natalia says, a smile appearing on her face as she rests the straighter on the counter.

"Hayden and I won't be happening, Natalia. We can't."

"Why not?"

"Well he has a fiancé. Second, we have too much trauma between us." "But something good can come out of it. You both could be happy."

Yes I'll be happy but will I be at peace?

Right now, life is peaceful with just Junior and I.

Other than all of the voices whispering in my head.

"Hayden and I are different people now. I have no clue who he is now," I try to explain.

I know Natalia just wants the best for her brother and me but sometimes people just aren't meant to be. I don't want to ruin a future marriage because Hayden or I can't control ourselves.

We've already fucked up.

"But I think that you could be really good for Hayden and make him happy like he was before. He needs you even though he won't say it."

I roll my eyes and walk out of the bathroom. Natalia follows me into the room.

"Why is everyone saying that? Hayden seems like he is doing okay on his own without my help. I mean he's rich, he has a fiancé who is rich, his career is off the charts, and he is one of the most famous fighters in the world. He is doing just fine." I want to almost laugh because I find it hilarious that people think that Hayden needs me. If anything, I probably need him even though I won't admit it out loud or sometimes to myself. "Are you ready to go? I'm pretty sure everyone is waiting for us," I ask Natalia, trying to be nice and not sound like a bitch.

I'm just over this conversation and Hayden.

I want, for one night, to just get drunk and pretend he doesn't exist anymore and like he didn't make my world fall.

Natalia sighs and grabs her purse. "You'll see, Jaclyn."

———

Natalia and I get to the bar where there's music playing on the speakers lightly and some people working the bar.

The boys are already at the bar as we walk up to them. Martin, Max, Chris, and Kayden are sitting while talking and sipping on their drinks.

Chris turns his head and smiles when he sees Natalia. "Hey, babe." He stands and goes to her to wrap his arms around her waist. "Lilah is with your parents," he says before kissing her.

Natalia kisses him back passionately before saying. "I know, my mom texted me. Where is Hayden?" she says, looking around for him.

"He stepped out to take a call from Rowan. He'll be back."

I sit down next to Max and smile at the bartender who comes up to me. "I'll get a double espresso martini."

He gives me a wink before walking away.

He's not bad looking.

Pretty cute and makes good drinks.

He looks young, maybe around my age, maybe older. Brown hair, dark eyes, and a light scruff on his chin and jaw.

"You still love those espresso martinis?" Max asks me.

I nod my head. "Yea. They taste good. I don't know how some people don't like them."

I look at Martin and Max together. They look like such a good couple. They match and compliment one another so well.

"So you and Hayden?" I hear a voice behind me say.

I turn my head and look at Kayden.

"Yeah, about that. You little stalker." I narrow my eyes at him. "I thought you went to a different part of the beach to take pictures?"

Kayden shrugs and sips on his drink. "I saw you guys and had to take some. Let me tell you, for two people who claim to not love one another anymore, you guys look pretty cozy in those pictures to me."

I shake my head lightly. "All of you are unbelievable."

"Well, we aren't wrong. You just can't admit it yet."

The bartender comes back and places the drink in front of me. "Vodka girl, huh?"

I smile at him and nod my head. "What can I say? They taste good."

"I hope you aren't paying for that drink yourself," the bartender flirts with a charming smile on his face. "No beautiful girl should be paying for her own drink."

I laugh lightly and before I can reply a deep voice cuts in and I see a familiar arm reach around me.

"Actually she isn't buying her own drink. I am." I turn my head, get a whiff of his cologne from his shirt, and meet those beautiful gray eyes.

Twenty-Seven

Present

I glare at Hayden as he hands his card to the bartender.

"Sorry bro, I didn't know she was with you," the cute bartender says while taking Hayden's card.

"I'm not his girlfriend. We aren't together," I say with a small smile as I try to block Hayden.

"Well in that case, I'm Jamie," Jamie says before giving me his hand.

I shake it. "Jaclyn." But then my hand gets ripped from his.

I glare at Hayden but he ignores it and he lowers his head to be at level with mine. "What the hell are you doing?"

"Having a conversation with someone?" I take my wrist out of his hold.

Hayden is about to say something but a voice cuts him off from behind. "Hubs!" I look behind him and see Nicole walking towards us with her group of friends behind her. Nicole walks up to us and she slides her arm onto Hayden's bicep. I try to ignore her hand on him and instead focus my attention on something else, anything else to distract me from her. "You look great," she says, smiling up at Hayden. He doesn't pay attention to her, instead his focus is on me. God's he's an asshole for doing that in front of his future wife. "Jaclyn, you look amazing too. Definitely will get a few guys up your dress tonight, right?" Nicole says before winking.

I put on a fake smile. "Yea, the bartender is so cute."

I notice Hayden's hands clench by his side and his jaw tightens.

Nicole smiles at me before looking at Hayden and next thing I know her lips are attached to Hayden's and I feel like throwing up.

My stomach churns and I look away from the moment between them.

"What the hell are you doing?" I hear Hayden say in a rough tone.

"Nothing, you just look so good. I had to have a taste," Nicole giggles while I just down my drink that Jamie made for me. "Enjoy your night, husband. I'll see you later."

Nicole leaves and I still have my lips on the glass, trying to erase the image from my brain and burn it.

God.

I turn my head to look at Hayden and he doesn't look too happy. He has a furious expression on his face and I have a feeling it's not from me.

"Why are you still here? Don't you have other people to talk to?"

Hayden leans closer to me until his lips touch my ear. "Princess, the only person I want to talk to is sitting right in front of me."

I shrug my shoulders. "Well I don't want to talk to you, so."

I don't even want to look at him.

He's not yours.

I know I have no right to say he can't kiss the girl he's marrying.

He's not yours.

I know it's my fault for coming to his wedding knowing he will be here kissing his fiancé.

He's not yours.

I know it's my fucking fault for leaving him and ruining what we had.

But God I hated that.

It actually broke my heart knowing that another girl's lips touched his.

Hayden sighs before walking away.

"Brother?" I look up and see Jamie looking at me while cleaning a glass.

"No, ex," I say, still holding onto the glass.

Jamie raises his eyebrows. "That's your ex? Isn't he a professional fighter?" I nod my head. "He lost an amazing girl then."

"I broke up with him," I say, while wincing. "Can I just get something else? Maybe something stronger?" I rest the empty glass in front of me.

Jamie laughs before taking it and walking away.

"You guys have to make things so hard." I turn my head and look at Max who looks like he is getting close to being blacked out.

His hair is a mess and his face is flushed.

Where is Martin?

How'd he get drunk so fast?

"Where is everyone?" I ask looking around.

"Chris and Natalia are dancing. Kayden left with Hayden to go see Hayden's other friends. Nicole and her friends went to the VIP area and Martin went to grab my wallet." Max scoots closer to me. "As I was saying, why are you making things hard?"

"Who?" I ask, furrowing my eyebrows.

"Hayden and you. You both have to be so complicated. You guys obviously want one another and are capable of love but you guys choose to do things the hard way. It's obvious you guys want one another."

"How so?"

"Well, Hayden likes to hide things so he can protect the people he loves and you are stubborn and maybe even a little scared which is why you like to run away from things that make you feel something. I think you might be scared of getting hurt.

"What does this have to do with anything?" I ask and Max opens his mouth but lets out a burp. I laugh and Max laughs too. Jamie ends up coming with my drink. "Still a heavy drinker?"

"A happy drinker, Jaclyn." Max gives me a drunk smile and I can't help but smile back.

Eventually Martin comes back and next thing I know Martin, Max, and I are downing shots. As I try to take a step back, Max yells "Peer pressure!" for me to keep drinking.

And after that, everything goes black.

Twenty-Eight

Hayden

"Why the fuck did you do that?" I ask Nicole as she leans back against the wall with her arms crossed over her chest.

I pulled her away from her friends because of that goddamn kiss. She never kisses me unless it's for publicity and I have not kissed her once, until now.

The one time I actually kissed a girl after Jaclyn happened to be right in front of her.

The last person I kissed was Jaclyn. I did have sex with a girl once to see if I could forget about Jaclyn and it didn't work. She tried kissing me but having sex with her felt all wrong and I knew if she tried to kiss me it just made me feel worse than actually having sex with her.

I fucking hated that night.

I remember being high out of my mind and Rowan carrying me out of the club because I was doing stupid shit.

He's a lifesaver, my angel of a brother.

"Because I wanted to prove a theory and I was right." Nicole smirks. "You care for that girl. A lot more than you should, husband." She laughs and shakes her head lightly. "I can feel the trouble coming."

"Don't kiss me again," I demand.

"Why? Don't want to risk Jaclyn seeing? Does she even know?" Nicole leans off the wall and raises an eyebrow at me. "Does she know the kind of person you are now? What you do?"

"It's none of your business," I say, leaning close to her face. "If you do stupid shit like that again or even think about starting trouble with her, I swear to God-"

"What?" Nicole smirks again. "You'll break off the wedding? Break off my dear old daddy's deal?" Nicole laughs, throwing her head back as if this is all some fucked up planned she made. "Remember, Hayden. If you don't go through with this deal then Killian won't get that alliance he wanted and then he's gonna be pissed at you because you work for him. You have to do whatever he says, last time I checked." Nicole's eyebrow raises and she walks closer to me until her chest is almost pressed against mine. "We don't want the truth to slip, do we? I mean that is what it's called right? *Codice di verità*?"

I push Nicole off me and she just laughs it off like the fucking bitch she is. "Stay out of it."

Nicole's eyes move away from mine and her smile slips. "Well you should go. Looks like Jaclyn will be going home with the cute bartender. He's kind of cute, isn't he?" Nicole says, mischief written all over her face.

I turn around and look at what she's talking about. I see Jaclyn talking and laughing with the bartender from earlier.

The one who was fucking hitting on her.

My jaw clenches and rage rushes through my body. My hands form a fist and all I want to do is grab that motherfucker by the collar and bang his head against the wall.

I ignore Nicole's light chuckles and go straight for Jaclyn.

"You know, bartenders usually aren't the ones I go for but you aren't bad, mister," Jaclyn says, giggling while touching his arm.

His fucking arm that I'm going to break off in two seconds.

Next thing I know I'm in front of Jaclyn, blocking her from the bartender. "Don't you know that taking advantage of drunk girls will cost you your life?" I say, making the bartender clear his throat as his face turns red. I wrap my arm around Jaclyn's waist. "Next time I see you around her or even breathe in the same air as her, you will first lose your eyes and then I'll cut you open and take out your lungs for breathing near her. Go back to your fucking job."

The bartender practically runs away as Jaclyn pushes herself off of me.

"You're such a dick, Hayden."

I turn to look at her.

Since she walked inside the bar, I haven't taken my eyes off her. She is actually stunning, so stunning I feel speechless and don't even know what to say.

She makes me lose my train of thought and I forget what to say or do around her.

The dress she's wearing tonight is a black dress that rides up her thighs. It makes her legs look long and beautiful.

I want those legs wrapped around my waist as I make her scream my name until she passes out.

God, she's drunk.

I can't.

Not yet at least.

"And the bartender guy wasn't?" I raise an eyebrow at her. "He was undressing you with his eyes, Jaclyn."

"Good." She crosses her arms over her chest making her breasts look huge. I can't help but look down at them and smirk. I love it when she's mad at me. It's such a turn on. "I was hoping he could take me upstairs for the night," she says before slipping out of my hold and walking away.

I follow her and grab her wrist, pulling her close to me and taking us to a hallway where it's empty.

"Why are you making things hard?" I ask while pushing her against a wall softly.

And like a switch, Jaclyn smiles up at me and runs her hand up my chest. "Because things are funner that way."

Oh fuck.

She has that flirty tone she usually has whenever she is a flirty drunk.

And usually when she is flirty and drunk, she is horny.

Jaclyn has five stages of being drunk.

1. Groovy and hyper drunk

2. Pissed off at everything drunk

3. Flirty drunk

4. Giggly drunk

5. Sad drunk

And then she passes out.

After almost five years of not seeing Jaclyn King, I still know everything about her.

"How much have you had to drink? Do you know if that guy even drugged you or not?" I ask in a serious tone but all she does is giggle.

"Stop being so serious. I only had a few drinks with Max."

"A few drinks with Max is like twenty shots. You know this."

She rolls her eyes before pushing past me but before

she can go too far I grab her by her legs and throw her over my shoulder. "Hayden! What are you doing?! Put me down!" she yells while slapping my back.

"Not happening," I say while walking towards the elevator.

Once we get inside, I put her down. She has a gorgeous smile on her face while staring up at me.

God I love her smile.

It's always made me want to smile. The way her eyes brighten when she smiles and how her cheeks turn up.

Jaclyn has always hated her cheeks and smile because she always thought it made her look chubby but I've always loved it, still do.

Even now, she is a lot skinnier, which I'm trying to get to the bottom of.

She has changed a lot in the past few years and I want to know why and how I can help her get back to her original self because the girl I'm looking at, even though she is drunk and smiling, she doesn't look happy at all.

She looks like she is having an inner battle with herself and I want to do everything in my power to fix it and bring her back.

"Why are you looking at me like that?"

"Because you're beautiful," I say, making Jaclyn blush and look away. I walk closer to her and turn her chin to make her look up at me. "Don't look away from me."

Jaclyn still smiles up at me with red cheeks. "You're

beautiful too." She trails her finger along my jaw and I swear blood rushes to my dick. "I love your eyes. They're my favorite thing ever."

I lean down and my lips graze her ear lightly. Jaclyn chuckles and pushes herself closer to me. "You're my favorite thing ever," I say before the doors of the elevator open. I step back from her and grab her hand, pulling her out of the elevator. We walk to her door, hand in hand. And it almost feels normal. "Where is your key card?" I look down at her and she just smirks up at me with glossy eyes.

Jaclyn holds a finger and giggles. She looks through her purse and pulls it out, showing it to me with a big proud smile on her face.

I unlock the door and we get inside as I hold onto her so she doesn't trip. I sit her down on the bed and she flops on her back and stares up at the ceiling. I look around her room and find her suitcase. I grab a t-shirt and shorts for her to wear and walk back to her. She is just watching me with a smile still present on her face.

"Stand up," I say, grabbing her hand and helping her stand up. "Can you change yourself?"

She smirks and pushes herself against me, going on her tippy toes. Her lips graze my ear and she says, "I want you to help me."

I swear I could give this girl the world if she said please.

And God, I want to help.

I want to do a lot more than help her.

"I don't think that's a good idea, princess." I narrow my eyes at her and she pouts.

"Please? I can't do it."

I nip my bottom lip and let out a deep sigh. "Okay." Jaclyn smiles. I motion for her to spin. "Turn around." Jaclyn turns around and I grip the black dress in my hands, trying my best not to just rip the thing off of her. I pull it over her head and her bare back faces me. I can't help but look down at her ass. She is wearing a black lace thong. I hold in a groan and look away from how perfect her ass is. I swear, one day this girl will bring me to my knees. Jaclyn stays still as I change her. She turns around and holds onto my shoulders as I put her shorts on. I then grab her by her legs and wrap them around my waist. I walk to her bathroom and rest her on the counter. "Where are your makeup wipes?"

"My bag."

I walk out of the restroom and look through her big makeup bag. I open it and immediately see a pink vibrator in a zip lock bag.

Images appear in my head.

Jaclyn on her bed, in the middle of the night. She's arching her back and her hand is playing with her nipple while the other is thrusting the vibrator inside her roughly.

God, the things I would do to see that vision come to life.

I don't just want Jaclyn, I need her.

Almost like I need air.

She is such an addiction, it's hard to simply just get rid of her. She is engraved inside my body and there is no way to get her out.

I put the vibrator back and go back to the bathroom, trying to calm down and focus on getting her in bed and then getting the fuck out of here.

I wipe Jaclyn's makeup off in silence while she just swings her legs back and forth and I try to think of anything, anything to get my mind of that vibrator.

She yawns a few times, making me know she's tired.

I grab her, once the makeup is off her face and I gently place her in bed and she stares up at me with those big brown eyes as I put the blanket on her.

I check my phone and go to the Dexcom follow app I still have on it.

After five years of not speaking or being in contact with her, I still have the app on my phone to make sure she is still alive and okay.

She doesn't know I have the app still on my phone.

Her blood sugar is 247.

"Did you do your Lantus?" She shakes her head no. I grab her purse and find her Lantus. "Is it still 31 units?" I ask her while prepping the shot and putting the needle on the pen. Jaclyn nods her head, still awake but her eyes are slowly falling. I pull the blanket down once the shot is prepped. I grab her arm, the one without the Dexcom, and push the needle slowly into her arm. Jaclyn doesn't flinch, instead she keeps her eyes on me while I take the shot out. "Didn't hurt?"

"No," she whispers.

I put the needle in an empty bottle and then her Lantus back in her purse. I go back to Jaclyn and lean down to press a kiss to her forehead. "Goodnight, princess," I whisper and am about to turn around but Jaclyn grabs my bicep. "What?"

"Please stay with me." I really shouldn't. I need to get out of here before I go insane and lose control. With this girl, I never have control. But instead of saying no and leaving, I take my shoes and jacket off before climbing in. While climbing in, I notice two orange pill bottles on her nightstand. I am about to grab one of the bottles but then Jaclyn turns around and says, "Can you hold me? I'm cold." I forget about the bottles, for now, and throw my arm over her waist and pull her closer to me. Her knee grazes my dick and I hiss but try to ignore it. "I can give you a blowie if you're hard, Hay Hay," Jaclyn whispers before giggling.

More blood rushes to my dick but I try, so fucking hard, to ignore it. "Sleep," I say, before resting my forehead in her neck and closing my eyes.

It's quiet for a few seconds before Jaclyn says my name. I open my eyes and see her staring at me. "Why don't you love me anymore?"

A pang of hurt strikes my heart.

She has no fucking clue.

Jaclyn happens to know all of my secrets even after all these years, except one. That I'm still madly in love with her.

She's drunk so it's not like she'll remember what I say.

"You have no clue how much I love you," I whisper. "The fact that I'm here with you in bed doing nothing rather than with her, shows how much I still love you. I wish I could tell you more but I can't. Not right now."

Jaclyn doesn't say anything, instead she leans up and presses her lips against mine.

I don't kiss her back, instead I just stay still and feel the movement of her lips on mine, taking her all in.

"Kiss me back," Jaclyn says and I can hear the hurt in her tone.

Instead of kissing her lips I kiss her forehead. "Go to sleep."

"Goodnight, Hayden."

"Goodnight, princess."

Twenty-Nine

Jaclyn

As soon as I wake up I fling the blankets off me and run towards the bathroom. I fall to the floor in front of the toilet, lift the lid and everything from last night just spills from my mouth.

Tears fall from my eyes as I throw everything up in the toilet. Once I'm done, I close the lid and go to the sink. I immediately brush my teeth to get rid of the god-awful taste in my mouth.

What even happened last night?

I walk back inside the room once I'm done and look around.

My bag is open and the bed is a mess. I look at my clothes and see I'm wearing just a regular baggy t-shirt and shorts. I walk to the bed and lay down, throwing the covers over myself. I rest my head against the pillow and immediately smell cologne.

I lift my head and stare at the pillow.

The smell is familiar.

Woodsy, warm, and fresh scent.

I know this smell.

Did I bring someone here last night?

What did I do while I was drunk?

Last thing I remember was Max and Martin taking shots with me. Kayden was somewhere in the mix. I remember the cute bartender and I flirting but that's it.

Shit.

Who the hell took me home and cleaned my mess?

Today I'm going to the beach with everyone. Natalia and Chris aren't coming though because they want to spend some time with Lilah and go shopping with her.

I clean up the room a little before I change into a blue bathing suit and jean shorts.

I'll call Junior and Brandon after Junior is done with school. I would call but they are probably already at work and school.

Even as I leave the room and go down to the lobby, I'm still trying to search my brain for what happened last night and who could have brought me back to the room.

Once I get to the beach, which isn't a far walk, I send

Kayden a text, letting him know I'm here. He said yesterday that he was going to go to the beach today because he wanted to take some pictures.

He texts that he's near the rock bridge. I walk towards that area and look around, trying to find him.

Kayden is down by the water, pointing his camera to take a picture.

I walk towards him and end up jumping in front of his camera and posing with a smile.

Kayden smiles before snapping a picture. "Jaclyn. Always a pleasure."

He lowers the camera and we walk towards his towel. I lay my blanket that I brought, next to him and sit down. "When are Martin and Max coming?'

"Probably in like thirty minutes. They just woke up now," Kayden explains, putting his camera to the side. "Max had a lot to drink last night but he always gets super fucked up."

"I bet he did." I chuckle. "I drank a lot too. I threw up this morning but being here is kind of making me feel, that's for sure," I explain. "Also, about last night, do you know who might have taken me to my room?"

"Hayden. Martin said Hayden saw you flirting with the bartender, and he took you to your room after that."

Shit.

And what kind of embarrassing shit did I do with him in my room?

"Oh," is all I say.

What the fuck am I supposed to say?

Hayden changed me so did he see the scar again? What was he thinking about when he saw the scar?

He probably saw how much my body changed too.

Did he see the pills on my nightstand?

What was he thinking?

He thinks you're probably crazy and need some serious help.

Did I say anything that might have gotten me in trouble or something?

God what the fuck happened?

"Why? Did something happen?" Kayden asks.

I give him a reassuring smile and shake my head. "No, I just woke up this morning and wondered how I got to my room."

"I mean, ask Hayden about it. I'm sure he'll tell you."

I smile and just nod my head.

No.

I'm trying to stay away from him.

Because being around him is just causing issues. He shouldn't be jealous of me flirting with a bartender when he has a fiancé.

He shouldn't be this friendly with a girl who meant everything to him as he claims I did.

Eventually Max and Martin come to our spot. They

brought some food with them, thank God because I haven't eaten anything this morning.

When Martin goes in the water, I decide to join him. We swim through the waves and then just relax in the water.

He told me more about how Max and him met and what he thought of Max. He mentioned how he wants to marry Max in the near future which I think is amazing.

I keep saying how perfect Martin is for Max because I genuinely believe he is. I can tell how much Martin loves and cares for Max.

We get out of the water eventually and go back to the blankets.

Max and Martin are leaving early because they have a date planned. So we all just decide to head back to the hotel.

"I'll see you around, Kayden," I say as I pack all my stuff up.

"Are you going to the bachelorette in a few days?" Kayden asks.

I nod my head. "Yea, Natalia said she wants me to go with her since she doesn't feel comfortable alone with Nicole and her friends."

Kayden nods his head. "Okay. Well I'll see you."

We hug before he leaves and walks off the beach.

I sit down on my blanket, trying to clear my head.

It feels like there is just so much going on in my head that I have no clue what to do anymore.

Everything gets so loud to the point where my head feels like it's just going to explode.

I sometimes wish everything would just take a pause or stop.

All my mind can think about is Hayden.

Thirty

Jaclyn

"Good night, hubs. Have fun." Nicole says before pecking Hayden's cheek with a fake smile on her face.

Hayden looks annoyed and like he wants to wipe the kiss away. He looks away from Nicole and at me instead.

Tonight we are going to Nicole's Bachelorette party. She told me to dress nice and meet in the hotel lobby. The boys are going to Hayden's bachelor party and I'm curious what they will be doing.

Tonight I decided to wear a dark blue dress with black lace that is sewn in the breast area. I put on my regular everyday makeup because I think that's the only kind of makeup that I look good in. For my hair, Natalia curled it so that my hair would be in waves.

Natalia and I got ready together, as we always do. I

love how we always get ready together. It's like a routine with her. We are going to have a sleepover in my room when we get back from the party.

I make eye contact with Hayden one last time before I follow Nicole as she exits the lobby with her friends.

For the past few days, I have been busy catching up with work, too scared to leave my hotel room and potentially face Hayden.

I haven't seen Hayden since the night I got drunk. I'm too scared to face him, especially when he keeps giving me those intense eyes like I should know something.

Kayden keeps telling me I can't hide from Hayden and eventually I will need to talk to him. Not just about that night but about everything.

It's almost like Kayden knows I'm keeping a big secret from Hayden.

It's just when I tell Hayden about Junior and what happened in that room, his reaction won't be pretty. It will destroy him.

We all get inside the limo and I sit next to Natalia while Nicole sits next to her three friends. There aren't many girls because most of the people here at the wedding are Nicole's family. All of Nicole's friends are models who are only able to make it to the actual wedding, not all the pre wedding stuff.

The wedding is in about a week and I am so scared

and nervous even though I shouldn't be because it's not my wedding.

I just happen to be watching someone who was my everything, kiss another girl at the altar.

"So, Jaclyn, where are you from?" Nicole asks.

"Southern California," I answer.

"Are you Russian or Middle Eastern? You look like you are."

I shake my head. "No. I'm Romanian."

Nicole nods her head lightly, like trying to connect the dots in her brain or something. "Interesting. I never really got along with Romanians. Always so stuck up."

I furrow my eyebrows and am about to say something but Natalia gets to it first. "Nicole, that's probably because they didn't like you." Natalia laughs. "Question?"

Nicole gives her a fake smile. "You always do."

"Are you finally jealous of someone?" Natalia asks and my lips part as I watch Nicole's face turn red. Her hands clench around her champagne glass and her friends raise their eyebrows in shock. "I mean I've never seen you so invested in someone's life before. You are just so pissed off at Jaclyn and I'm trying to figure out why."

Nicole sits up and makes her friend hold her glass. "You should learn to mind your own business." Nicole points her finger at Natalia while Natalia just smirks at her. I'm just watching all this unfold as a smile wants to force its way onto my face. "You keep opening your mouth like that and there will be consequences. Watch it."

Natalia looks anything but scared at Nicole's threat which is just embarrassing for her.

The rest of the car ride is mostly silent. Natalia only talks to me and Nicole only talks to her friends.

I want to grab Natalia by the shoulders and hug her because I've never had anyone stand up for me like she just did. I missed her and forgot what a good friend she's always been. It makes me pissed off at myself for losing her friendship for some boy.

But God, that boy did a lot of damage.

When we get to the destination we all get out of the car. I look at the building and see that we're at a strip club.

Okay.

Cool.

Never been to a strip club in my life but there's a first for everything.

I just didn't expect a strip club.

"Have you ever been to the strip, Jaclyn?" Nicole asks as we walk in.

"No. Have you?"

Nicole shrugs and says, "I've worked a couple."

Oh.

I didn't expect that.

Mostly because Nicole doesn't seem like the type and

also because she has money too so I didn't think she worked at all.

But I'm not judging.

She probably just likes dancing or something.

We walk inside the main room and the song "Haunted" by Beyonce is playing which is somewhat perfect for a chill vibe but also this kind of environment. It's kind of sensual and slow which makes it great. There are pink and blue LED lights on the walls and where the bar is.

There are three poles in the middle of the room and sofas surrounding them.

Three guys, who are only in white boxer briefs, with oiled up muscles and props, walk in.

God, what did I just sign up for?

Thirty-One

Jaclyn

This morning I woke up with the worst hangover.

I usually don't get hangovers but after the club, Natalia and I had an afterparty of our own in the hotel. We smoked a little weed that she got from Max and we were still a little drunk from the club.

I was a wreck this morning. Natalia woke me up saying we had to go to breakfast with everyone since Nicole made reservations.

I had fun last night though. It was definitely an interesting experience going to a male strip club. Nicole got a private dance from one of the strippers and I saw them making out a couple times which I was a little shocked at because I thought she maybe liked Hayden a little or respected him.

I know for a fact that Hayden doesn't give two shits because he keeps trying to make a move on me.

But they have no respect or love for one another at all.

So then why the fuck are they getting married?

It keeps nagging at my brain as I watch Hayden across from me at the table and Nicole sitting next to him. They aren't touching one another or looking at each other. Nicole is talking to her friends while Hayden has his eyes on me.

I'm sitting in between Max and Kayden. Martin is sitting next to Max and then Natalia and Chris are sitting next to Kayden. Across is Hayden, Nicole, and her friends.

Hayden looks annoyed, I can tell by the way his jaw keeps clenching.

Meanwhile I'm sitting across from him, wondering so many things because nothing seems to make sense.

This morning I talked to Junior and as usual he always reminds me of Hayden because of how similar they look.

Junior misses me and I told him I'd be back soon and that I miss him. He's been taking his meds, he told me. I told him that when I come back I'll have a lot of presents for him that I got here. I can't help but buy him clothes and everything cute for him.

I love spoiling my boy.

My heart and body aches for Junior because I've never been away from him this long. I trust Brandon to watch over him but God, all I want to do is hold him.

Looking at Hayden makes me feel closer to Junior, just because of how similar he is to him.

They are literally twins.

I mean that's why I called Junior, Junior. He is a mini version of Hayden, looks-wise for now.

"Water, miss?' the waiter asks, making me look away from Hayden.

"Yes, please. Thank you." I smile as he pours water.

"How was last night?" Kayden asks.

"Good. We had fun."

"What'd you guys end up doing? I heard you came back late."

I shrug. "We went to a club."

"Sounds fucking boring. We went to a party at Killian's. He has such good whiskey. Need to hang out with that guy more often." Max says.

"Wasn't boring for Jaclyn," Natalia says and I look at her as she smirks my way. "She got a stripper's number."

"What?" Chris and Hayden say at the same time.

Chris looks at Natalia with a confused look and then Hayden is glaring at me with his jaw still clenched.

"Oh, you pulled a stripper?" Kayden says, looking between Hayden and I with a stupid smile on his face.

"Is he hot?" Max asks.

"Wait, you guys went to a strip club?" Chris asks, still looking at Natalia.

She got herself in trouble.

That's what she gets.

"Yes, and we didn't even touch them, just drank, and danced. Calm down," Natalia says while running her hand down Chris's chest.

"Wait, you got a stripper's number?" Chris says, looking at me now.

My cheeks turn red and I can't help but smile shyly. "Yea."

"Are you going to call him?" Max asks, now looking at Hayden and back at me.

God, what are they all doing?

I shrug. "I don't know. He seemed nice."

"Nice," Hayden mutters while shaking his head lightly.

"What does he look like?"

"He's good looking. Brown hair, brown eyes, and tall."

"Is he fit?" Max asks.

Nicole rolls her eyes. "Of course he's fit. He's a damn stripper, Max," she says before talking to her friends again.

I forgot she was even here for a second.

"Damn, okay Jaclyn." Kayden smirks.

"What's his name?" Martins asks.

"Ethan. He wrote it down for me."

"Oh my god! He gave you a note? So romantic!" Max

says, looking at Hayden before looking back at me again. "What did it say?"

I shake my head lightly. "I'm not going to talk to you guys about this." I try not to smile, from how embarrassing this is.

A chair scrapes against the floor making everyone at the table startle. I look up and see Hayden walk out of the room and towards the entrance.

"Damn, he must really care about you?" Nicole chuckles as she smiles watching Hayden walk away.

I look at Natalia, Max, and Kayden. "Really?"

"Just needed a little push." Natalia shrugs with a happy smile on her face.

"It's just getting started," Kayden mumbles before drinking water.

Thirty-Two

PRESENT

I'm in my hotel room watching the movie, *Freedom Writers*.

Today has been a long day.

After breakfast this morning, Natalia and I went shopping.

The whole entire time we were together I kept lecturing her and asking her why she did what she did at breakfast and all she kept saying was to wait and see.

Wait and see for what?

It's going to end in a disaster like last time.

Hayden and I can't happen and that's what I told her but she just shook her head at me and continued looking at clothes to buy.

Natalia doesn't understand the demons that Hayden

left me with. He left me with so much overthinking, worse than before. Although while being here, I haven't gotten any nightmares, mostly because of the meds I think.

Most nights I just replay the memories between Hayden and I that I wish I could forget.

Remembering the good things between us hurts my heart because I know we are ruined.

Hayden and I were doomed the day we met in that alleyway. But the universe just keeps pulling us closer together.

No matter how hard I try, Hayden will always be a factor in my life. I won't be able to rid myself of him.

Coming to this wedding was a mistake because I'm just digging myself into a deeper hole with Hayden and it will just continue to grow bigger.

I can't forget about Junior either. He is the priority and he needs to meet his father but God, I'm so scared.

I'm scared of growing attached to Hayden again and eventually getting hurt because with love comes pain and heartbreak.

A knock on the door makes me look away from the TV.

I get up and walk towards the door. When I open it, I see familiar gray eyes that are heated and almost look furious.

Hayden looks mad.

So royally pissed off probably from the show that Max, Kayden, and Natalia pulled this morning.

Now I have to deal with the aftermath.

"You know, since I've laid my eyes on you in that alleyway, I've never been able to understand why I was so obsessed. Why, out of all people, did I become obsessed over a girl who doesn't give two shits about me?" Hayden says, walking inside. I back up and Hayden closes the door behind him and locks it, sealing our fate almost. "Every second of every day I think about you. It's like my mind is addicted to you and the only way to control this addiction is to be with you." We stand in the middle of the room as energy pulls us closer. "I sometimes wish I hadn't met you so I wouldn't know what falling in love meant. I wouldn't have to be fucking vulnerable."

"Then why did you? Why'd you continue to pursue me if you didn't want this to happen?" I ask, a tear falling from my eye making me realize that I'm crying. "Why did you have to start all this?"

Hayden puts his hand on my jaw and tilts my head so I can get a better look at him. "Because somehow the universe wanted me to end up with you. Even if we destroyed each other five years ago." I shake my head and remove Hayden's hands from my face. "You promised me you would stay."

"That was before!" I say, tears streaming down my face as everything in that fucking room replays in my mind.

"That was before I got fucked up! That was before they fucking broke me, Hayden!"

"You never told me what they did in there."

I shake my head as my heart speeds up. "Please don't make me tell you."

An image of Eric flashes in my head.

Eric walks closer to me, a menacing smile on his face with a knife in his hand.

"Won't hurt much, sweetheart. I'll go easy on you."

And when he finally puts his hands on me, I scream.

Hayden walks closer to me and I step back, screaming.

I don't mean to scream but I can't stop.

Hayden still walks towards me and he wraps his arms around me as I sob into his chest.

"Please, please don't make me. I don't want to go back there," I cry while pushing my face into his chest more.

Being this close to him feels like home but when will these images of Eric, Marco, and that room pass?

When will it all go away?

"It's okay. You're okay, you're going to be okay. I've got you."

I shake my head in his chest. "No it's not. It's all going to end in a disaster again."

Hayden runs his fingers through my hair and rubs his thumb against my cheek softly. "Just give me a chance."

"You're getting married," I mumble and lean away

from him to stare at his face. "Whatever you and I want to happen, can't. It's wrong and not who I am."

"You're the only one I want and if I can't have you then I don't want to have anyone. I told you so many times that I'm obsessive and almost addicted. My heart is dedicated to you. My fucking heartbeats are dedicated to you."

"Then why would you marry someone if this is how you feel Hayden?"

Hayden pushes a strand of my hair behind my ear. "I can't tell you. Not yet," Hayden whispers. "Make my world fucking stop, Jaclyn," he says, turning my head so that I can look up at him.

His eyes are heated again and they almost look daring.

"Hayden," I say as a warning but my mind is telling me to shut up.

"Stop my world again, princess. Destroy my heart and everything that makes me Hayden Night. I'm begging you."

And as I look at Hayden, who almost looks desperate, I can't help but lean forward and kiss him.

His lips connect with mine and my eyes automatically close. Hayden's lips feel smooth and warm against mine and so familiar.

It's like he sucks all the negative air out of me and breathes in love. His kisses will always have this kind of effect on me. Kissing him makes me smile against his lips and wrap my arms together around him.

Hayden instantly grabs my cheek and his other hand is on my waist, squeezing and gripping me tighter.

Hayden sucks my bottom lip and I breath out heavily before connecting our lips again. The spot between my legs pulses and my heart feels like it's going to burst out of my chest.

He has a way of melting every part of me without even trying.

We can't.

He's still getting married.

Whether he loves her or not.

I lean away from him and rest my forehead against his. "You're still engaged," I whisper.

Hayden sighs and presses his lips to mine. "I'll take care of it."

"You also have a ring on you finger." I say, looking at that goddamn ring, just wanting him to take it o! at least. Hayden sighs and takes o! the ring and giving it to me.

I take it hesitantly. I look on the inside of the ring and see my initials.

"I've been wearing that ring for almost four years now. It's always been you, Jaclyn."

Thirty-Three

Jaclyn

The room is dark.

The only time light actually comes on is when the door opens and Eric turns on the lights. They chained me down to the point where I can only reach the bucket they put near the bed for me to go to the bathroom in.

The clothes I'm wearing are loose and they feel like I have no armor on. They can so easily take the shirt and shorts off, baring me for them to look at.

The only one who's done serious damage is Marco.

It replays in my mind every night. I can't stop the memories or the visions.

Sure Eric did major damage but Marco is the one who broke me.

He came in wearing a black hood as if he could read my mind.

As if I was dreaming and seeing a black hooded man all along.

My nightmares came true and they are only beginning.

I can't keep track of the days.

Eric drugs me every night and God knows what else. I wake up feeling achy and sore everywhere. It's like they are tearing down my body and breaking me slowly and painfully.

There is only so much I can take before I take these chains and wrap them around my throat.

But something's stopping me.

I don't know why I can't do it. I came close last time I was awake but then a boy, someone who looked similar to Hayden, told me not to.

He told me to keep going.

So every time one of them comes in to feed me or scare me, I remember him.

I feel disgusting.

I hate using the word disgusting because it feels wrong to say. But in this moment I've never felt so used and nasty.

I've never felt like a discarded toy that someone uses constantly. It's the fact that I'm not even awake which makes me even more disgusted.

The only time I was awake was with Marco. He made sure to have me remember every little detail.

Every nasty touch, every degrading word, and every fucking moment of those ten minutes and thirty-seven seconds.

Those are ten minutes and thirty-seven seconds I will never forget or get back.

A knock sounds on the door making me look up. Eric walks in, with a menacing smile on his face but my eyes go to the knife in his hand.

I've learned to put a mask on my face when they come in. Most of the time I just block everything out and pretend I'm somewhere else.

The drugs help.

I wish I would fucking have a seizure or pass out from high blood sugar but the one time my diabetes decides not to act up, it's right now.

I have been low from not eating but they make sure to force food down my throat.

"Hey, sweetheart." Eric closes the door behind him and locks it. "Just me and you today. Got my own personal agenda I need to take care of before Marco comes back."

Marco has gone on a business trip and that's why I haven't seen him since that first day.

Eric has been the one traumatizing me with his buddies but they usually drug me up a little bit.

He walks closer to me and I move back until my back is against the wall. "Now don't worry, sweetheart, won't hurt much. I'll go easy on you," he says before putting his hands on me.

I scream.

I flinch away from him as he removes the shirt so it's dangling on my arms and my breasts are free. Cold air hits my nipples and goosebumps rise on my skin.

When the pointy end of his knife touches my skin that's when I freak out. I try to kick him but he digs the knife deeper.

Block it out.

Block it out.

Block it out.

"No! No! NO! Let me go! Let me go! Please!"

I'm sobbing at this point.

Screaming to the top of my lungs for anyone, anyone to hear me and save me.

I want it all to stop.

Make it all stop.

I claw at his hands on me but he presses me against the wall with a hand on my neck and the other carving my side. Eric is getting scratch marks and I think he might be bleeding a little from how desperately I'm rapidly scratching.

There's nothing I can do to stop him or make him stop.

I'm defenseless.

It's painful, the things that are running through my mind.

Not even the knife that's cutting me is distracting me from the pain inside my head.

"Almost done," Eric yells loud enough for me to hear through the screaming.

I become limp against the wall and close my eyes while still screaming.

Eventually Eric stops and he releases me.

I choke on air and my eyes go down to my side.

There's blood everywhere.

And the tattoo, the one I got for Hayden, it's gone.

"Now, Night knows not to fuck with me in the future," Eric says before walking towards the door and slamming it closed.

All you see is blood on the bed and on my ribs.

I cover my side with my shirt and cry as I put pressure on the wound.

"It's okay. I'm going to be here. You'll have me," a little boy with brown hair and gray eyes says. I smile down at him and suddenly I'm at the beach as he stands in front of me. He grabs my hand and pulls me towards the water. "Just come with me and everything will be okay."

Thirty-Four

HAYDEN

PRESENT

Jaclyn wakes up with a jolt in my arms, breathing heavily. Sweat is running down the side of her face as she whimpers in my hold.

"Hayden-"

"I'm here," I say instantly. I wrap my arms around her tighter and pull her closer to me. "I'm always going to be here."

"He, he was out to get me, again. He's always there."

"Who?" I ask, rubbing her shoulder to calm her down.

Jaclyn leans into me and rests the side of her face against my chest as she calms down her breathing. I can feel how fast her heart is beating against my chest as she turns her body towards me.

"The man in the black hood."

I furrow my eyebrows and look down at her. "Man in the black hood?" How long has she been having these nightmares? Did they start before everything happened or after? Jaclyn looks up at me, with tears in her eyes from the nightmare she woke up from. I look at the clock behind her and see that it's 5:44am. "How long have you been having nightmares?" I ask after letting her calm down a little bit.

"About the black hood or that night in general?" she asks.

So, there are two different nightmares that she has?

I think she notices me tense up from her question because she runs her hand down my arm to hold my hand. She leans into my chest more and we both just lay back down against the headboard.

"I've had nightmares about the black hood ever since we started getting stalked by Eric."

"Why did you never tell me about them?"

How did I not fucking notice?

"Because I knew you would worry about me." Jaclyn looks up at me.

I wipe the dry tears from her face. "I'd rather worry about you than you just keeping everything in." Jaclyn nips her bottom lip and nods her head. "What about the other nightmares?"

"The ones about that night, I got the day we last saw each other. That's when they started and they stopped after a while. Every now and then they'll come but it's been a while since I've had a bad one. It's just always the black hooded man."

I stroke a strand of hair and push it behind her ear.

Hearing this makes me want to punch a fucking wall.

I already killed Marco and Eric but God, I wish I kept them alive so I could torture them forever.

I had to have Killian pull some strings to be able to get them out of jail so I could deal with them.

Rage blinded me when I killed them.

Killian watched me kill them and my brother was the one who pushed me back and said it was enough. Killian was enjoying the show and letting me take it all out because he knew I needed it.

He's all about losing control when needed but my brother, he likes to always be in control, no matter what. He is very calculated and calm which is almost scary because you never see him coming.

But Killian, you have to really piss him off or do something to make him get out of control.

I've heard from my brother that Killian went out of control only once, killing anyone in sight. I still don't know why because Rowan said that the only person who should tell me is Killian.

"You don't ever have to worry about Marco or Eric."

Jaclyn turns her head and looks at me. "Why?" I narrow my eyes at her but don't say anything. She knows I killed them. I mean I did promise her I would kill Eric. "Hayden-"

"You think that after they touched you, after they touched what was mine, I'd let them live?"

"No but-"

"No buts. Anyone who lays a hand on you, I. Will. Kill. Them. No hesitation." Jaclyn's eyes widen as she stares at me. This is probably one of those overthinking moments she's having. She's most likely thinking whether or not she should run like last time or stay. "You might not agree, but I will do anything to protect the people I care about."

The people I love. And I love you.

"Okay," Jaclyn says.

"They are already dead. There is nothing I can do."

Jaclyn nods her head. "I never told you what they did in that room because I was scared you were going to do something to them and I didn't want blood on my hands since you would do it for me."

"Princess, I would do just about anything in the world for you," I say, sitting up and pulling her on top of me so she is sitting on my lap, facing me. "If you asked me to burn the entire world down, I'd do it in a second, no questions asked. You didn't make me do anything. You didn't ask me to kill them. I did that because they hurt what was mine and for that the only reasonable punishment was death. I'd kill them all over again and go to hell just so I could make their punishment last a lifetime. You didn't make me do anything," I say, holding her face in my hands and reassuring her.

Jaclyn doesn't say anything, instead she leans forward and kisses me on the lips.

I close my eyes and enjoy the feel of her lips on mine. I make the kiss deeper and trail one of my hands to hold her neck. She moves her hips slowly on top of mine and I swear she is slowly killing me or testing my patience.

I thrust my tongue in her mouth and she moans gliding her tongue against mine. Her tongue against mine feels soft and makes the kiss sensual. An overwhelming feeling bursts in my chest, which always happens whenever I'm with her.

But kissing her is just a different type of pleasure.

Jaclyn pulls away and her breath hits my lips as she tries to calm down her rapid heartbeat.

I push a fallen strand behind her ear. "I want to tell you everything," she whispers, her lips lightly bumping against mine from how close we are. "I just hate having to retell every detail."

"I don't want to rush you. That's the last thing I want. I know they fucked you up in there and I wish to God it's not as bad as what I'm thinking but I'll wait for you.

However long you need, I'll wait for you whenever you're ready to talk about it."

Jaclyn smiles down at me softly and she runs her finger softly on my cheek. "Thank you."

"Always."

Thirty-Five

Hayden

After Jaclyn's nightmare and the talk we had, we went back to sleep. I just held her in my arms in silence as she fell back asleep.

I myself didn't end up falling back asleep because I couldn't stop thinking or staring at her.

I kept my eyes on her as she was cuddled up against me and I would notice the way her lips parted at times or goosebumps would randomly appear on her skin making me wonder what she could be thinking about.

There is still so much we both need to talk about.

And one of these days we will. We have to if we want this to work and God, I want this to work.

But priority right now is breaking things off with Nicole and then talking to Killian about it.

I'm not worried about breaking things off with Nicole and how pissed her dad will be. I'm worried about how Killian will react.

Yes, I am Rowan Valentino's brother and practically a part of the family as they say but, actions speak louder than words.

Rowan may have found me and helped me but Killian is the one I work for and who I answer to.

I've done everything Killian has asked me, no questions asked. But this is the one thing I just can't move forward with.

I'm currently walking to the restaurant in the hotel, because that's where Nicole and her friends are having breakfast.

Before I left Jaclyn's room, I told her I was going to be back late tonight to see her and that I had a lot of things to do today, but didn't specify what. But she understood. I kissed her, of course and then she pulled away when it started getting heated which she always does but in a teasing way making me want more.

Eventually I end up near Nicole's table. When I walk up to her, her back is to me as her friends look up at me and stare with confusion.

"Nicole-"

"What do you want Hayden? I'm busy," she says in that bitchy tone.

I look at her two friends again. "Leave."

They do it, no questions asked, because they know exactly who I am and what I can do.

I walk around and sit in the chair facing her. "Can't wait until the wedding, husband?"

"Don't call me that," I say, making the smirk wipe off her face. "Wedding's off. I won't be going through with it."

Nicole's eyes darken and her jaw clenches. She looks like she is going to start throwing that tantrum she throws with her dad whenever she doesn't get what she wants. "You can't do that. You and Killian made a deal."

"I'll deal with Killian. But you, I don't need to do shit for you."

"My dad. He'll be pissed."

"Again, I need to deal with Killian. Killian will deal with your father. But you and I, it's done, Nicole," I explain and all of a sudden she just starts laughing and shaking her head.

"So you finally got her huh? After five years of obsessing over this girl, you finally got her back? Seems a little easy if you ask me."

I glare at her. "You don't know shit. I don't remember asking you for your opinion on her or me."

"I was trying to fucking get something out of this but you had to go in and ruin it all," Nicole sneers, her good mood vanishing. "I was supposed to get my cut of his company, making me set for life."

I shrug. "Not my problem. Figure out your own shit."

"You better hope and pray that my dad or Killian don't fuck you up for this."

"As long as they don't touch Jaclyn, then we shouldn't have an issue."

Nicole licks the inside of her cheek and crosses her arms over her chest. "You really care about this girl more than yourself or your own life?"

"Yes."

God, I love her.

I've never loved or been so protective of someone before. But Jaclyn, she was always it.

She was never and never will be just some girl.

She is the girl.

My girl.

Nicole scoffs. "Pathetic. Watch her run away like last time. Like you told me, she doesn't even know who you are. You aren't the same guy I met five years ago. You weren't ruthless or controlled. You were impulsive and easy to read. No one knows what you'll do or what moves you'll pull."

"People change and I happened to change for the better.

"Yes you did," she says while giving me a once over. "You aren't that weak boy you were when Killian and Rowan found you. What will Killian think? His best friend betrays him for a girl? Gonna be one hell of a show."

"I know how to handle him." I get up from the chair. "I'm done now. You can enjoy your breakfast and the rest of your trip. I only needed to tell you that. I'll take care of canceling everything and it will be as if this wedding and trip was never meant to happen."

"My dad will ruin you and then he will destroy Killian right after he's done with you," Nicole says with a straight face.

I almost laugh because she has no fucking clue.

I put my hands on the table and lean close to her. "Do you know who Killian's family is? Who his father is? What he and his family can do to you if you simply disrespect them? If they heard what you just said right now, you would have been dead a minute ago. Keep your mouth shut. Understood?" Nicole's face goes red again and she clenches her fists on the table. "Do you understand, Nicole?"

"*Codice di verità*," Nicole mutters.

"Good," I say before turning around and leaving.

Thirty-Six

Jaclyn

Present

"How's Italy treating you?' Brandon asks over the phone.

Junior is still sleeping and I'm not surprised because it's Saturday so Junior always sleeps in and gets up around 8 or 9.

It's 11am over here in Italy and since Hayden is out doing whatever it is he has to do, I decided to call them now.

I call Brandon and Junior every morning so that I can see Junior's face and so he can tell me everything he wants to tell me. And when he gets home he calls too because he wants to tell me about his day.

Brandon told me he cried a few times and had a

tantrum recently because he missed me and it made my heart hurt.

I told Junior over the phone that I'd be home soon and right when I get home we can get cinnamon rolls from this really good bakery down the street from the apartment.

He loves cinnamon rolls and every time he does good in school or just whenever we want a sweet treat, we'll go to the bakery.

Saying we'll go there put him in a much better mood for sure and made things a tad bit easier for Brandon.

Brandon has learned to handle Junior's mood swings and tantrums. He has a temper just like his dad and it's funny because they've never even met.

"It's good. Definitely getting a good tan, that's for sure," I say as I sit on the bed and stare at the view out of my window.

It still smells like Hayden was in here because you can smell his lingering cologne and scent.

This morning I pushed my face into the pillows and blushed.

I do deja vu when I did that because in the morning I would do that in Hayden's room from when we were in college. He would leave me in bed on the weekends when he went to work out and I would smell the pillows.

"New York makes you pale as fuck so it's good that the sun is treating you well."

I roll my eyes at Brandon because he always likes to tease me about how pale I am.

"I'm not even that pale. I just need a light tan."

Brandon laughs. "How are things with Hayden?"

Whenever we talk on the phone, Junior is around so I haven't been able to talk about Hayden with Brandon at all.

Hayden told me this morning he needs to take care of some things but he wants to talk tonight again.

He and I have a lot to talk about.

His career, his brother, his friend Killian who I suspect is not in a good crowd, his wedding, so much more of what's been happening with him.

For me, there's what happened in that room, what I've been doing to myself in the past five years, and Junior.

Junior is the main one that he probably cares about the most even though he knows nothing about him.

I don't know whether I should tell him that piece of information first or what happened in the room.

Either way he'll be pissed so does the order really matter?

I know we have months to talk and catch up on what's been going on and it will take time so we don't have to talk about everything at once.

I just feel like we have such little time and I need to tell him everything soon before it's too late and something happens.

"Things are good. We talked last night a little bit and he told me he wants to see me."

"Even though he has a fiancé?"

"Hayden was never the type of guy to play games with other girls when it came to me. I trust him, even after so many years," I say, backing Hayden up.

"I hope you're right. I don't want to see you get hurt. You're still trying to heal from the past and Hayden unfortunately is the past."

"I know. I'm scared, Brandon," I admit. "He knows I am too but he's trying so hard. I want to let him in, I want to tell him everything but God, the past scares me so much."

"Is he forcing you to tell him everything?"

"No. He just tells me he wants to know but is willing to wait."

"Does he know about Junior yet?" Brandon asks and I stay silent. Brandon sighs over the phone. "Jaclyn-"

"I know. I know I need to tell him."

"The reaction he'll have won't be good but if you keep waiting until he finds out himself, he will be even more pissed off," Brandon explains.

"I know. Junior needs to meet him too. I know Junior won't be mad, maybe in the future he might but I have to think about him too."

"Junior isn't calm like you. He may be your son and you may have given birth to him but he acts like you only a little while he acts like Hayden a lot. That's saying something because I've never even met Hayden and you would always say, "Oh Hayden used to do that. That's what his dad did" and Junior doesn't even know."

"Brandon, I know. I just hope the outcome isn't as bad as what I think it'll be."

"You just need to trust that Hayden won't leave again. If you truly trust him not to leave or just to still be there for you and support you, then you shouldn't worry. I may not like the guy that much because of how much pain the past with him caused you but I still think he is your literal soulmate and will always be there."

I lay back on the bed and close my eyes.

Everything I feel for Hayden is overwhelming, it always has been.

I remember the nights I would cry to Brandon or my mom about him. I never cry to my mom about a guy but Hayden wasn't just any guy.

He was the guy who stopped my world and made it his. He took my heart and held it in the palm of his hand to keep safe.

"I still love him, Brandon. Even after all these years and it hurts," I say as tears start forming in my eyes.

"No one ever said love was going to be easy."

"I just wish I hated him sometimes so I wouldn't feel like this," I say as I start to cry to Brandon. "I hate realizing how much he still affects me and how much I care and love him. I'm so fucking scared, Brandon."

"I know. But you'll be okay. Whatever happens with Hayden, I'm always going to be here."

"Thank you," I say, after a while of silence. "I don't know what I'd do without you."

"Probably end up in the bathtub every night crying while drinking red wine to get drunk."

And we both start laughing lightly because he's probably right.

Thirty-Seven

Hayden

I'm sitting next to my brother with Killian in front of us.

We are at Killian's house here in Gaeta. He lives in Lombardy where he grew up but he has multiple properties around the world. I've been staying here instead of the hotel because I like having privacy and this is a big piece of property with a private beach too.

Killian is wearing his usual attire. Black trousers and a dark blue shirt. He is always wearing some sort of blue with every outfit, it's something odd I've noticed about him.

He also has his regular jewelry on. A thin chain necklace on his neck, an expensive Bulgari watch on his left wrist and then some rings. Only one ring on his left hand which looks like a band on the ring finger.

He never mentioned he was married but the one thing he never talks about with me is women. So I know not to question it.

My brother is next to me in his usual attire. A black fitted t-shirt with some jeans. Rowan is always dressed casually because he thinks it's not necessary to be wearing a suit all the time since he doesn't need to prove himself to people.

Killian was born wearing suits, he told me he's used to wearing a suit all the time. I've seen him in casual attire from time to time but he still dresses with class.

"Why am I here, Hayden?" Killian asks, leaning into his chair.

I'm pretty positive that Killian already got word of what I did.

He knows I fucked up but he also knows I don't care.

Rowan is here because with me and Killian being the two hotheads, we need one calm person to make sure things don't get out of hand but at the same time I've never seen Killian really lose control or get crazy.

He's always been calm with a stern voice. What he says goes and no one questions him because they are too scared to see what might happen.

His dad is completely different, I heard.

You never know what Ace De Luca is going to do. He

doesn't waste time killing someone. He lights their ass on fire and says, "*Saluta Satana da parte mia.*"

Ace De Luca doesn't care who's in his way. If you say one bad thing about him or his family, if you don't obey him, he won't even think twice about killing you.

Everyone is replaceable to him except his wife.

"You know why. I'm sure Earnings called you about it."

"He wasn't happy, Hayden. You caused an issue that I have to fix now. He was going to be a great investment."

"I know. I know I fucked up."

"So, when were you planning on telling me you were going to do this? You just decided to do all this and ruin this deal on your worn without discussing things with me first?" Killian raises an eyebrow at me.

"I'm telling you now."

Killian bites the inside of his cheek and shakes his head lightly. He looks at Rowan. "Who's worse? Me or him?"

"Right now it's still you. He's not as crazy as you," Rowan answers without hesitation.

Killian looks back at me. "And all this for one girl?"

Killian doesn't understand because he loves nothing and no one. Killian told me he used to love a girl but she died and from what I heard, after that, he changed. He's colder and doesn't care about a single thing in this world.

"Yes," I say.

"You threw away a multi-million dollar deal because of

a girl?" Killian repeats, making me frustrated because he has no clue how important Jaclyn is to me.

If I had to, I'd choose Jaclyn over Killian any day.

I'd die trying to kill Killian if it meant saving Jaclyn.

"Yup," I repeat, leaning in my chair. "I wanted to tell you about my plan-"

"When? Because it sure as fuck wasn't going to be today."

"It was going to be today."

"You should have told me when you started even thinking about calling off the wedding."

I roll my eyes. "What do you want from me, Killian?"

"I like you Hayden. You are like the brother I never had and my family even trusts you which is a shock knowing who they are." Killian sits up in his chair. "So because you cost me this deal and I have to pay Earnings an absurd amount of money to keep his mouth shut about this whole thing, I am promoting you."

I raise an eyebrow at him. "Promoting me for what?" Killian looks at Rowan making me look at my brother. "What does he want?"

"He wants you to be his second in command. He needs one and doesn't trust anyone other than you," Rowan explains.

I look at Killian. "You're kidding me?"

I'm not exactly happy about this because it puts me in a fucking deeper hole that I wanted to get out of.

I don't want to constantly be looking over my shoulder, worrying about someone killing me or Jaclyn or possibly our future children.

I don't want to endanger anyone I care about.

Sure Killian is powerful and his name can fucking protect us but that doesn't matter when Jaclyn would be in a position where a gun is to her head without me there.

"I told you I didn't want to do that. I can't risk my family being in danger like that. If it was just me I wouldn't care but now that I have Jaclyn, I can't risk that or her getting hurt."

"Rowan, how has Jane been since her accident?" Killian asks my brother.

"She's fine. She has me."

"But Jane has been in this life since she was born, not Jaclyn. She has no fucking clue who I am now or what I do," I explain to Rowan and Killian.

They both don't get it because they were born into this.

I wasn't.

I have a family who is somewhat fucking normal.

Carter is the only one who I think is a little deranged like them.

"Jaclyn and your family will be under the De Luca protection. You also have your brother's company to help you as well. You and Jaclyn are protected all around. You need a specific bodyguard for Jaclyn, easy. We'll get you one."

I look at my brother, trying to figure out what he thinks.

I trust Rowan, he's my brother.

I've grown so close to him in such a short time period and I know if he says I can trust him and do this, then I will.

Rowan cares about me and my interests, he's never made me question that.

Killian, on the other hand, always does things that benefit him.

If he needs to fuck me over he will.

His loyalty lies with no one, not even his family.

Everyone is a pawn on his chess board.

"You can trust me. I won't let anyone hurt or touch her," Rowan says, making me nod my head at him.

I look at Killian. "Anything, and I mean anything happens, I'm out. I don't care what you'll do or say, I'll be out if anything happens to her."

Killian nods his head and thrusts his hand in my direction to shake it.

"Deal."

I shake his hand, sealing my fate with him forever. "Deal."

Thirty-Eight

Hayden

My palms sweat as I knock on the door.

I mean I could just open it but at the same time it's not really my hotel room.

Killian and I eventually came to an agreement after many negotiations from both sides. Rowan spectated and made sure things didn't get out of hand or we started fighting.

You would expect me and Rowan to fight, which we sometimes do, but Killian and I fight more, but it's because we are so alike.

But as soon as that meeting was over, I bolted out of the house and sped to the hotel where Jaclyn King is.

The door opens and I see her.

She's wearing sweatpants and a sweater that says New York on it.

Suddenly I'm back to being 21 and she's opening the door to her house for me to come in so we can do a project.

Back when I openly hated her but secretly was obsessed.

Jaclyn and I never had to force love, we were drowning in it since the moment we met.

She wore that same sweater but with shorts.

After five years I still remember every detail of every moment we've had together from that year.

I walk inside her room and she lets go of the door and backs away from me. I close the door and walk towards her.

"For more than five years, I have been so obsessed with you, that it's become an unhealthy addiction. I wish I didn't feel like this," I admit. "But I can't help it. When I look at you, I can't help but fall in love all over again, and that's exactly what happened at the fight. You have no clue how fucking happy and in love I still felt even after you destroyed my heart that night."

Jaclyn shakes her head. "I didn't mean-"

"I'm not done," I say, walking closer to her but this time she stays still and just stares up at me. "You don't understand the butterflies you still give me. How bad I want to pull you closer and just kiss you. I want to give you everything again. My passion, my love, my heart, everything." Jaclyn's lips pull in a soft smile that makes my heart almost burst. "I ended things with Nicole. It's done, I'm not with her anymore. I never was with her. I only want you."

It's quiet for a few seconds, her heart bumping against my chest making me realize we are chest to chest.

And like God's answering my prayers, she goes on her toes and reaches my lips, kissing me.

I smile into the kiss because I love it whenever she makes the first move because she rarely does.

I grab ahold of her face and pull her closer to me if that's even possible. I just wish we could be closer, where there's no barrier between us. I nip her lower lip making her moan. With my other hand I clutch the back of her neck to pull her closer.

My tongue slides against hers, tasting her. She melts easily against me and I swallow every moan she gives me.

Jaclyn and I move towards the bed and I lay her down before standing up in front of her. She looks up at me, all flushed and out of breath. Her thighs are rubbing against one another.

I take my shirt off while Jaclyn stares up at me as if I'm her god. I lean down and kiss her, grabbing ahold of her neck and licking the seam of her lips.

She opens her mouth for me again and deepens the

kiss as our tongues dance together. "You're so perfect," I say against her lips.

She wraps her legs around my waist and says, "I want you."

I lean back, still holding onto her. "What?"

Her hands reach for my jaw, her fingers playing with the hair on the back of my head. "I want you, Hayden."

I smile down at her and then can't resist the urge to kiss her.

Her sweater comes off and I kiss my way down her body while taking her sweatpants off slowly. I throw the sweatpants somewhere behind me and then hook my fingers on the sides of her underwear, slowly pulling them down as Jaclyn rubs her thighs together.

"Impatient?"

"After so many years, yes." She breathes heavily.

I throw the underwear behind me, probably near the sweatpants and sweater. I kiss her thighs and my hands reach up to grab her breasts. My forefinger and thumb pinch and pull at her nipples causing her to squirm under my touch.

"You have no clue how long I've waited to taste you again," I say, looking up at Jaclyn and seeing her stare down at me.

I lean in and lick her gently, almost teasingly.

Jaclyn moans softly and her hands immediately make

their way into my hair. Jaclyn tastes just how I remember she did.

Like an addiction and a sin.

I lick her up and down, making her even more wet. She caresses my hair as I play with her clit, getting her close but not enough to the point where she's able to release.

I lap my tongue over her folds making her head go back as I watch her from between her legs. I suck so hard that she starts shaking and moaning louder. I release one of her breasts and bring my hand to her pussy. I thrust one finger inside her and she shifts her hips away but I hold her down with my arm.

"Hay," she moans my name and grips onto my hair harder, pulling me closer to her.

I repeat that same movement with my finger and flick my tongue against her clit for a good minute before her hands grip my hair and her legs close around my head as she cums around my finger and on my tongue.

She spasms and her legs shake around me. I continue licking, sucking, biting, and thrusting my finger inside her in the same motion.

She moans loudly, her chest rising and falling with every heavy breath.

I remove my finger and mouth from her. I climb my way up her body and then smash my lips against hers. She breathes heavily in my mouth, barely even kissing me from how spent she is. I take my jeans off as I kiss her and then throw them behind me.

Jaclyn thrusts her hips to meet mine, making my cock slide against her pussy. She's still wet from me tasting her.

I trail my kisses down her neck, sucking on a spot making her moan. "Let's see how well your body remembers how to take my cock," I whisper in her ear, before thrusting inside her.

Jaclyn wraps her legs around my waist tightly and screams.

So loud I'm pretty sure everyone on the floor can hear her.

I stay inside, not moving, letting her adjust to my size.

She is so fucking tight, just like I remember. She clenches and unclenches around me as she breathes heavily in my neck. I grab her hands and hold them against the bed over her head.

She throws her head to the side and moans while lifting her hips to move against me. Her doing that, does things to me.

Bad things.

I pull out and thrust back in and Jaclyn throws her head back and moans softly.

"Only you." She breathes out. "Only you can feel this good."

I drop my forehead to hers, our panting breaths

mixing together as I stare down at her. Her eyes are closed, lust written all over her face while I move inside her.

I go faster, making the bed hit the wall multiple times. Jaclyn screams and moans.

She feels so perfect, warm, wet, and all mine.

She was mine back then and she's mine now.

Nothing changed.

And there's no way in hell I'll let her go again.

She thrusts up to meet my hips, desperate to cum as I feel her walls squeezing around me.

"Fuck you make me insane. I love how you wrap around me. You know you're mine and always will be, don't you princess?'

"Yes," she moans, throwing her head back. "I'm close, Hayden." That's the only motivation I need to go faster, pounding into her harder making her choke on her air. I release my hold on her hip and reach down to press on her clit and play with it. "Ahh," she moans, making me lean down and press my lips against hers.

She moans into my mouth, almost screaming as she cums around me.

I shoot my load inside her as we continue to kiss.

"I love you so much. You have no clue," I mumble against her lips as she stays silent.

She knows and that's all that matters.

Thirty-Nine

Jaclyn

Strong hands and a warm tongue trail up my thigh, slowly waking me.

I keep my eyes closed as Hayden makes his way to the spot between my legs. I spread my legs wider, urging him to come closer.

"Does it ache?" Hayden mumbles and I take the blankets off and see him lying there, between my legs and looking up at me like he needs me.

I nod my head, unable to say anything.

Hayden keeps his eyes on me as he leans forward and finally places his lips on me. His eyes are filled with lust and the way he grips my thighs causes goosebumps to spread across my body. His tongue flicks and swirls around my clit, hitting that same spot, over and over.

I feel like I might pass out from him doing that. All I can do is grab his shoulder with one hand and grip his hair with my other.

My hips move against his mouth, faster than he's licking me. I force myself closer to him, feeling empty and wanting more.

Hayden knows because he adds a finger inside me. I gasp and grip onto his hair.

"Fuck you're tight, even after so long. You were made for me, I swear," he says against my clit, sending vibrations through me. When I move against his tongue and I feel him smile. "That's it, princess. Ride my face and take it." All I can do is moan. I'm a mess, sweat forming on my body as I grip and pull his hair to make him come closer. My eyes are clenched shut as I feel my release slowly coming closer and closer. "Eyes on me."

At that I open my eyes and lift my head, watching him stare at me while I clench and unclench around his finger. My eyes want to shut so bad but I also love seeing pleasure take over Hayden's face as he makes me feel good. The way his finger slides in and out of me, reaching so deep I swear I can feel him everywhere.

Last night he made sure that it was all about me and how I felt. I missed him and his touch, I fucking craved it and more last night.

He ended up waking me up in the middle of the night, from doing exactly what he is doing right now, and then he slid inside me and I swear I blacked out from how many times he made me cum. He still has the same stamina, if not better.

"Get out of your head and cum for me," he mumbles and I swear, like clockwork, I cum all over his tongue.

My eyes squeeze shut and I try to close my legs around his face as he keeps going, not stopping for one second as his finger slides in and out of me at a fast pace. My legs shake around him and I grip his hair so hard, pulling him closer.

He slows down his pace as I come down from the high and I release his hair and the grip on his shoulder. I cover my eyes and try to calm my breathing down.

Jesus, he's still crazy.

I don't know how he's the only one who's able to do it.

I don't ever remember being able to cum like this with anyone except Hayden.

He knows my body and how to play with it so well.

He knows me in general so well.

Hayden unwraps his arms from around my legs and climbs his way up my body. He uncovers my face and I open my eyes to stare up at him.

His finger goes towards my eye, not the one he touched me with, and he wipes a tear that I didn't even realize has fallen. "Why are you crying?"

I laugh because I have no clue why. It's not like I'm overthinking so there's no reason for me to be crying.

I just miss him and how he made me feel so much.

I shake my head at him. "I just missed you," I say, truthfully.

One of the main reasons why I think I was so unhappy over the years, was because after all this time I was missing him, even though I pretended I didn't.

Hayden smiles down at me, a genuine smile. "You have no clue how much pain I was in without you for all these years." His fingers trail through my hair. "I was a mess without you. Killian and Rowan had to be there to pick me up and put me together because I couldn't do it without you."

"How did you meet your brother?"

Hayden never told me the story but that's only because we just started this thing again.

We have a lot of things to talk about.

Junior.

Hayden doesn't answer me. Instead he moves and gets comfortable on the bed before pulling me on top of him so I'm sitting on his lap.

"We met at this fight that Kayden took me to a few months after we broke up. It was a special kind of club for very important and wealthy people. I met Rowan and after that he just started showing up more until he asked me to move to New York."

"And Natalia and Chris followed you?"

Hayden shakes his head. "Not really. Chris got an offer for football so they were moving to New York anyways. I just followed Rowan."

"Are you guys close?"

"Yea." Hayden nods his head. "He is great. I definitely want you to meet him," Hayden says as he runs his hand down my hip and rests it there. "He told me a lot about our dad and how he wasn't the best person."

Hayden told me his mother was a drug addict and he doesn't care about her or the memories that include her.

He always wondered how his dad was.

"Why's that?"

"Because he was a bad guy. He was affiliated with the mafia."

The mafia.

I always knew that the mafia was a thing but I didn't think they were still active or that I would ever know if they were actually real or not.

"The mafia is real?" I ask, looking up at Hayden.

He nods his head. "Yea." He is silent for a few beats before he says, "I'm working for the Italian one."

He's working for the Italian one.

He is in the Italian mafia.

Hayden, the guy who is currently holding onto me and running his hand up and down my hip, is a part of a group that kills and tortures people and God knows what else.

I don't know how to react because for some reason I just can't believe him.

All I can think about is Junior.

How will this affect him?

Junior is the only concern that comes to mind.

"Say something," Hayden whispers and kisses my forehead. "I hate when you're quiet."

I shake my head lightly. "I don't know what to say. That's a lot to process, Hayden."

"I know, I just need to know what you're thinking."

Junior.

Junior.

Junior.

Junior.

That's all I can think about but I can't say it to Hayden.

My heart is beating so hard and fast to the point where I feel like I'm going to pass out.

"I need time to comprehend what you told me. Because I just can't imagine the kind of danger you'll get yourself into. I already know how the underground fighting was for you and now the Mafia. That's insane."

"I know." Hayden turns me around so that I can look at him. "I just need to know you won't run. I just thought you should know. I'm trying to be honest with you because I wasn't before. You deserve that."

"I know. I appreciate it, but Hayden, you said 'mafia' as if it's some normal thing. The mafia is a big deal. How will it affect me or you?"

Or Junior.

"I don't know. All I know is that no matter what, I don't want to lose you and I will keep you safe no matter what." Hayden grabs my face and rests his forehead against mine. "I'll protect you. All you have to do is trust me."

But trusting Hayden destroyed me.

"I want to. I'm just scared."

Hayden nods his head. He wraps his arms around me and makes me rest my head on his chest.

We don't say anything as I rest against Hayden. I try to clear my mind but all I can think about is what I'm getting myself into with him again.

Forty

Hayden

"How did you end up working for Killian?" Jaclyn asks as we walk around with my arm around her shoulder.

We are at a mini festival that's being held near the beach. There are booths and some food carts. There is also a giant Ferris wheel too which is in the center.

Jaclyn is holding my hand as it rests around her shoulders while looking up at me with curiosity.

I thought taking her here on a date would be fun and relaxing. We wouldn't have to focus on the issues between us or what's actually going on. We can pretend for a few hours that we're back to being in college where we had no ugly past or memories.

When everything was okay.

"Rowan ended up introducing me to him after a

while. Killian had heard of me and my fighting. He was impressed and wanted me to win some fights for him. Eventually it all just escalated and I dug myself in a hole with him."

"Is it like Marco and how he was?"

I look down at Jaclyn and I swear fear is present in her eyes. I know she is worried about this whole thing with Killian and a new lifestyle, especially with how it'll affect her. Plus her overthinking just makes it worse because she thinks about every scenario which isn't good.

I know she is scared of getting hurt again but things are different, especially with Killian. He isn't like Marco at all.

Marco was dirty and didn't care about anyone but himself and money. Killian on the other hand has a family that he stands by. He knows that he has loved ones to protect so he isn't the type to fuck you over without a valid reason.

"No. Killian isn't like Marco. He may seem colder and harsher but he's loyal and never goes back on his word. If you fuck him over then he'll fuck you over. He is more of a 'treat others how you want to be treated' type of guy," I explain as I caress her bare shoulder.

Tonight she's wearing a red summer dress with small white flowers on it. It's not too cold out tonight so she isn't cold, but if she is I have my jacket that I'd love to give to her.

"Killian is the leader I'm assuming."

I nod my head. "Yes. He is the main guy."

"Who are you and Rowan?"

"I'm the second in command. So like Killian's assistant although he likes to joke around and say I'm his little bitch." I smile down at her in a joking way. She gives me a small smile back while still looking up at me. "And then Rowan isn't a part of it. He has his own organization that I help with sometimes."

I honestly have no clue where we are going or where we are headed. At this point we're just walking and catching up.

"Don't you have to be in the mafia for a while to be able to have that kind of position?"

I shrug because I have no clue. "I don't think so. I think it's just up to whoever is in charge and he is the one who appoints them. I don't think that Killian has to run anything by anyone. Not even his dad."

Jaclyn nods her head, understanding. Although I'm not 100% sure what is going through her head and what she's thinking. I look ahead and see the ferris wheel entrance. I take my arm off Jaclyn's shoulder and grab her hand to pull her towards the entrance.

I want her to get out of her head for a few minutes and forget everything I told her because I can tell it's causing her a little stress.

I pay for one ride each and he lets us on. He closes the

door behind us and Jaclyn immediately goes to the opposite side of the cabin with a shy smile on her face.

A ghost smile makes its way to my face and I am itching to close the distance between us and grab her so she can be closer to me.

The cabin starts to move up as the wheel turns and now Jaclyn looks away from me and instead looks around the cabin and outside of it.

I admire her from afar and think to myself, "Holy shit, I have her back again. Jaclyn King is mine again."

Although part of her is still wary of me and completely unsure, I am still with her. She is still here, willing to give this another try.

But I made a promise to myself, once I have her in my arms again I'm not letting her go.

"Princess," I say, making Jaclyn look at me. "Come here." She shakes her head, a smile widening on her face. "I'm not going to ask again. If you make me ask again, I'll come over there and make you scream so loud the people on the ferris wheel will hear you."

Jaclyn's face turns beat red but she makes her way to me, standing between my legs. I grab her waist and she falls on my lap with a small laugh.

I can't help but smile up at her because her laugh is one of my favorite things in the world as well as her smile because I swear no one has a smile like her.

I lean towards her and press my lips against hers.

Her eyes close and mine follow as I enjoy the feel of her lips. I thrust my tongue between her lips and Jaclyn opens her mouth for me wider. She breathes heavily in my mouth and I slide one of my hands up her spine and grab the back of her neck, guiding her through the kiss.

She tightens her arms around me and pulls me closer to her.

The cabin moves but I don't pay attention to that, I pay attention to how the kiss heats up, especially as Jaclyn rocks her hips against mine.

Kissing her is the closest thing to feeling like a god. I can't control my breath and everything is hot.

But I don't want to stop, I want to keep going and give her everything she wants.

I grip her waist in my hands and move her against me making her moan. I do that again and she grips one of my arms and moans again.

My head is spinning like crazy and I swear my legs feel like jelly. The taste of her on my tongue, I never want that to go away. I trail my kisses down her neck and I feel her pulse as I press my lips tenderly against her sweet spot.

I give attention to her neck, slowly getting her ready while she rocks her hips against mine. I smell the perfume she's wearing, like a vanilla musky floral scent. It smells mature and feminine, and just like Jaclyn.

My hearts racing as I trail my hands down her waist

and to the spot between her legs. "Touch me already," she mumbles against my mouth.

I bite her bottom lip before smiling. I give her exactly what she wants and move my hand to the spot between her legs.

I move her dress up her thighs and move her underwear to the side. Her body tenses in my hands and then relaxes when I stroke my fingers through her folds and rub her clit. "Jesus," I moan before taking my lips off her neck and connecting our lips. "So wet and ready for me, princess. Your cunt knows exactly who she belongs to."

I thrust a finger inside her and she bucks against me and moans in my mouth. I rub her clit with my thumb, getting her ready and close but not to the point where she'll release.

She'll get off with me inside her and not a moment earlier.

Jaclyn's moans echo in the air as I press my lips all over her neck and the cabin moves around but it's hard to pay attention where we are when I have her in my arms. "Hay-Hayden." I suck on her neck and thrust my finger inside her faster as my thumb gives attention to her clit and rubs it side to side. Jaclyn's legs tense around me and she grinds against my fingers. I lean back and watch as her face fills with ecstasy and her eyes fill with euphoria. "Oh my God."

I take my fingers out and move my hips to get out of my jeans. They feel so tight and I just need a release.

"Spread your legs and lift your dress to your chest. I want to see how your pussy welcomes me home." Jaclyn does as I say and holds her dress to her chest with one hand while the other rests on my thigh behind her. My pants and boxers are at my feet and I stroke my cock a few times before pushing inside her. Jaclyn moans and squeezes her eyes shut and her lips open wide. "That's it princess. Scream so loud so everyone can hear who owns you."

Jaclyn's face is red and flushes as she grinds against me. She moans, all while still holding the dress to the top of her chest.

I thrust in and out of her, moving her up and down as she clenches and unclenches around my cock. I know she's close by the way she tenses around me as I hit that sweet spot inside her.

"I'm-I'm close, Hayden. Please."

"Eyes on me. I want to see how you come for me," I demand. She shakes her head and suddenly releases the dress before holding onto my shoulder. I grab her by the throat making her eyes open wide. She tenses around me and opens her mouth wide. I press my lips against her as she screams in my mouth. Her whole body tenses against mine as she comes with me inside her. "Good girl, look at you. You feel how much your body craved me? You feel like mine."

I thrust inside her a few more times before I feel my balls tighten and I release inside her. Ecstasy runs through my veins and I can't control my heaving breathing in Jaclyn's mouth. She holds me against her as my cum floods inside her.

"I wish we were at the hotel," she whispers in my ear.

Same, so I could show her just how much I missed her in the last five years.

I smile and press my lips to her cheek and then her jaw. "You have no clue."

Forty-One

Jaclyn

"And then Brandon also got me a toy car from Mini Soa. It looks like a race car and he said that we'll race with this car and one of my other cars. Whoever loses has to do the dishes," Junior says, his smile is bright and genuine on the screen.

It almost reminds me of his dads smile.

Hayden is at the convenience store a few miles away right now. I told him that my doctor put in a prescription for me for some new meds. I called him a few days ago to tell him I was running out of insulin and close to running out of Lantus too. He told me that he'd put in a prescription for some and that I just need to pick it up at the closest pharmacy.

I told Hayden about it this morning and he offered to pick it up for me. He left about twenty minutes ago so I decided it was the perfect time to talk to Junior. We've been on the phone for not that long, or at least I think we haven't.

This whole weekend, Hayden and I have spent every moment together. I saw Natalia and the boys the day we went to the small festival. I got to talk to them for just a few seconds before Hayden pulled me away.

He said, "They've had you this entire trip while I've waited five years to be with you. I'm spending every minute I can get with you."

Then when we got inside the hotel, he spent the entire night making me scream his name and see stars. I swear I blacked out a few times which just made Hayden laugh.

I guess what happened on the ferris wheel wasn't enough for him and he had to get his fill of me some more that night.

He said he loves giving me pleasure and just making me happy in general. He also said that he'd do anything to see me have a smile on my face, even if it meant doing something unethical.

"Why are you smiling, mama?" Junior asks me, making me focus back on him.

I smile wider. "I'm just happy to see you baby. I miss you and I can't wait to see you," I say, not necessarily a lie.

More so, not the whole reason why I'm smiling. "I got you a few presents from here so if you continue being good, like Brandon says you're being, you'll get them right when I get back."

"What'd you get me?" Junior screams on the phone while pushing his face closer to the camera. His smile becomes the only thing I can see. "Mama, tell me. You gots to tell me what you got me! I can't wait."

I laugh and shake my head. "I'm coming back soon baby, don't worry. You can wait."

Junior pouts on the screen and then his eyes go to something behind me. "Mama, there's someone behind you."

My stomach drops and I lower the phone, turning my head.

Hayden is standing, facing me with his fists in his pocket making him appear calm but the clenched jaw reveals that he is anything but.

"Hayden-" I start to say before Junior cuts me off.

"Who's that mama?" Junior says on the other line.

I hang up and throw my phone facedown on the bed. Brandon will talk to him. He'll take care of that.

I stand up from the bed and start to walk towards Hayden as he watches me and says nothing. "I can explain, what that was-"

"Who is he?" Hayden says in a low, calm voice.

I don't know how to react to Hayden acting so calm. I'm used to the Hayden who screams and gets frustrated, who demands answers. Not this Hayden.

This one is unpredictable, I don't know what he'll do when he talks in a calm voice because I know Hayden is mad, I can tell by the way he is trying to conceal it.

"Hayden-"

"Who's fucking kid is that?" Hayden says, still looking down at me as a tear finally falls from my eye.

This isn't how I wanted to tell Hayden. This isn't how I wanted him to find out about Junior.

But this is what I get for waiting too long.

Hayden deserves to know he has a kid. He doesn't deserve to find out like this.

Things were going perfect but something always ends up happening, causing chaos.

And this time I am the one who caused this.

The chaos.

I lick my bottom lip before forcing out, "Yours. He's yours." Hayden nods his head and licks the inside of his cheek. He backs away from me and I swear I feel like someone is squeezing my heart. "I was going to tell you-"

"When? When you went on a plane back to New York, to never see me again?" Hayden says, his whole body tense as his voice gets louder. "I have a fucking kid that I never knew about and you fucking knew that!"

More tears start to fall from my eyes. "I didn't want to tell you because I was scared!"

"Scared of what, Jaclyn? You didn't care about my feelings that night because you're too fucking selfish to care about anyone but yourself! That night when you left me and didn't come back showed me that, but I didn't give a single fuck because I still loved you! I was scared too, but did you care? No, you left me on my fucking knees to protect yourself," Hayden yells, pointing at me before running his hands through his hair.

I cry harder.

What he's saying, it's true. I left to protect myself and although I did care about Hayden, I cared about myself more. What I did was shitty but like I said five years ago, the girl who went through what she went through in that room, who was going to save her? Because it sure wasn't going to be Hayden.

"I left because I needed to heal, Hayden. I didn't want to leave but your face was a reminder of that night. I needed to be on my own for a little while because I knew I couldn't love you while feeling absolutely nothing." I wipe the tears on my face. "I couldn't love you because they took all that love and fucking killed it in that room. The only reason I'm here right now is because of that boy on the phone."

Hayden shakes his head again. "I understand why you left me but the fact that you didn't even tell me I had a fucking kid was fucking selfish. Because like I said, you cared too much about yourself to care about me and my feelings."

"I'm sorry. I should've told you. I was going to tell you I just was scared of this reaction. I knew you'd be mad-"

Hayden cuts me off again and says, "Mad? I'm not mad, Jaclyn. I'm furious, enraged!" he says while pointing to his chest but still backing up from me. "I have a son and I didn't know until now. I feel like absolute shit. And it's because you didn't care about my feelings. You fucking knew I wanted to have a family, with you out of all people but you still didn't care to tell me I had a son."

I shake my head, tears falling from my face as guilt makes its way through my body. My stomach feels like it's going to just drop and my heart hurts so much to the point where I think it will stop beating.

Of course I feel like shit.

I know not telling him was shitty and I should have told him before but God, I was scared. Even now, spending time with him, having sex with him, and talking to him again fucking scares me. I'm terrified that it'll end up in chaos between Hayden and I because that's how things always are for me.

"What's his name?" Hayden asks, not looking at me.

"Junior. Hayden Junior Night," I say in a quiet tone.

Hayden nods his head, runs his hands through his hair.

Next thing I know he is leaving out the door.

And then I scream with tears running down my face.

No one is there to hold me or protect me from the dark.

No one is there to silence the demons in my head.

Forty-Two

Rowan

PRESENT

I've always been the big brother in the family.

I'm used to the role and to always having to be the fixer in situations because that's what I've been doing since I got into this whole certain business that I'm currently running.

But with Hayden, my little brother, it's always been different with him.

Maybe it's the fact that he's the youngest of all the siblings, maybe it's because he and I are full brothers and not half like the rest of my siblings, but all I know is that I've always been closer and more protective of Hayden.

He's destructive and impulsive. Completely different from me who is in control at all times.

Ever since I met him, I just keep learning new things

about him, like how he has a short temper. I know his trainer taught him how to control it and he does it well when it comes to fighting.

Fighting is the only way for Hayden to let those demons lose.

Everyone needs an outlet. Fighting just happens to be Hayden's.

My eyes find his figure at the bar. He is sitting on a stool with a crystal glass in front of him. It's half empty and looks like an old fashioned.

I sit next to him but he keeps his eyes on the drink. He doesn't look drunk, plus I've been watching him for a good thirty minutes and after a few sips he just stopped and started to stare at the old fashioned instead of drinking it.

"About time you stopped being a stalker," he mumbles before taking a sip of his drink.

"Well, you were kind of just sitting and staring so I thought I'd figure out what's going on."

Hayden pushes the drink away and leans in his chair instead of resting his arms on the bar. He looks tired, like his mind has been running 100 mph for the past who knows how long.

Overthinking causes a lot of damage. It can make you drained and tired without you actually even doing anything.

Your mind constantly running like that is kind of like

a car. Eventually it gets tired and runs out of oil which makes it all suddenly stop.

He doesn't look at me as he says, "I have a kid and I didn't even know."

I can't help but widen my eyes a little because I didn't see that coming.

I knew about Jaclyn King and her issues with my brother but I didn't keep an eye on her because I wanted to respect my brother's relationship with her.

But after knowing this piece of information, I should have.

"Don't know what to say?" he says, downing the rest of the old fashioned and then slamming the glass on the table. He looks at me, his jaw clenched and rage filling his eyes. "Yea, that was my reaction except I was a lot more pissed off. Thing was though, I wasn't allowed to act out and fucking punch something because then that would have scared her away." Even though Hayden is older now and a lot more responsible and controlled, he has more anger in him. He just knows how to control it at certain times. "I have a fucking son and I didn't even know."

"How old?"

Hayden laughs dryly. "Fuck if I know." Hayden shakes his head lightly, still staring at the glass. "Hayden Junior Night. That's his full name."

"Want me to get information on him?"

Hayden looks at me, no he's glaring at me. "He's my

son. I shouldn't have to ask you to get information on him."

"How'd you find out?'"

"I was getting back to the hotel from getting Jaclyn's meds and then when I walked in, I heard a little boy on the phone. I stay for a few seconds and keep hearing him call her mama. I walk in and the kid stares at me." Hayden looks at me. "The kid has such familiar eyes. He had these dark gray eyes and I swear I was looking at myself. He told Jaclyn there was someone behind her and then she hung up before telling me he was mine."

"Did she explain why?"

"Yea. She told me she was scared and that's why she never told me. I don't understand why she was scared because I would have been there for her. I would have helped her and held her hand every step of the way. I would have been in that fucking delivery room with her, telling her how good she's doing and that she was going to be a great mother. But no, she did it all by herself because she was scared." Hayden runs his hands through his hair. "And the shitty thing was that I didn't care she was scared because I'm fucking hurt. She didn't think about my feelings with this and I know it's shitty that I'm mad at her but-"

"You should be mad at her, Hayden. But you should never make her feel guilty for it because she had a valid reason." Hayden looks up at me instead of at his hands.

"You have no clue what she went through in that room, right? You don't know what they did to make her scared of being with you. They fucked her up in there. Thank God Jane didn't go through what Jaclyn went through instead. Because if Jane did, I'm not sure I would have gotten to her. Jaclyn is fucking strong for taking care of a whole child by herself while also facing her demons."

"She's strong," Hayden agrees. "I just wish things were easier for us."

"God gives the worst situations to people who he knows can handle it and Jaclyn is strong. She can handle it and still come out okay. She just needed a little time. I think if she was still scared of you and the possibility of you she wouldn't be here right now," I explain. "Like I said, be mad at her but don't make her feel guilty for it because she was just protecting herself and your kid from the possibility of all that trauma happening again."

Hayden rests his head in his hand. "And I left her in the hotel room screaming."

I shake my head and shove his shoulder. "Then why are you here drinking instead of talking to her and making everything better?"

"I didn't want to do anything that I would later regret." Hayden takes his head out of his hand and looks at me, regret all over his face. "Fuck, I just keep fucking up."

I shake my head. "You can still fix it. You just need to

talk to her and understand her side of the story. She knows what she did is wrong but she was thinking of herself and her child."

Hayden nods his head. He is about to throw a bill on the bar to pay for the tab but I shake my head at him. "You sure? You just gave me your wisdom and now you want to pay for my drink?" Hayden raises an eyebrow.

I nod my head. "Just big brother things." Hayden rolls his eyes and is about to turn away before I say, "You love her, Hayden, and she knows that. She is just scared that she loves you too much to let you go. Take your time with her, that's what I did. Let her come to you."

Hayden nods his head before walking away.

My phone rings and I see the name "Fawn" pop up. A smile makes its way to my face as I answer.

"Fawn."

"Where are you? It's late," Jane says from the other side of the phone.

It sounds quiet which probably means the kids are asleep.

"I had to be with Hayden," I explain to Jane. "He had a situation."

"He always does. Is he okay?"

"Yea. He found out he has a kid so he's taking it kind of rough."

I explain the whole situation to Jane while she just listens and gives her input every so often.

After a while we just talk about our days. When she's talking, I can't stop smiling because hearing her voice is one of my favorite things. She has no clue how that sound gives me such a huge wave of euphoria. She talks about the kids and how their day was but I'm honestly just happily drowning in the sound of her voice for the rest of the phone call.

Forty-Three

Jaclyn

Ever since Hayden left, I haven't been able to stop crying. It's like the tears won't stop no matter how much I try to forget about Hayden and his words.

The guilt is eating me up and makes me feel like shit.

I know what I did was wrong and Hayden wasn't lying when he said all that.

It just hurts to know how much I affected him by not letting him meet Junior earlier.

I'm standing in the shower trying to forget all about the whole situation that happened with Hayden. I just need a minute or at least a second where my mind is quiet and not running 100 mph.

I wish it would all stop again.

I took some pills just to quiet my mind down and

Brandon started calling me a few minutes after Hayden left but I left it ringing.

I don't have any more pills either. I ended up taking the last of my dosage which means I'm technically done with them.

As water runs down my chest I suddenly feel strong and familiar arms wrap around me. I can't help but flinch and turn around quickly, only to see Hayden staring down at me.

"You're okay. It's just me," he says softly as he caresses my hair. I rest my head in his chest and cry.

I cry because I wish things weren't so hard between Hayden and I. I wish things weren't always a disaster waiting to happen.

I just wish love was easier.

Hayden and I are quiet as we stand underneath the shower in one another's embrace, the boiling water pouring on us. I rest my eyes and relax in his arms while hearing his heart.

His heart's rapidly beating but he appears so calm and collected.

I'm still definitely not used to Hayden's calm and collected composure because he is the type of person to act out and if he's mad, he'll show it.

"I'm sorry," I whisper, not knowing what else to say.

Everything he said, broke my heart and made me know for a fact that I can still feel something in there.

Because God, when he said those words, there was no way to stop the crying.

I feel bad because Hayden lost so many years and memories with Junior and I'm the reason for that, because I was too scared to get broken again by Hayden Night.

Hayden has no clue what I went through though, so he has no clue how I feel or why I couldn't have Junior meet him yet.

It's not because Junior wasn't ready, it's because I wasn't ready, especially to tell Hayden what happened that night but eventually he needs to know.

"I'm so sorry," I say as I start to cry in his chest again.

Hayden doesn't say anything. He just places his lips on my forehead and holds me as I cry.

We stay like this for a while, to the point where my whole body feels rough and soggy from the water.

Hayden gets out first and grabs my towel, holding it out for me. I get in the towel and he wraps it around me before putting a towel around his waist.

We both get ready for bed silently, him drying his hair and putting on his briefs and sweatpants. I put my hair in a braid and then put on some shorts and a big t-shirt that happens to be Hayden's.

When I'm done I walk towards the bed where Hayden is sitting on the edge, almost like he's waiting for me.

I go to sit on my side of the bed, resting my back against the headboard. Hayden doesn't turn to look at me, he stays in that same seated position, looking down at the floor.

My eyes go to the crown tattoo on the top of his back.

He always said he wanted to get a tattoo for me but I beat him to it. I never thought he'd actually do it, especially after everything that happened.

"When Eric kidnapped me he put some syringe in my neck and I passed out in the car," I start saying, and Hayden turns his head slightly. "When I woke up, I was in a dimly lit room. One cot, one sink, and a bucket near the bed. The walls were concrete, same as the floor and there were no windows. Pretty sure I was in a basement." Hayden now fully turns around and faces me, scooting closer so he can hold my hand. "On the first day, Marco came in, I wasn't drugged up anymore so I was fully aware of everything that was happening."

Ten minutes and thirty-seven seconds.

"It was one of the worst moments I've ever experienced. Ten minutes and thirty-seven seconds," I say, a tear falling from my eyes as the moment starts to replay.

Him ripping my shirt.

Me screaming at him to stop.

Me begging and pleading.

And then the little boy at the end telling me to hold on.

"I-" I shudder, making Hayden scoot closer and wrap his arms around me. He whispers in my ear that I'm okay and that I can stop whenever, but I keep going. "Eric and the others eventually had their shot at me but I wasn't awake for any of that. They drugged me up so much to the point where I was throwing up every night. But they managed to keep my blood sugar from going too low or high because they wanted to make sure I was still alive and breathing. They wanted to make sure that you could still see me and the damage they inflicted on me."

Hayden's arms and whole body tenses against me. I rest my head on his chest, the tears still slowly falling. "And then the scar on my side was from Eric. I was stone cold sober when he did that."

"Hey, sweetheart." Eric closes the door behind him and locks it. "Just me and you today. Got my own personal agenda I need to take care of before Marco comes back."

"He took a knife to my side and carved out the tattoo I got for you. He skinned me because he still saw me as your property and he didn't like that."

"No! No! NO! Let me go! Let me go! Please!"

I'm sobbing at this point.

Screaming to the top of my lungs for anyone, anyone to hear me and save me.

I want it all to stop.

Make it all stop.

I laugh through my tears and look at Hayden.

His eyes are so red and full of rage to the point where tears are starting to fall slowly from his lids. "And it's the fact that it was all because of some fighter who just wanted to be good," I say as more tears start to fall. Hayden licks the tears that fell onto his lips. "It's the fact that being with you caused me all that damage. And that's why I had to leave you Hayden," I explain. Those ten minutes and thirty-seven seconds weren't the worst moments of my life. Leaving you was because nothing could hurt more than losing your love."

I start crying more and Hayden cries with me. He holds my face in his hands and rests his forehead on mine.

We cry together and block the outside world again.

I've never seen Hayden cry, ever.

I've seen him mad, so mad to the point where he broke a mirror in his room because his family was being rude to him, I've seen him mad about Eric to the point where he almost beat him to death, but I've never, ever seen him cry.

Even the night I left him, he was close to crying but he didn't shed a tear.

"I didn't want to cause you this pain but I had to protect myself because after all that, all I could see was that room when I looked at you Hayden." I lean away from him and lick the tears from my lips. "I had to leave you so I could heal myself and having Junior did heal me."

Hayden caresses my hair and puts a strand behind my ear. "I just wish I was there to help you."

"I know. But I needed to be alone. That's how I heal."

Hayden nods his head. "I understand. I know and I shouldn't have said you didn't care. I just was hurt not knowing about Junior. I wanted a son and you knew that."

"I didn't mean-"

Hayden cuts me off by kissing me.

I still feel guilty.

I still feel like shit knowing I caused Hayden so much pain to the point where he starts crying.

Does he still love me?

After I betrayed him and caused all that chaos?

Does he still want a future with me?

Is this it?

"I want to meet him," Hayden says after pulling away from me. "I want to get on the plane tomorrow and go to him."

I knew this was going to happen someday.

I just wished I had more time and didn't have to rush Junior or this whole process.

But it has to happen sooner than later.

I nod my head. "Okay."

Forty-Four

The flight felt long, especially since I was ready to go back home to Junior.

Hayden is coming back to New York a little later just because he still had some work to do in Italy.

Mafia work.

He's probably killing people as we speak.

But I can't think of that. I have to distract my mind by the fact that this is all happening.

Too quickly?

Yes, but it's happening.

I can't deny Hayden seeing his son.

So he booked me a flight, first class even though I tried to tell him I was fine with economy. Hayden wouldn't budge though. He dropped me off at the airport and kissed me goodbye. I already texted him that I landed because he told me too.

Things since Hayden found out about Junior have been weird. It feels like we're both walking on eggshells around each other. After that night, all we seem to talk about now is Junior. It's only been two days since I told him about Junior and he doesn't stop asking questions about his son. I love how much Hayden wants to know more about his son.

He hasn't pushed me at all to talk about that night with him and I'm glad because I hate reliving that day and having to talk about it.

I feel like ever since I told him everything about that night and Junior he's been more in his head. Constantly thinking and wondering. I just wish he would act normal so I don't constantly feel like there is something wrong with me.

I know he's still mad, and I feel like he's always going to hold a grudge over that, which is a valid reason but I hate it.

I just wish things were easier for us.

A familiar boy appears in my line of view making a smile appear on my face. I bend down to his level and once he's close enough, Junior jumps into my arms and wraps his tiny arms around me. He places a big fat kiss on my cheek and starts laughing when I smother his face with kisses.

"I missed you so much baby," I whisper while hugging him as if he'll disappear. I smell his hair and it makes me want to just get in bed and cuddle with him.

I've always loved how Junior smells, he reminds me of home and after being away for so long, I've missed it.

"I missed you more," Junior leans back to look at me and smile, a familiar sparkle in his eyes that reminds me of his father.

I raise my eyebrows at him. "Really? How much?"

Junior jumps off me and he opens his arms really wide. "This much, mama!"

I widen my eyes and continue smiling at him. "That is a lot of missing me, bud." I look around and see Brandon walking up to us.

He grabs my bags from me before wrapping his arms around me for a hug.

"Your son is a menace. He would not stop running away from me when we were trying to find you. And once he saw you, he basically forgot about me and ran to you."

I laugh and look down at Junior smiling. "He has his priorities straight."

"What's a priority?" Junior says, pronouncing 'priority' wrong which I can't help but chuckle at a little.

"It means that you value something that's more important to you than something else."

"Oh," Junior says before nodding his head like it all makes sense.

I look at Brandon. "How was the flight?" he asks.

"So long, so let's get to the car. I'm ready to go home."

"I mean your flight was like ten fucking hours long so I bet."

"Brandon said a bad boy word!" Junior points at Brandon which makes Brandon glare at Junior.

"You're such a little snitch now that your mom is around."

"That's my boy," I say before picking him up and kissing his cheek.

We all get in the Uber eventually and we put my bags in the back.

I'm so ready for a long shower and then some rest.

"So where is he?" Brandon asks as the car starts moving.

"He is still in Italy. He said he'll fly out tonight and come over tomorrow. He just had to take care of some stuff before leaving," I say before looking at Junior who is slowly falling asleep in my lap.

When I told Brandon about Hayden meeting Junior, Brandon was a little skeptical because in a way, Brandon is an important male figure in Junior's life. He may not be his father, but Brandon is the only guy I've let Junior around.

Hayden doesn't even know this because I know how Hayden is.

He's possessive to a fault and if he knows that

someone else was his role in Junior's life in any way, he won't be happy at all.

"How are you guys going to break the news?"

I shrug and nip my bottom lip. "I have no clue. I think we'll just go with the flow because with Junior and how he is, there is no certain way you can tell him or have a plan on how to tell him. You kind of just have to go with the flow."

"How are you feeling about all this?"

"Does it really matter how I feel? I'm the one who caused all this."

"Don't say that." Brandon narrows his eyes at me.

I look down at my hand, playing with the bracelet around my wrist. "But it is. I'm the one who didn't tell Hayden and kept Junior from him so it is my fault."

And I feel guilty about it all.

Like, will Junior be mad at me for keeping him from his father in the future? Will Hayden eventually be so mad at me to the point where he leaves me and tries to take Junior?

All of these negative thoughts are running through my head and all the overthinking always ruins everything for me. I just wish the voices would stop.

I'm pretty sure it's because I have no one to talk to about all this.

I need to talk to Patience now that I'm back home.

"You had a good reason, Jaclyn. You needed time and

you needed to heal on your own. If Hayden doesn't understand or accept that, then he isn't who I thought he was. You deserve someone who would wait a lifetime for you."

"I know, it's just-"

"You and your stupid mind." Brandon raises an eyebrow at me.

I chuckle. "My mind isn't always stupid. It comes up with great stories."

"My stories are better. Even Junior thinks so."

I roll my eyes. "Junior will tell anyone anything to get what he wants."

"True."

Forty-Five

Hayden

I've met millions of celebrities.

I've been in more than hundreds of fights in my life.

I even met my biological brother and grew a relation-ship with him.

But I've never been as nervous as I am right now.

Jaclyn told me she wanted to do this at her apartment.

She asked me what I wanted to do today with Junior. I first asked her what kind of stuff he likes and she told me he likes going to the aquarium a lot in Brooklyn.

So we're all going to be going to the aquarium as a family.

Like we should have been all along.

I got in from Italy about five hours ago. I couldn't

sleep the entire flight because I was nervous as well for today.

Right when I got to my penthouse, I worked out and then took an hour nap before heading over to Jaclyn's apartment.

We both live in Manhattan, probably a twenty to thirty minute walk yet I've never seen her around. I still find it crazy how she was right under my nose, she could probably see my penthouse from her apartment but we haven't run into one another since the fight.

Yesterday, I was busy doing some stuff with Rowan and Killian. I wanted to come to New York with Jaclyn but Killian and Rowan said I should give her some time with Junior before tagging along.

But since Jaclyn told me everything about that night, I've been overthinking non-stop. I feel like shit knowing I'm the one who blamed everything on her when in reality, what she went through was something she couldn't control. Her mind wasn't in the right place and she couldn't see me after everything that happened.

We both still need to talk about a lot of things, for one, the pills she's been taking, why she's barely eating, because I notice she isn't, and then her mental health overall. But one thing at a time.

When she's ready, she'll tell me.

I knock on the door, hearing laughing from a familiar voice and then a little boy, coming from the other side of the door. The laughing stops and a few seconds later, the door swings open.

Jaclyn is wearing dark blue cotton shorts and a white tank top. My hands start to feel clammy instantly.

After not seeing her for two days, my mind feels calm suddenly. Another thing I've been worrying about since she told me about that night, was if she is in any danger.

I feel like I should be with her at all times to make sure she's protected and safe.

I just want to make sure she comes back to me this time.

That's why I hired a personal guard and driver for her because there's no way in hell I'm ever leaving her alone again, not making that mistake again. If I'm not there, I sure as hell am having someone with her, someone that I trust.

We haven't really talked about that yet but it will be happening, especially now that I'm more involved in Killian's world.

Jaclyn gives me a nervous smile. "Hi."

"Hi," I say before licking my bottom lip.

"Are you ready?"

"I'm scared," I admit.

Jaclyn steps out of her apartment and closes the door softly. She puts her hands behind her back and her chest rises and falls with every breath she takes.

"Everything's going to be fine," she assures me.

"Junior is an amazing kid and he's going to love you. If anything, he'll just need time with you."

Jaclyn did show me a bunch of videos and photos of Junior because I was curious about him and what he's like. Jaclyn told me everything there was to know.

It made me even more excited to see and meet him.

I nod my head. "How are you feeling?"

Jaclyn shakes her head. "It doesn't matter." I narrow my eyes at her.

Does she really think her feelings don't matter or something?

"No. I'm going to ask again." I take a step closer to her. "How are you feeling?" I hold her face in my hands to make her look up at me.

Jaclyn takes my hands off her face and steps back. "I'm fine. Junior's waiting," Jaclyn says before opening the door and holding it open for me. I continue to worry even as I walk in and see a boy, who looks so similar to me, jumping up and down on the couch while laughing. "Junior, what did I say about jumping on the couch?" Jaclyn says, walking past me and towards the couch.

Junior looks at his mom with a guilty look on his face.

I put my hands in my pockets, not wanting him to see how my hands are sweaty.

God, I'm fucking nervous.

I feel my eye twitching and my stomach clenching. My

heart is beating against my chest hard and fast and I feel like it's going to burst.

"Who's that, mama?" Jaclyn helps Junior off the couch and she grabs his hand as she walks towards me.

Jaclyn looks at my hands in my pockets, glaring at them making me take them out. She looks at me and mouths, "You okay?"

I nod my head before kneeling in front of Junior to be at the same height as him.

Junior looks at me skeptically. "Is he a stranger?" Junior asks, moving closer to Jaclyn.

"No baby, he's safe." Jaclyn kneels with me and she looks at Junior. "Baby, you know how everyone has a mama and a papa?"

Junior nods his head. "Sometimes people have two mamas and two papas."

Jaclyn nods her head. "Yes, that's right. But everyone has two parents. Sometimes it's two mamas and some-times it's two papas. Most of the time it's a mama and a papa."

Junior nods his head before looking at me. "Well, I just have you and Brandon."

Brandon?

My eyebrow raises and I look at Jaclyn. Her body tenses but she doesn't look at me.

Who the fuck is Brandon and why is he spending time

with my family and why did Jaclyn not mention this to me?

"Yes baby but you also have a papa."

"Where is he?" Junior furrows his eyebrows and tilts his head a little bit.

Jaclyn looks at me.

I clear my throat, my nerves starting to sky rocket and my anxiety going crazy. "Well, I'm your dad."

Junior shakes his head. "No you're not. If you were my papa then where have you been?"

I look at Jaclyn this time while Junior stares at me with confusion.

"Well, your papa, he didn't know how amazing you were until recently. He's been wanting to meet you for a while."

Junior looks at his mom with a smile. "Really?" Jaclyn nods with a smile. "So you want to be my papa?" Junior asks me.

I give him a small smile. "I do. I am your papa, but I want to be in your life."

"Are you and my mama married?"

Not yet but I'll get there, just be patient.

"No. But I want to be a part of your guys' life. You and your mom."

"How did you guys have me if you aren't married then?" Junior asks, looking at his mom this time.

"Well baby, things happen a certain way and we just

had you. But the point being is your papa wants to start seeing you and he wants to have a relationship with you."

"So I have someone new to play with?" Junior questions and Jaclyn nods her head.

"Yea. I would love to hangout with you and get to know you better if that's okay?" I raise my eyebrow at him. "I was thinking that maybe we could all go to the aquarium today? Your mom said that you like going there, right?"

Junior nods his head and smiles widely. "Do I call you papa?"

I look at Jaclyn and she gives me a small smile and nods, making sure I know that I'm doing alright.

"I mean, I would love for you to call me papa but I know that's probably weird, especially since you just met me right?" Junior nods his head. "So you can call me Hay or Hayden."

Junior's face brightens. "My name is Hayden too!"

"I know, it's a pretty cool name, isn't it?" I say, not able to contain my smile.

Junior nods before looking at his mom. "I like him."

Jaclyn smiles at him, a genuine smile that I feel like I haven't seen in a while. Last time she smiled like that was in college when she was genuinely happy.

"So you ready to go to the aquarium?" I ask Junior and he nods his head excitedly.

Junior looks so much like me there is no doubting that he's my son.

I can't believe I have a fucking son.

Forty-Six

Jaclyn

Watching Hayden hold Junior on his hip as they point to all the fish does something to me. Even seeing Hayden smile so wide when Junior yells at him to look at a certain fish or whenever Junior runs towards another exhibit and Hayden runs after him to make sure he doesn't get lost.

Hayden has always been the protector type.

I, out of all people, should know.

Hayden would look over every so often and he would have a wide smile on his face showing me how much fun he's having.

I can already see Hayden slowly starting to fall in love with Junior. It's so easy to fall in love with Junior and his unique personality.

Seeing Hayden fall in love with Junior and show his protective side with him makes me want to fall in love with Hayden all over again.

I can't stop smiling at them but inside I still feel guilty for having them be apart for so long.

I'm trying to make it up to not just Hayden, but Junior as well.

"How's it going?" Brandon says as he walks up to me.

"Good. Junior is keeping him on his toes."

Brandon wanted to give us some space in the morning for Hayden and I to tell Junior the news. He told me he would meet us at the aquarium a little bit later, which is now, making me realize how long we've been here for and how long I've been watching them and following them around.

We ate lunch before coming here. Hayden took us to a nice brunch place down the street from the apartment that he told me he would always go to.

"He looks happy," Brandon says as he stares at the two of them. "It's crazy how similar they look."

"There's no denying that he's his son. His personality is also another indicator."

"Junior looks like he's having fun."

He is.

But after all the meetings and hanging out with Hayden, what will happen?

That's another thing I can't stop overthinking about.

What will happen with Junior and I? What will happen between Hayden and I and the role he's now playing?

There is still so much baggage and history that Hayden and I need to talk about and I know that it won't be a pretty talk.

Hayden still doesn't know about Junior's condition with his VSD or how he has to take meds.

It's not a bad thing that he has his condition but Hayden should know.

And what will happen when Hayden eventually becomes more and more involved, especially with his lifestyle?

Do I want Junior to live the kind of life filled with people wondering about your every move or taking pictures everywhere you go?

"I can't stop staring at them," I admit. "It's weird seeing them together. It makes me feel even more guilty with how happy both of them are."

"You shouldn't feel guilty," Brandon says but I don't take my eyes off Hayden and Junior.

"I know, but after the conversation with Hayden, it opened my eyes to how selfish I was for not letting him know about Junior. I should have told Hayden."

"You needed time to heal. If you told him, who knows

what could have happened. It's good that you both took time away from each other because that's what you guys needed. Hayden may not agree because he doesn't like spending time away from you but he needed that break too."

"I know. It's just hard to think that after seeing them together and how good they both are with each other."

Hayden turns his head to me again and instead of smiling wide it drops and he's glaring.

Shit.

Brandon.

"He doesn't look very happy that I'm here."

Even being far from him with people walking around us, I already know he is clenching his jaw.

Hayden puts on a mask and turns to Junior, asking him something. Junior looks up and smiles when he sees us.

Junior waves at Brandon making Brandon wave back.

"I never told him about you," I admit. I look at Brandon and he's now looking at me. "Sorry."

Brandon sighs and nods his head lightly. "I have a feeling he's going to threaten me or something."

I shake my head. "I won't let him. You're my friend Brandon and a part of Junior's life. Hayden will understand that."

"I just don't want him to think I'm taking his position."

"He won't. Trust me." I look back at Hayden and Junior but instead of pointing to different fish, they are now walking up to us. I force a smile on my face. "All done playing baby?" I ask as they walk up to us.

"Yea. I'm tired and want to eat," Junior says as he walks up to me and wraps his tiny arms around my legs.

"I did promise you cinnamon rolls, didn't I?" I say, touching the strands of his hair once he's close enough.

Junior smiles and jumps up and down. "Yes, yes, yes! And watch a movie! Spiderman!"

I look at Hayden and see him smiling down at Junior. But it's not genuine. He's just doing it so he doesn't worry Junior.

"Okay, then we'll head out."

"Brandon!"

Junior runs towards Brandon and hugs his legs while Brandon hugs him back. I look at Hayden for a second but I swear in that second, I can see and almost feel how pissed off he is.

He's glaring at Brandon and his jaw's clenched.

"Let's go, baby," I say, moving away from Hayden to hold Junior's hand.

We eventually leave the aquarium in Hayden's town car. I asked Hayden if we could give Brandon a ride since he lives in my complex.

Hayden didn't like hearing that at all but then he looked down at Junior and said 'yes'.

Hayden was still giving Brandon the stink eye while staying silent during the drive back to the apartment. Only talking and smiling to Junior.

"Can my papa come?" Junior asks once we get to the building.

I look at Hayden and see him staring at me. "I don't think so, baby. Your papa has things to do for the rest of the night."

"I'll be here again tomorrow," Hayden says, making Junior cheer and hug Hayden.

"You guys go inside and I'll meet you up there," I say to Junior and Brandon.

Junior lets go of Hayden and goes to Brandon. "Bye, papa! See you tomorrow!" Junior yells while waving goodbye.

I turn to face Hayden and see him glaring down at me.

Him glaring always reminds me of our times in college when he had a mad or serious expression on his face.

Or when he used to hate me and gave me these specific looks filled with lust but also hate.

"Brandon's a friend. You don't need to worry about him."

Hayden shakes his head and walks closer to me. "I'm not worried about him."

I furrow my eyebrows and my head tilts slightly. "Really?"

Hayden nods his head. "I know what I have and what he doesn't. You and Junior are both mine and nothing will change that. I'm just not very happy with the fact that he probably got to experience what I should have been experiencing before me." I'm about to say something but Hayden continues. "I know you needed to heal and to be away from me but I just hate the fact that I couldn't experience Junior with you and growing a family. But that guy did," Hayden says.

"I'm sorry," I say, for the thousandth time this week. "I feel awful, Hayden, you have to believe me." I look down at my feet, afraid to meet his eyes.

Hayden puts his hand on my cheek and makes me look up at him. "I know, Jaclyn. But I still can't help but not be completely happy. Don't get me wrong, I love Junior. I loved Junior before I even found out about him but I'm just not happy that I couldn't love him or show him that love sooner." I lick my bottom lip and nod my head lightly. "It's going to take me time."

I furrow my eyebrows and almost feel my heart break.

What does he mean by time?

He needs time to what?

To decide if we're worth the trouble or the heartbreak?

He needs time to make sure I'm not going anywhere?

God, I hate the way he makes me feel, like I'm needy

and desperate for his love and attention when I'm the one who fucked him over.

But instead of questioning him, I nod my head and take his hands off me.

"Goodnight, Hayden."

Forty-Seven

Hayden

Waking up alone in my apartment is what I've become used to after not living with people for a while.

I will say, it's more peaceful and the mornings go by slowly which means I'm able to just relax and enjoy them.

But I'll also admit that I miss someone waking up next to me.

A warm, specific body next to me to wake up with.

I could already imagine waking up next to Jaclyn in the morning and then a few minutes later, our children running into the room and jumping on our bed. Making breakfast and just spending the whole day together.

Being with her is a dream itself.

But I also can't help but still feel pissed off that a

motherfucker named Brandon had the chance to be a "father" figure to Junior instead of me.

The bag in front of me swings fast as Freddie tries to hold it still.

"What's on your mind?" Freddie asks as he holds the bag. "Your punches seem nasty."

Freddie doesn't know about Junior or what the fuck happened in Italy with Jaclyn.

I haven't talked to him since I left for Italy.

I stop punching the bag and try to control my breathing.

Every Friday morning, Freddie and I train together. Usually he is in Utah with his family but he flies out every Friday to check in on me and train.

I think I talk more to Freddie about things than I do with Carter.

I take off my gloves and walk towards the bench where my phone's at. I unlock it and go to the camera roll, clicking on the most recent picture and showing it to Freddie.

He takes the phone and furrows his eyebrows at the photo I took of Junior when we were at the aquarium.

"His name is Hayden Junior Night. He is mine and Jaclyn's kid."

Freddie's eyes widen as I expect them to and he looks up at me with a shocked expression. "Really?" I nod my head and take the phone from him.

"Yup. And I didn't know about him until about four days ago." I sit on the bench. "I'm pissed off about it. I want to be mad at Jaclyn for keeping him from me and allowing another guy to be a father figure in his life but at the same time I can't. The whole reason why she couldn't be with me or see me is because she was scared of me. After everything she went through five years ago, she's scared of the danger I come with."

"That's understandable. I mean I feel for both of you." Freddie sits down next to me on the bench. "It's not fair for you to not be able to meet your child but I also understand why she would want to keep her distance. Son, I have no clue what they did in that room so I can't really say much about her feelings."

I nod my head lightly. "Yea. I just don't know how to feel. My emotions have been all over the place. Sometimes I want to argue with her and ask why she would keep me from having the family I've always wanted and then whenever I actually see her, I want to hold her in my arms and just protect her from everyone, including myself."

"Did she tell you or did you find out yourself?" Freddie asks.

"I found out when I walked inside the hotel room and heard her talking to him."

"Tell me about him."

And I do.

I tell Freddie everything I learned about Junior when we were talking at the aquarium.

Junior's favorite color is dark blue.

He loves cars which I'm not surprised about since his mother likes cars too.

He loves whenever Jaclyn reads him bedtime stories.

His favorite superhero is Spiderman.

His favorite movie is The Lion King, just like his mother.

Junior loves pasta, especially pasta that has cheese on it.

He has three friends in school. Matt, Josh, and Kyle.

My son has a crush on a girl already even though he is only four years old.

Her name is Scarlett and she has blonde hair. He told me he plans on marrying her and I just laughed at him when he said that.

He likes clownfish although he calls them Marlin because of the fish from *Finding Nemo*.

Freddie listens with a small smile on his face while I tell him all about Junior. I even have a smile myself that I didn't even notice while talking about him.

I just love talking about Junior and the fact that I have a son.

Jaclyn and I talked about kids when we were together in college. Our plan wasn't really to have kids right away.

We were going to graduate, I was going to propose, then travel and enjoy life by ourselves before having kids.

"I want 3 girls and one boy. The boy first so that he can protect the girls," I explain to Jaclyn.

We're in bed right now as I hold her hand in mine and she is laying on my chest. I'm comparing our hand sizes because her hands are so fucking small compared to mine. I know Jaclyn loves how big my hands are because sometimes when she looks down at them, she'll blush before looking away.

"I don't think you can decide which is first, Hay." Jaclyn looks up at me with a teasing smile.

"Well I happen to be a lucky person so I'm not worried."

"I won't be having four kids, Hayden."

"We'll see about that. What do you want?"

Jaclyn thinks for a little bit before replying with. "One boy and one girl."

"Any name ideas?" I ask, kissing her shoulder.

"I like the name Sydney a lot. I also like the name River or Easton too."

"Sydney is pretty."

Jaclyn looks up at me again. "What about you?"

"I like the name Isabelle, Belle for short."

"Like Beauty and The Beast."

Because I can't help it, I lean down and kiss her.

"Jaclyn and I talked about having kids. I just loved

thinking about the future with her. I liked the fact that she was going to be pregnant with my kids and living in a house together just enjoying life." I explain to Freddie. "I guess I just jinxed it."

"The universe is a very weird thing and fate is even weirder. You guys were put in this position for a reason. You don't ever know the reason but it happened and you both are trying to do better for each other and Junior. What do I always tell you?"

"Everything always happens for a reason," I mumble while rolling my eyes.

Freddie always tells me this.

Whenever I win a fight, get in my weird moods when I met Rowan, etc.

Freddie always told me that everything had a reason.

Now looking back at it, Jaclyn told me her doctor told her the same thing when she found out she had diabetes.

Everything happens for a reason.

And sometimes we may never know the reason.

"Exactly. The universe or God or whoever is in charge of this life, they have a plan. Jaclyn and you are both strong. You both love each other so much. I can tell, Natalia can tell, your family, everyone who has met you guys can tell. I'm not worried and neither should you."

I nod my head. "What if she doesn't love me anymore? What if she leaves again?"

"She won't. And if she does then she's just scared. Just be patient and trust that everything happens-"

"For a reason," I repeat with him, making him nudge my shoulder as we chuckle.

Forty-Eight

Jaclyn

"How was your vacation? We missed you here," Jules says.

She's sitting across from me in her chair with a notepad in front of her. I have mine laid on my lap.

It's my first day back in the office and right when I walked out of the elevator, Jules' assistant told me that Jules wanted to see me.

She probably wants to go through the article with me in depth and then my next project.

"It was good. I had a good break from work and just regular life I guess," I say with a kind smile on my face.

"I heard the wedding got canceled on the news. Any clue why? No statements were put out, TMZ just stated that Nicole and Hayden's wedding was canceled."

I shrug my shoulders. "No clue. My friend just told me that they were sending everyone home," I lie, straight through my teeth.

I think since the moment Hayden saw me at the fight, that wedding was doomed.

Nicole stood no chance because of Hayden seeing me and I may not know for sure if Nicole liked him or not, but I still feel horrible and guilty that Hayden canceled everything and did all that for me.

Hayden and I haven't talked about what will happen after he grows closer with Junior or if he will be revealing he has a son to the public.

I think that Hayden revealing he has a son is his decision but revealing that it's Junior is something completely different.

I know I'm already pretty well known, not A-List celebrity well known, but journalist well known while Hayden is known by almost everyone in the world. So, everyone who knows Hayden would know who Junior is and me.

Which means, no more privacy or peace.

Let's not forget about the fact that Hayden still comes with history.

Plus, he has no idea who I've become since leaving that room.

"Jaclyn," Jules says, making me look at her.

"Yes? Sorry, I spaced."

"It's fine. I was asking how you even got invited to Hayden Night's wedding. Who's the friend who invited you? I just can't believe they even let a journalist join."

"My friend is Hayden's sister. We were friends in college and just reconnected recently. We aren't close or anything." I lie.

Jules raises her eyebrows in shock. "Why didn't you tell me this?"

I shrug again. "I didn't think we would ever talk again. It didn't seem important."

Jules nods her head, still wanting to ask questions but she stays silent. "Well, I'm glad you had fun, nonetheless. If you do end up finding more information on Hayden Night and Nicole Earnings let me know," she says, but I won't. Mostly because I want to respect both of their privacy. I'm not a paparazzi. I'm a journalist who likes writing stories and learning more about people that I talk to and meet, not by finding out myself from online. "For now, here is your next project. I already emailed this CEO about a meeting, and he is trying to find time in his schedule. A lot of people are just wanting to know how he got so successful and wealthy at a young age. Pretty easy and basic." Jules slides a folder my way about the CEO.

I take the folder and smile before leaving her office quietly.

I walk into my office and Brandon is sitting across

from my desk. I place the folder on the desk and start to get to work.

I just need to quiet my mind, especially from all the thoughts of Hayden.

"Everything okay?" Brandon asks.

He's been wanting to know what Hayden said to me after he dropped us off at home yesterday. I wasn't in the mood to talk to Brandon, so I sent him home. I honestly don't feel like talking to anyone about Hayden.

My mind thinks about Hayden enough.

"Yea, everything's fine. Just getting back to work," I say quietly, not looking at him.

"Bullshit. You're anxious. You're trying to distract yourself. Talk to me. Is it about him?"

"No. I'm just tired, that's all. Jet lag," I lie.

I just don't want him to worry about me.

Plus, Hayden is my problem. I don't want Brandon to worry about Hayden and I or just Hayden in general.

Hayden and I are the ones who need to figure out our shit, with no one else involved.

My phone starts buzzing, making me look down.

Hayden's name pops up on the screen and I sigh. Brandon looks at the call and gives me a worried look. I ignore him and answer the call.

"Hi."

"Hi," Hayden replies. Us saying 'hi' was our thing. He

would say a simple 'hi' making me smile and say it back. I don't know why a simple 'hi' from him would always make me nervous or blush. "What are you doing?"

"I'm working right now. What's up?"

"Nothing much. I finished training with Freddie. He told me to tell you he said 'hello'."

"I'll have to catch up with him one of these days," I say as Brandon watches me talk to Hayden on the phone.

"Yea, about that. I wanted to ask if you and Junior wanted to come to Utah for the weekend. I want my family to meet Junior and I want Junior to meet more of his family," Hayden asks.

Is he fucking serious?

He is the one who wants time.

He needed time to process him being mad at me for keeping Junior away from him and now he wants to fucking go to Utah as a family?

He told me that not even 24 hours ago.

Is he okay or something?

"No. It's too fast. I don't want Junior meeting so many people at once. I need him to get used to being with you and the fact that you're his father now."

"I've always been his father," Hayden argues.

"Yes, but you are now in his life, and he needs to be comfortable with that and grow a relationship with you before meeting more people from your side. He all of a sudden can't just have this whole other family after four years of not having one."

"I want my son to meet my family."

His son?

Is he kidding me?

What the fuck is his problem?

"I'm not saying no, Hayden, I'm just saying to wait for a little bit. Let Junior process his time with you and enjoy being with you."

I can hear Hayden sigh over the phone making me assume he is a little frustrated.

"Okay. When are you off work?"

"5:30."

"I'll be at your place at 6:00 for a movie night," Hayden says before hanging up, not even giving me the chance to say no.

I toss the phone on the desk and rest my head against my chair before closing my eyes.

He's making things so hard.

Why does everything have to be so hard?

I swear the pills weren't making me feel this crazy.

It has to be the pills.

"Wow, you are in love. And it's scaring you."

I look at Brandon and furrow my eyebrows. "What?"

"You're still in love with him. That's why you're being mean to him and pushing him away. You don't want to love him or have these feelings, but you do. And you hate it."

I shake my head and lick my bottom lip. "You're wrong."

"I'm not. And you know I'm not." Brandon stands up and he leaves my office without another word.

God, I wish he was wrong.

Forty-Nine

Jaclyn

Hayden is over right now.

Right when Hayden walked through the front door, Junior pulled him through the apartment, and they went to his room to play.

Junior loves having a new play buddy. When he saw Hayden, he got so excited and jumped up and down on his little feet. Hayden smiled right when he saw us too. I also noticed him looking behind me, probably expecting Brandon to be with us.

I'm a little annoyed with Hayden being here because I just don't feel like talking to him after he said what he said the last time we saw each other in person.

How he needs time to not be mad at me for keeping his son away from him.

I get it.

I know I fucked up and I keep fucking up, but doesn't he understand how hurt and broken I was when I left him?

"Let's watch *The Lion King*! It's mama's and my favorite movie!" Junior cheers as he walks out of his room with Hayden trailing behind him.

Hayden is wearing a casual fit tonight. In Italy, he was always wearing fancy pants and shirts but here he is just wearing a black sweater and gym shorts that show off his muscular legs. I can't lie and say when his shorts go up a little bit, I don't stare at his thighs because how could I not?

"Your mom still likes that movie a lot?" Hayden asks, his eyes going to me for a second before looking at Junior.

"Yup. She always wants to watch it," Junior says as he jumps onto his side of the couch. Hayden sits next to him while I dump the popcorn into a bowl.

Kettle corn for me and Junior and buttered for Hayden since he doesn't like kettle corn. He thinks it's too sweet.

I remember him saying that whenever we watched a movie when we were together in college.

I walk away from the kitchen and turn off the lights before going towards the couch where the boys are and sit down next to Junior. I hand Hayden his bowl of popcorn and give Junior the bowl to hold ours.

"You still like kettle corn?' Hayden asks.

"Yea. I got your son on it too," I tease as I pick up the remote.

"Kettle corn is the best popcorn ever," Junior agrees, nodding his head while smiling.

"What about fruit on pizza?" Hayden asks Junior while eating some of his popcorn.

Junior grimaces which makes me laugh a little. "Mama likes it, but I think it's weird."

"That's my boy." Hayden high fives Junior and I just roll my eyes at them.

I can already see how they'll be ganging up on me.

"Sweet and salty go hand in hand. Pineapple on pizza tastes good. Any other fruit doesn't belong on there though," I explain which makes Hayden shake his head a little and laugh.

"Princess, you are one of the pickiest people I know yet you have some weird taste in food," Hayden says, and I click on the movie, ready for it to play.

"Why do you call mama 'princess'?" Junior turns his head to Hayden.

I look away from the TV to look at Hayden.

"Because your mama is a princess. She's pretty like a princess, everyone in the castle envies and loves her."

"What princess is she?" Junior asks.

Hayden looks up at me. "She's her own princess. Your

mama is strong and beautiful. She doesn't need to be another princess from a movie."

"Who's her prince then?"

"You and me, bud," Hayden says, a small boyish smirk on his face appearing when he moves his eyes to me.

My heart melts.

Because Hayden isn't wrong. Hayden's always been my knight in shining armor and Junior has been my little prince.

Hayden and I stare at each other for what feels like an eternity. He has this soft glint in his eyes that makes him always look like that boy from college. The one who was soft and was in love with me.

I know Hayden still loves me, it's just hard for me to break down my walls for him even though he is desperately trying to break them down himself. And he is so so close.

Hayden, Junior, and I are quiet as I start the movie.

Halfway through the movie, Junior starts to get more comfortable and yawns as he lays on Hayden's chest. Hayden looks down at Junior, not really knowing what to do before he rests his arm on Junior's back and gets more comfortable, sinking into the cushions on the couch.

I wish I could take a picture of them two but I don't want to make it seem weird, especially since Hayden and I still have no clue what we're doing and we still need to figure it out.

The movie continues to play and eventually Junior ends up falling asleep on Hayden. I end up laying next to Junior, my body behind his and my arms wrapped around him. Hayden's still sitting on his side of the couch but his arms are still on Junior, itching to go closer to me.

We're at the part where Simba is saving the Pride Lands from Scar and the hyenas.

I think my favorite part of the whole movie is when Nala and Simba find each other after so many years. I am a romantic at heart and the old Disney movies make the romance aspect of their cartoons so good.

I feel a hand lay on my shoulder. I look up at Hayden and his attention is on the TV. He is drawing small circles on my shoulder, somehow calming down my rapid heart.

Eventually the movie ends and Hayden still has his fingers drawing circles on my shoulder. I don't want to get up because I feel so comfortable and at peace with us three cuddling like this.

But I know Junior has school in the morning and I have work. I have no clue what Hayden's plans are but I know he probably has some stuff for work going on.

"Do you want to put Junior to bed?" I sit up and turn to Hayden, realizing we are so close from how all of us were laying together.

I notice Hayden's eyes move down to look at my lips, which I can't help but lick.

Hayden meets my eyes again and nods.

Fifty

Present

I've been watching Jaclyn sitting on the floor, looking at a box of God knows what, for a good five minutes.

She hasn't noticed me since I leaned on her door frame and started watching her. Junior is dead asleep. Didn't move an inch when I laid him in his bed.

He's a heavy sleeper like me, that's for sure. Jaclyn told me one time in bed, when we were in Italy, that Junior has a lot of my characteristics. He doesn't just look like me but he also acts like me a lot. Since I've met him, I've noticed how he is the perfect mix of me and Jaclyn.

He does have her cheeks, thank God. I'm working on getting Jaclyn's cheeks back since her face slimmed down from doing God knows what. He has my drive and confidence. He won't ever take no for an answer. He does this nose scrunch thing that Jaclyn always did in college, still kind of does now, when he grimaces or when he's thinking really hard about something.

He also picked up on some of her habits. Like in his room he has a pile of clothes on the floor that he just throws when changing into his pajamas. He loves water like his mom. He doesn't like soda or any other flavored drinks, thank God. He does like juice but only apple juice, orange juice, and Capri Sun since that's always in the fridge.

There are so many more things that I've noticed about Junior and I only hope to learn more.

I walk inside Jaclyn's room and she turns her head when she hears my footsteps. "Junior stayed?"

I sit on her bed while she stays seated on the floor in front of the bed, with the box in front of her. "Yea," I say quietly before looking down at the box. "What's that?"

Jaclyn hands me the box instead of telling me.

There are petals from flowers that look familiar, small notes, tickets to some stuff, and a tiara necklace that I never got back.

These flowers are ones I gave Jaclyn just because.

The notes are just small notes I gave her. Some of them were notes I would give her in class to make her blush.

You look so pretty after taking my dick like a good girl this morning.

I can see you squirming in your seat. Are you wet, princess?

God, look at how pretty and perfect you are? Did you wear that dress today for me princess? Just wait until I get you in the car.

Jaclyn loved my dirty mouth in college and I know she still likes it now too.

I wrote her other notes too, not just dirty ones. I left her notes on her bed with a dress and told her to get ready for a date.

I always loved leaving her notes because they made her smile.

And then the last thing in the box that really grabbed my attention was the tiara necklace.

I still can't believe she kept it after all these years.

She never gave it back so I thought she just got rid of it. She only ever gave back my clothes, nothing else.

"You kept all this?" I ask Jaclyn, looking down at her.

She's staring up at me with worry in her eyes like she's scared of my reaction to seeing all this. "Yea. I don't know why I did. It was probably stupid now that I-"

I shut her up by leaning down and placing my lips on hers.

Goddamn.

Her body goes limp and I get down to her level on her floor and hold her face in my hand. I rest my other on the floor behind her as we slowly lower ourselves to the floor.

This kiss, just like every other kiss, I feel it all the way down to my toes. Jaclyn's kisses were always the ones that would ruin me but not in a bad way.

The only person I wanted to be ruined by was her.

"Hayden," she rasps against my mouth and I can't help but kiss her all over again. I lower my hand from her face down to feel her body melt against mine.

She molds perfectly against me and I never want to stop touching her. My tongue slides between her lips and I savor the taste of her in my mouth.

I swear my eyes roll to the back of my head as I feel her tongue glide against mine. I slide my hand down to where the top of her shorts begin.

Jaclyn shivers against me as I slip my hand beneath the thin cloth material. Jaclyn feels nice and hot down here even though her body is covered in goosebumps as if she's cold. "How bad do you want me, baby?" I ask against her lips.

Our lips are touching but we stop kissing, now we're just breathing each other in. Jaclyn's hips reach up for my hand but I pull my hand back so it won't touch her.

Not yet.

"Hayden, please?"

I move my lips away from her and start kissing

towards her neck. "Tell me, princess," I whisper against her neck, giving her soft and sensual kisses. "Tell me how bad, princess." I start trailing my kisses down her neck to where her nipples are poking through her thin tank top.

"Oh my God," Jaclyn whispers, moving her head to the side and closing her eyes shut. I bite her nipple through the tank top and she arches her back and presses her breasts against me.

"You really did miss me, huh? No one knows your body better than I do." I nip her nipple. "Tell me what you want me to do. Tell me how bad you want me to make this pussy mine all over again."

"Touch me, Hayden. Please, I-I can't. I need you," she begs as I finally spread her lips and press my thumb on her clit. "Oh," she moans, each time I rub her clit. Her hips rock against my hand. She was so ready and desperate to come, for me to give her an orgasm.

I thrust one finger inside her and she sucks in a breath, her face filled with pure ecstasy. Jaclyn is soaked and I easily slide in another finger, going so deep past the knuckles. I use my other hand to cover her mouth as I take her nipple in my mouth again. I bite her nipple making her squirm and moan in my hand.

"Oh God, Hayden," she mumbles against my hand as I play around with her g-spot, going deeper and forcing my fingers even farther just so I can bring her to where I need her.

She is still the same girl from college. I still know how to show her the world and even the stars. Playing with her body always used to be my favorite pastime in college.

I realize I should never take Jaclyn for granted ever again.

Because I could one day lose her and never get her back.

I lean up to her lips and take my hand off her. I press my lips against hers and say, "I need to feel you come."

"I'm close," she says against my mouth.

"Yea?"

"Yes," she moans before I take my hand away from her pussy. "No, Hayden!" she yells.

I take off her shorts and underwear. I shove her black underwear in her mouth. "Keep that there. Can't risk Junior waking up." I take off my shorts and sweat-shirt, throwing them somewhere on the floor behind me.

I would move us to the bed but I'm too impatient to feel her.

I need to feel her wrapped around me, desperate to come.

I settle between her legs and part them further, holding them against the floor. I look at her and see her staring at me with a lustful look in her eyes, a desperate look that says to just start fucking her.

The moment I thrust inside her, all the way in, Jaclyn

clenches onto me tightly and screams, or at least tries to with her underwear in her mouth.

"That's it," I moan, pulling out and thrusting back in harder, pounding into her as if she's some doll but I can't help it. "Your pussy knows exactly who she belongs to, princess." I squeeze her hips and Jaclyn holds onto my arms, her nails digging into my arms, probably digging deep enough to make me bleed.

Jaclyn clenches onto me tightly. I remove the underwear from her mouth and lean down, smashing my lips against hers. Jaclyn's orgasm catches up and she comes around me with a muffled scream against my mouth.

"Hayden, Hayden, Hayden," she repeats my name as if it's a prayer and I'm her god.

Her whole body is tightening and her nails are digging into my skin deeper. I thrust into her faster, my orgasm slowly coming up.

I pound into her through her orgasm, hitting that spot over and over. It doesn't take long for me to shoot my load inside. I trail my kisses down Jaclyn's neck as she closes her eyes and takes a minute.

She's always been like that with sex, taking a minute to come down while I just kiss her wherever I see fit. Sometimes putting hickeys on her while she doesn't notice or have the energy to tell me to stop.

I pull out of her and look between her legs seeing my cum dripping out of her. I press my thumb to her pussy, massaging her clit and our cum mixes together before thrusting it back inside her. Jaclyn shudders and moans softly.

"I like when you do that," she whispers. I look at her face seeing that she's flushed and there's some sweat on her forehead. "Pretty sure that's how I got pregnant with Junior when you did that."

"I don't want you to miss a drop." I lean down and press my lips on hers. "Plus I'm trying to get you pregnant again so I can experience it with you."

"We aren't having four kids."

"Wanna bet?" I smile through the kiss.

Fifty-One

Hayden

I feel a featherlight touch on my cheek making me stir. I push the hand away but keep my eyes closed. I turn towards Jaclyn's warm body and wrap my arms around her.

The poking doesn't stop though and I end up hearing giggling shortly after.

I open my eyes and turn my head to look behind me. Junior has a guilty look on his face with a small teasing smirk.

Fuck, what time is it?

I look over Jaclyn and see her clock reads 7:32.

Doesn't she have work at like eight or eight thirty?

"We're gonna be late and mama hates being late," Junior whispers. "Why don't you and mama have a shirt on?" he asks, tilting his head to the side and furrowing his eyebrows, looking just like his mother.

I look at Jaclyn, the covers are up to her chest thankfully so Junior can't see anything.

"Go to the living room. I'll be there to make some food for you," I tell Junior and he runs out of the room, not closing the door behind him.

I kiss Jaclyn's shoulder softly and take a strand of her hair between my fingers. I wish I could just stay in bed with her forever but I know she would want to go to work. I also know that I could easily provide for her and Junior and she wouldn't even need to think about working.

But it's not my choice, it's up to Jaclyn and what she wants to do with her career. I know she's always loved writing and being a writer so I would hate for her to quit her passion just cause I can provide for her.

Jaclyn's always been super independent. From the moment I met her she never needed a prince charming or someone to help her.

But that doesn't mean I don't want to help her or be there for her.

After staring at her for too long I whisper, "Jaclyn," while running my fingers through her hair. "You've got to wake up." I kiss the spot below her ear making her stir.

She moans softly, making my dick twitch.

We already went at it like three times in total last night.

Once on the floor, the other times in her bed with her on her hands and knees and ass in the air, and then her laying on her side, too tired and spent with me thrusting in her fast and hard.

I can see why she's tired. I wore her out last night, not giving her a single break but I just missed her. I missed the way her body would cling onto me, desperate to have me and never let me go.

"It's about to be 7:40. You need to wake up, princess," I whisper again and that seems to make her open her eyes and look at the clock.

"Shit." Jaclyn gets out of bed and throws the covers off her. She gets out of bed and closes the door. She goes to her closet while I get out of bed and walk towards her. "I'm going to be so late. I was supposed to wake up at seven. I need to make breakfast and get ready and then take Junior-"

I cut her off by grabbing her chin to make her look at me. "Calm," I whisper, keeping eye contact with her. "I'll get Junior ready and make breakfast. You just get ready. If you need me to take Junior to school this morn- ing, I will." Jaclyn stares at me not saying anything, worry still present on her face. I know she would always worry about being late. She never liked being late; only, always on time. "Understand?" she nods her head and because I can't help it, I lean down and kiss her softly. "Stop being in your head and worrying so much." I get away from her before I decide to make her even later for work.

Plus Junior is here and awake so I don't want him thinking I'm killing his mom or something.

I put on my shorts from last night and then my sweater.

When I walk out of the room I see Junior standing in front of the TV. Jumping up and down while watching some dog movie.

"What do you usually have for breakfast?" I ask while walking into the kitchen.

Junior runs over to me. "Well, when mama is running late I have cereal. Usually though Brandon comes over and helps mama out with feeding me while she gets ready. He always likes making sure she eats."

Why would that motherfucker come over to have to make sure Jaclyn eats breakfast every morning?

I remain calm so Junior doesn't see my change in mood. "Where's your cereal?"

Junior points to a cupboard near the fridge. "I also need to take my medicine. I have to take it every morning before I eat. Mama says if I take medicine with no food it's bad for me."

"Why do you take medicine?" I ask, now worried and a little pissed off that Jaclyn is hiding even more from me.

What could she possibly be afraid of that she feels the need to constantly lie to me?

"Something's wrong with my heart," Junior says. "My medicine is in the very top cabinet," Junior says pointing to another cabinet on the very top.

I open the cabinet and it looks like a regular medicine cabinet with first aid stuff and some pill bottles. "Your mama takes medicine too?" I ask, looking at one of her pill bottles. Some of them are labeled Lexapro and others are labeled Prozac.

Junior nods his head innocently. "She said it's so she doesn't feel sad anymore."

So she doesn't feel sad anymore?

Why the fuck does she take these? It's basically poisoning her.

Now I also can guess why she lost so much fucking weight and looks so dead most of the time.

She's probably back into those old habits she told me she was on when she was in high school.

Over my dead fucking body that I'm going to let her ruin herself like that.

I put the bottles back and instead look for Junior's pills. I find some with his name on them. On the bottle it says, diuretics, which is fucking heart failure medicine.

What the fuck?

The more I keep finding in this stupid medicine

cabinet the more pissed off I'm getting. "You only take one pill or two?"

"Just one. And then I take another at night," Junior says as he seats himself on the chair at the island.

I give him a small cup of water and then his pill. He takes it easily which I worry about because no kid should be taking pills this young.

I make Junior a bowl of his favorite cereal which is Cocoa Pebbles. Jaclyn eventually comes out wearing dress pants that have a flare on the bottom and a black vest over a white button up.

She looks goddamn beautiful but I am still pissed.

Jaclyn can tell because she furrows her eyebrows at me. I don't do anything. I lean against the counter as she walks inside the kitchen.

"Morning, baby." She kisses Junior before going towards the medicine cabinet.

Junior smiles at his mother. "You're coming to my school tonight right? My teacher said that I've been good and I want you to know," Junior asks while looking at me.

"I promised I would, right?" I tell Junior, making him smile.

I want to smile back at him but I can't.

I'm so mad to the point where I feel a blood vessel might fucking pop or something.

I thought everything after last night would somehow be okay. Watching a movie, doing absolutely nothing with

Jaclyn and Junior was my definition of a perfect night. I would dream about nights like that.

But this morning, fuck it's like a bunch of overwhelming information that you don't want to hear just shooting at you.

Jaclyn opens the medicine cabinet. "I already gave him his meds," I mumble and Jaclyn looks at me, her eyes slowly starting to tear up. "Sit down. I'll make you something to eat."

"I have to go to work-"

"Sit down," I demand and Jaclyn's tearful eyes turn into a glare. "I already told you I would take Junior. I can have my driver take you to work. You have time to sit down for a few minutes and eat."

Jaclyn doesn't argue with me, she just forces herself to sit down on the chair next to Junior.

The rest of the morning is spent in silence.

As I make Jaclyn breakfast, change Junior into an outfit, and drive her to work.

She doesn't say one word to me. The only words exchanged are with Junior.

Don't worry, we'll be having a very long talk after Junior's conference tonight.

Fifty-Two

I knew today was going to be a bad one when I woke up late. Although waking up next to Hayden was nice and reminded me of old times, I hate whenever I feel rushed in the mornings.

Being late always gives me major anxiety, whether it be for work or lunch with friends, I always like being on time.

After I finished getting ready I still had to worry about getting Junior dressed and fed before going to school. Everything started to feel hectic but then I walked out of the room and saw Hayden leaning against the counter while watching Junior eat.

Hayden's arms were crossed and his whole body looked hard and tense. Then he looked at me and I knew, I just knew every good thing that came out of last night had crumbled down. Hayden and I didn't talk the rest of the morning and Junior tried to have us both talk during the car ride to my work but neither of us said anything to each other.

Hayden would only talk to Junior while I stayed silent, fixing Junior's hair.

I let Hayden drop me off at work first so that I wouldn't be late and he could drop Junior off at school.

Work today has been as normal as it could. Brandon bothers me, a meeting with Jules about the CEO article, and then just emails about other stories I needed to look over.

Currently I'm waiting in my office lobby for Hayden's car. Brandon is with me because Hayden is going to send Brandon home with Junior while we both are at the conference tonight. Hayden mentioned last night he would pick me and Brandon up but after this morning I wouldn't be surprised if he just bailed.

He is trying to do better though.

I need to stay positive.

"He's here," Brandon tells me as if Hayden himself heard my thoughts.

I wipe my sweaty palms on my dress pants and take a deep breath.

I know why Hayden's mad at me.

It's because I didn't tell him about his son's medical

condition. He probably saw all the med's in the cabinet and he got worried.

But it's fine.

I'm handling it.

I've been doing okay and just fine without him or his support.

Brandon and I walk outside as Hayden gets out of the car.

"Brandon, we never exchanged names or met properly," Hayden says, putting out a hand towards Brandon.

Brandon shakes his hand. "Nice to meet you, officially. Glad you're finally able to be a part of Junior's life and experience him."

Hayden nods his head, his jaw clenching. His eyes go to me and yup, he's still pissed. "Yea, looks like you're no longer needed."

"Hayden," I say, making him look away from Brandon and glare at me.

"What? I'm just saying the truth. He's not Junior's father so Junior isn't his responsibility. I'm allowing him to hang out with my son since you and I will be busy."

My hand clenches around my bag. "Brandon, can you wait in the car for us?" I say, keeping my voice calm while glaring at Hayden. Brandon gets into the Escalade before I go off. "What the fuck is wrong with you Hayden? Brandon's my friend and he doesn't deserve your stupid jealousy."

Hayden walks closer to me until we're about a foot away from each other. "I told you, I'm not jealous. I can't be jealous of someone when they have nothing I want. You and Junior are mine so I'm making sure he knows his fucking place with you two," Hayden says.

"Brandon is Junior's friend. He will be coming over still and hanging out. You can't just stop someone who is important to Junior from coming over and showing Junior love. I'll let whoever loves Junior around him because that's all that matters. So tone down the protective bullshit and quit the attitude."

Next thing I know, Hayden's hand slides onto me to hold the side of my throat, gripping it. Not tight enough to make me scared because I could never be scared of Hayden.

But tight enough to know who's in control here.

"I'm not the one who keeps fucking lying and hiding things. I'll make you a deal. You start telling me shit and stop hiding things that I should know from me, and I'll back off on that piece of shit in the car."

I push Hayden's chest and move past him to go to the car.

Fuck him.

———

"So I know I've spoken with you, Ms. King, about Junior a few times but this is the first time I'm meeting you, Mr. Night," Junior's teacher, Ms. Johnson says.

The entire car ride here was spent in silence. I sat in between Hayden and Brandon so that there wouldn't be any chances of Hayden nagging Brandon.

Brandon knows how to take care of himself but I just don't like the fact that he has to when Hayden is acting like a child. When we got to the school, Brandon went to get Junior while Hayden and I walked to his class in silence.

Now we're here. Sitting in two tiny desks with our son's teacher in front of us.

"Yea, Junior asked me to come and I know he's a good kid from what I've learned. I just want the chance to meet the teacher properly."

"I would have never thought you'd be a single dad, Mr. Night. I mean the fights and everything must be hard and a lot of work for a man like you," Ms. Johnson says with a small smile.

I raise an eyebrow and that green monster slowly rises as I stare at her.

What's with that tone and those comments?

Is she serious?

Right in front of me?

And she's making it seem like I'm not here and Hayden's doing all the work.

I swear I'm going to smash this bitch's head-

"I'm not single Ms. Johnson. But I appreciate the concern," Hayden replies politely.

I look at him and raise an eyebrow.

Since when did we decide we were together?

"Please, call me Robin." Ms. Johnson smiles sweetly at him. Doesn't she have a damn boyfriend? Why does she have to flirt and talk like that to Hayden when she already has someone at home. As if Hayden could sense me getting pissed off and starting to overthink, his hand covers mine under the table as he stares at Ms. Johnson. "Well let's get started shall we? Junior is a spectacular kid. I mean knowing who his father is now, I know why. I must say your fights are impressive."

I bite my bottom lip to keep from saying something because I swear I'm about to go off on her.

Why the fuck is she being so unprofessional all of a sudden?

Hayden is just a fucking fighter, not the Bachelor from season one of *The Bachelor*.

She is prettier than me anyways.

I mean look at her and those curves.

Maybe Hayden is into her too.

Or maybe, just maybe, I should fucking make her lose her job for talking to Hayden, my Hayden, like that.

"I appreciate the comments, Ms. Johnson, truly but I'm here for *our* son. I could care less what you think of me. So if we could go on with the meeting without mentioning my fights or career that would be great," Hayden says while running a thumb over my hand.

Ms. Johnson blushes and nods her head. "Of course, Mr. Night. I apologize." Ms. Johnson put her notes together from Junior's folder. "Junior is doing really well with all his letters and spelling. He's a very bright kid. Only thing he's struggling a bit in is some of his math."

Ms. Johnson starts to go on about Junior and how he's doing in school and with the other classmates.

She says he is one of the friendliest kids here with a good heart. Hayden listens throughout the whole time and asks questions every now and then to learn more.

Hayden holds my hand the entire time while listening to her while I hold his hand back.

"Overall, Junior is doing great."

"Can you tell at all if he'll need special ed or anything for math?" I ask, wondering if he's like me in school, struggling.

Ms. Johnson shrugs. "It's too hard to tell now. We'll have to wait until he's a bit older. But I wouldn't be worried, Ms. King. He is doing well. You should be very proud of him." I smile and nod my head. "Well that concludes this meeting." Ms. Johnson gathers her papers together. "I have to talk to my next parents but it was lovely talking to you both."

Hayden and I both stand up. "Nice meeting you,

thank you for doing everything you do for our son," he says and I swear that the green monster is about to come up again until he says, "Let's go, princess."

"You go, I'll catch up," I say to Hayden quietly.

Hayden raises an eyebrow, questioning me but I smile and nod my head. Hayden lets go of my hand and smiles at Ms. Johnson before walking out the door. I look at Ms. Johnson and walk up to her desk.

She looks up at me with a raised eyebrow. "Is there an issue Ms. King?'

"Yes. Look at and talk to my husband like that again and I'll get you fired so quickly you'll regret doing that," I say, keeping my composure calm.

Ms. Johnson's face turns red and she laughs nervously. "Ms. King, it wasn't my intention to threaten you. I didn't even know you were married."

We aren't, but I'm sure with Hayden's dedication we will be. "We are and I hope me telling you this is a lesson for you not to do it next time I come in with my husband. Know your place, which is being my son's teacher. That's all you are to Hayden and all you'll ever be. You'll be smart to keep that in mind. Understood?"

Ms. Johnson nods her head. "Of course."

"Good. Have a good rest of your day, Ms. Johnson," I say before leaving out the door.

Fifty-Three

Jaclyn

"I don't understand why you're mad," Hayden says as we walk through the front door of the apartment.

Junior is at Brandon's house right now because I know Hayden wanted to talk as soon as we walked through the front door of the apartment. I told Junior to just sleep over there and then Brandon can bring him back in the morning.

I just know that Hayden and I need to talk about everything.

My jealousy, Hayden's job and what that means for us, what exactly we're doing, Junior's health, and probably more.

"If anyone should be pissed off it's me," Hayden says as I put my stuff on the counter and walk into my room, with Hayden following after me. "You don't tell me about Junior, you don't tell me about Junior's fucking health condition, and then don't even get me started on the pills and starving yourself."

I furrow my eyebrows, acting shocked about the last statement even though anxiety is running through my veins.

How does he know?

How does he know?

How does he know?

I ruined the girl he loved and now he's pissed.

I'm not perfect in his eyes anymore and he can see that, can't he?

"No I don't. What are you talking about?"

Hayden's hands clench and he licks his lips.

I can see how calm he's trying to stay. "You fucking take pills, anti-depressants to make yourself skinner. You forgot that you told me that you used to do that shit in high school. You would take your prescribed antidepressants and use those to lose weight. You didn't care if they helped you or not, you were addicted to them and how they would make you not hungry. Or was that another girl I dated in college that told me that?" Hayden yells.

By the time he's done a tear rolls down my cheek and his face starts to become blurry as I try not to let another tear fall.

He knows.

He knows.

He knows.

He knows.

Hands grab my face and more tears start to fall. "I don't give a fuck what you look like. Big thighs or not, flat fucking stomach or not, I never cared, Jaclyn. I only ever cared if I got to see that genuine smile on your face. I only ever cared that you were healthy and happy. Why can't you understand that?"

I shake my head, more tears running down my face. "They made me hate myself," I whispered. "Having Junior made me hate myself even though I love him to death."

"Why? Just cause you gained a little weight during pregnancy."

"I hated looking in the mirror and seeing the same girl who was supposed to die in that room. I didn't want to see her or be reminded of how happy she was so I continued to kill her after Junior was born. And then just losing the weight naturally was hard especially since, with my diabetes, it felt impossible. I got addicted to taking those same meds I took from high school because my therapist prescribed me those pills to help with the nightmares and overthinking. But then she stopped recently and it's just hard, knowing I won't look perfect in your eyes."

Hayden wipes away my tears from under my eyes, his eyes starting to water "Princess, I could care less about the weight you put on. In my eyes you'll always be perfect. This body carried my son for nine months, you think I won't love you or think you're not perfect for doing just that?" I try to take my face out of his hands but he doesn't let me. "No, tell me."

"I'm just scared."

"Scared of what?" Hayden looks in my eyes, still holding my face in his warm and strong hands.

God, I've always loved him holding me like this. I've always felt safe and loved whenever he did that. It almost makes me want to cry because I haven't felt this way in such a long time. I haven't felt loved in so long and I miss it.

"I'm just scared."

Hayden shakes his head lightly. "You're scared of the way I make you feel because you don't want to feel anything for me at all." Hayden raises an eyebrow and I swear I fucking feel my heart shatter. He is so on point that it scares me. He knows me so well even after five years. He can read me like an open book. "Right? You're scared to fall in love with me because of the way I make you feel. I bring out that girl that I fell in love with during college, and you hate her because of that night." Hayden puts my hair behind my ears and wipes my tears again. "Baby, that night changed nothing and never will, I promise you that. That night doesn't make me see you any different. You're still the same girl that I fell in love with in that alley way when we were teenagers, still the same girl I fell in love with in college when you were putting me in my place, still the same girl who had my kid and didn't even tell me," Hayden says with a chuckle, making me smile at him, feeling guilty.

"I still feel awful for that."

"I understand why you had to do all that. I know you needed to protect yourself," Hayden says softly, looking at my lips before meeting my eyes. "I wish you told me sooner but things happen and you just have to make do with it."

I nod my head and lick the dried tears from my lips. "I'm sorry. I will do whatever I can to make it better."

"Then stop hiding things from me. If you struggle, I want to struggle with you. If something is wrong with Junior, I want to know. If you're scared about me leaving, don't be. I don't ever plan on leaving you or Junior. You guys are it for me."

I nod my head.

Hayden leans down and he kisses my tear stained cheeks, forehead, and then presses his lips on mine softly. I inhale and kiss him back passionately. Hayden uses one of his hands to hold my hair while the other stays on my jaw.

Even though the kiss is soft and passionate I can feel Hayden's control dripping off him. The way he holds my hair, his hand on my jaw angling my face to deepen the kiss, and the way his chest brushes against mine.

My head is in the clouds whenever I kiss Hayden and it seems like my mind shuts up.

Hayden has always been the boy to make me feel all types of emotions I never thought I would feel. I never thought, in my entire life, that I would feel so much for someone like I do for Hayden.

His love for me and my love for him are unexplainable yet it makes so much sense.

"I love you," I whisper against his lips.

Hayden stops kissing me and looks at me. "What?"

I blush and smile. "I love you, Hayden. I never stopped."

Hayden smiles before smashing his lips against mine and saying, "I love you."

Fifty-Four

Jaclyn

Present

It's been a few days since Hayden and I talked about things. He comes over every night to watch a movie with Junior and I. He falls asleep with me in bed every night while playing with my hair.

While I work and while Junior is at school, he's busy with work.

He tells me that he talks to Rowan and Kayden during the day sometimes. He says he wants me to meet Rowan's family.

Today is Saturday, Junior and I went to the mall with Natalia and Lilah.

Hayden had things to do today with his brother and Killian. I guess they are in New York. He said after he was done he would come over.

He gave me his card today and told me to go crazy with it and buy whatever I want and whatever Junior wants.

I told him that I would only buy stuff for Junior since I don't need anything but Hayden said if I don't then he'll have Natalia shop for me or he'll take me shopping.

I only bought two things for myself with his card which were a nice summer dress and a pair of sunglasses. I got more stuff for Junior since he saw a lot of things he liked.

"What are you doing tonight?" Natalia asks as the driver pulls up to my apartment.

Now that Hayden has a more important role in this whole mafia thing he wants us to have a guard and driver. I don't disagree with that because it honestly makes me feel safer and I know that it will keep Junior safe as well.

"We're gonna see my papa!" Junior exclaims in his car seat next to Lilah.

He and Lilah got along and it was their first time meeting today. They wouldn't stop talking about Paw Patrol.

Natalia smiles at him. "Really?! That sounds like so much fun. What are you guys going to do?"

Junior laughs mischievously which I raise my eyebrows at. "It's a secret."

Natalia smiles and looks back at me. "So how are things going with Hayden?" Natalia asks.

"I can honestly say that things are better," I say with a small smile that Natalia is proud of.

I feel like the weeks are slowly passing by with how much time we've spent with Hayden. I'm not complaining about it and neither is Junior because he loves seeing his dad everyday. Our driver pulls up to our building. I get Junior out of his car seat and we say 'bye' to Natalia and Lilah.

"I'll take the bags up, miss," the driver tells us through the cracked window and I just nod my head and thank him.

Junior holds hands with me as we walk to the elevator. When we're inside the elevator I look down at Junior.

Whenever I'm looking at him I always see his father. "Would you be happy if your papa were to stay here with us, Junior? Or we live with your papa someday?"

Junior looks up at me with an excited smile on his face. "Are we going to live with Papa?"

"No, not now at least but someday if you're up for it?" I say with a small smile.

Junior nods his head repeatedly and I laugh at him before kissing his chubby cheeks. I think that might be the only thing he got from me because Hayden's jaw is slim and strong while mine is round and a little chubby.

Or at least was.

Hayden is doing everything in his power to make my

cheeks come back whether that be feeding me so much food I might barf or feeding me sweet treats.

The elevator dings before the doors open. We walk towards the apartment as Junior goes on and on about how he would love for us to live with Hayden.

I unlock the door and open it. Junior runs in as soon as I put my bag down on the island. I walk towards my room and my eyes go to the bed that is covered with pink flower pedals and a black box placed in the middle of the bed. There is also a huge bouquet of pink peonies.

Peony season just ended so how did he get them?

"Look what papa did for you mama!" Junior cheers as he stands next to the bed, jumping up and down with a happy smile on his face.

I walk towards the bed and grab the card that says my name on it.

> *Be ready by 8:30. We have dinner reserva-*
> *tions. Junior is staying with Brandon for the*
> *rest of the night. I love you, princess.*

"Mama, you're smiling weird."

I look up from the note and look at Junior. "No I'm not," I say, wiping the smile off my face. "Did you know about this?"

Junior nods his head. "Papa told me to keep a secret because I was spending the night at Brandon's place so I promised not to say anything. I was so excited but I couldn't say anything," Junior exclaims. "You know how hard it was?!"

"Thank you, baby. I love you," I say and Junior hugs me as I kiss his forehead.

"Love you too, mama," he mumbles before pushing me away and running towards his room to go play.

He gets distracted so easily.

The dress Hayden got for me is a light pink silk dress that ends maybe around the mid thigh area. It's gorgeous and has lace on the neckline.

"Junior, Brandon is going to watch you tonight, is that okay?" I yell so he can hear me from the other room.

"Gots it!" he yells back.

That's all I need for me to start getting ready.

I take a quick shower while Junior is occupied with his toy cars and the show I put on for him. I shave everything and make sure to also exfoliate everything.

Suddenly I'm a little girl again who is all giddy, feeling butterflies in my stomach over a crush.

But Hayden was never just a silly little crush, he's everything.

By the time I'm done with my shower and working on my hair, it's 7:15 pm and Brandon walks in. He entertains Junior while I continue to get ready.

I straighten my hair and do my makeup naturally because that's how I feel like I look best with makeup.

After I'm done getting ready I have ten minutes to spare.

I clean the petals up and put them in a bag. I put the black box and flowers on the desk.

I look in the mirror, making sure I look good. Brandon comes in and leans on the doorframe. I see his eyes go to the gift Hayden got me on the side table.

"He really loves you."

"I'm afraid that I feel the same," I admit.

Hayden already knows though.

And I still can't help but not get over the overthinking but Patience says it will take time.

"Love has always been scary. But you deserve someone to love you like Hayden does. Don't ruin what you guys have because you're scared." I nod my head and lick my bottom lip, taking my strawberry lip gloss from my lips. My phone buzzes and Brandon looks at it on the desk. "He's waiting for you downstairs."

I grab my phone and look at the text.

Come down, princess.

I suddenly get deja vu from all the times he would do this sort of thing for dates. He would always give me a note, telling me the time he'll pick me up and then texting me when he's outside.

I say goodbye to Junior and he tells me to have fun but not too much fun.

I laugh and promise him I'll be okay.

My nerves sky rocket as the elevator goes down to the ground floor. I wipe my clammy hands on my dress and take a deep breath as I walk through the lobby.

The door man tells me I look stunning while he opens the door for me. I smile and thank him before my eyes go to a familiar set of eyes that always happen to steal my breath away.

Hayden is leaning against a black 458 Spider.

Hayden knows that I've always dreamed of having this kind of car, along with a BMW M5 Competition.

I told him all my dreams and wishes. He always told me that he'd someday make that happen because he loves me that much.

He walks up to me and grabs my hand. "You look beautiful, as always."

I can't help but blush. "Thank you." I look behind him at the car. "Nice car."

"I got it for you." Hayden pulls out the key. "I'll let you drive if you don't make me wait until after the date to kiss you."

I smile and chuckle lightly. "Tempting."

"Is that a yes?" Hayden raises an eyebrow at me and I just nod my head.

I would hate to wait until after the date to kiss him.

He leans in and steals my breath and makes my whole body heat up. He grabs my waist and pulls me closer to him. I hold his jaw in my hand and kiss him back.

It's a soft yet passionate kiss. Hayden keeps it tame and forces himself away.

"Just wait until the end of the night. The whole city will know my name," Hayden whispers in my ear which sends shivers down my spine. "Here." He puts the key in my hand. "Go crazy."

I can't stop the jittery smile on my face as I walk to the driver side of the car.

Fifty-Five

PRESENT

I pull up to the valet and then put the car in park.

Hayden is staring at me with adoration and pride in his eyes. My heart is pounding from the speeds I went on the highway.

Hayden leans over and places his lips on mine for a quick kiss. "How do you feel?"

"Alive," I mumble before pulling away.

Hayden continues to smile at me as we get out of the car. I hand the keys to the valet and then Hayden takes my hand and opens the door for me.

The restaurant where we're at is outside of Manhattan and has an Italian vibe. When we walk in it's quiet with soft romantic music playing.

Hayden says something in Italian to the hostess and

the way he talks so smoothly impresses me. I never knew he learned how to speak Italian. He never told me. I've always loved Italian, it's so romantic and beautiful.

She nods her head and grabs two menus before she walks off. Hayden grips my hand in his and follows her.

She takes us towards the back of the restaurant where it's more quiet. We walk through the balcony doors and she takes us past all of the tables where people are dining. We walk upstairs and end up in a private section of the restaurant. There is a table placed in the middle of the balcony separate from the other tables. A giant peony bush is behind the table and there is a clear view of the city in front of us.

"Hayden," I whisper so low that he probably can't hear me. The hostess places the menus on the table before saying something in Italian and leaving. Hayden pulls me towards the table, pulls out my chair so I can sit. He takes his seat in front of me and grabs my hand over the table. I take a look around us again to admire the setting. "You did all this?"

Hayden nods his head. "You deserve only the best and I want to give you that without you being scared."

I smile at him and run my thumb against his fingers on my hand. "I'm not scared of you. I'm scared of the past happening again, but this time worse."

"I won't let it. Things are different this time. Working with Killian has given me a lot more security and I trust

Killian like a brother because essentially he kind of is one to me."

It's like I'm falling in love all over again with Hayden but at the same time did I ever stop?

Those butterflies in my stomach have come back and it feels like I'm always smiling whenever I look at Hayden and Junior.

"I want to believe you. It's just hard sometimes."

Hayden nods his head. "How'd you like the car?"

"It's fun. Is it yours?"

"Yea. Whenever you want to go for a drive, I'll give you the keys anytime."

I raise an eyebrow at him. "You trust me?"

"I trust you with my life, princess. I can trust you with a car."

A waiter eventually comes to our private balcony. He is holding two waters and he starts speaking in Italian. Hayden and him speak to each other before the waiter nods his head, takes the menus, and leaves.

"I didn't know you could speak Italian," I say to Hayden before taking a sip of my water.

"I learned it over the years from Rowan and Killian. They both taught me. They said if I was going to be a part of the family I had to learn it along with other languages."

I smile before asking, "Say something to me in Italian."

Hayden smirks at me before saying, *"Ti amerò per*

sempre. Che si tratti di questo o di un milione di altri. Che tu ti ami o no, ti amerò per entrambi. Niente al mondo potrà mai farmi smettere di amarti. E non vedo l'ora di farti la proposta un giorno, così capirai che sono qui per restare per sempre, " with a smooth tongue.

I have no clue what he said but I swear it made my core pulse and my stomach fill with even more butterflies.

"What did you say that was so long?"

Hayden leans back in his chair and stares me down with lust in his eyes. "You look very beautiful tonight."

"That was a lot of Italian words for not a lot of English words," I say, making Hayden's smirk widen just a little, almost turning it into a smile. The waiter eventually comes back with two plates of food. He slides a rigatoni bolognese my way and then what looks like steak and gnocchi in front of Hayden. "You already took our orders?"

"Yeah, when he brought the water."

"But we didn't even look at the menus."

"When I was looking for restaurants I was also looking at menus to see what you'd like and I saw they had rigatoni here and a nice setting so that's why I chose this place. I already knew what you were going to get so that's why I already ordered that for you."

"And what if I didn't want rigatoni?" I ask with a teasing smile.

"You love rigatoni. Every time we went to an Italian

restaurant you would always order rigatoni with a side of ricotta cheese."

My jaw wants to drop because of how much effort he put into this and also how much he still knows me after so long.

The fact that he made this set up and even took time to look at all the menus to make sure I'd like what they have is mind blowing.

I would never think someone would care about me this much.

It makes my heart ache and yearn for him.

"Why are you looking at me like that?" Hayden asks.

"Like what?"

"Like you're falling in love with me all over again?" Hayden leans towards me and grabs my hand to hold it in his.

"Because I am."

Hayden smiles and then starts eating, making me smile back.

Fifty-Six

Hayden

Once I finish paying the bill my eyes go to Jaclyn who has a subtle but flirty smile on her face. After I spoke Italian to her she has been giving me these eyes. God, her damn eyes kill me. They could bring me to my knees if I wasn't in a public setting.

I think if she asked me for anything right now, I'd give it to her, no questions asked.

I'm hers, my heart, body, and soul if she wants that too.

"Ready?" I ask her, standing up.

She nods her head and gets out of her chair. I take her hand in mine and pull her close to me as we walk away from the table.

Once we get to the car that the valet pulled up, I give

her the key. "You want me to drive again?" she asks, raising an eyebrow. I nod my head and open the driver door for her.

She gives me another heart stopping smile and gets in.

I close the door and get in the passenger seat. The car vrooms to life making Jaclyn smirk a little at the sound.

She pulls out of the valet area and zooms out of the parking lot. I smile and rest my hand on her bare thigh making her clench her thighs together but she keeps her eyes on the road.

I tell her the directions for getting to my penthouse. Brandon is watching Junior for the night so I'm going to take advantage of that and have Jaclyn to myself for the night.

During the ride to the penthouse I occasionally grip Jaclyn's thigh lightly making her press the gas harder. She went as fast as 100 mph along the highway. I could make her go completely undone with my touch but then that would probably end with us at the bottom of the cliff.

And when we pull up to the front of the building, I get out of the passenger seat and go to the driver side as Jaclyn gets her bag and turns the engine off.

I open the door for her and just pick her up bridal style.

She laughs in my arms and holds onto me as I walk to the front of my building. I toss the keys to the valet before walking in.

The elevator up feels like it takes forever especially since a neighbor of mine is in there so I can't do what I want to do to Jaclyn in the elevator.

We eventually get to my floor.

I kiss Jaclyn's neck softly and let her walk in.

She smiles at me and stays still for a second before turning around and running towards the stairs.

I let her run upstairs as I take off my suit jacket and rest it on the table in the foyer.

I follow her, not running or quickening my pace.

I go inside my room, where the door is open. I look around and see her bag on one of the side tables next to the bed. My eyes roam the bed and closet but hands cover my eyes, or at least attempt to due to our height difference.

I turn around and push her against the wall that's behind her, near the door.

I immediately put my lips on hers. She moans into the kiss and I hold her jaw and waist in my hands, somehow trying to pull her closer to me.

I swear there is like this magnetic energy trying to pull us closer. I don't ever want to leave her arms.

Jaclyn claws at my back and she moves her hips against mine in a slow rhythm. She's so responsive and desperate for my touch, I fucking love it. Her tongue rubs against mine and I can't help but groan into her mouth.

I taste every inch of her mouth with my tongue

wanting more and closer. I know she does too by the way she is gripping onto me.

I slowly start to kiss away from her mouth and across her cheek, down to her neck. I give attention to her sweet spot and look at her face seeing her eyes close and mouth open wide as she moans softly.

"Turn around and close your eyes," I say and she does, turning around to face the wall.

I grab the black bandana out of my pocket. I put the bandana in front of her eyes and then tie the back in a knot. She reaches up and touches the fabric as I lean down and whisper "Does this feel familiar?"

Jaclyn turns around, the bandana covers her eyes. "Our first kiss in the closet."

I push her back against the wall and press a kiss to her neck. "Do you understand how goddamn beautiful you are? I could literally go on my knees for you."

"Then do it," she whispers softly.

I do it.

No hesitation.

I kiss my way down her body, not missing a spot. She arches her body for me as I caress her breasts through her dress. When I get on my knees I push her dress up her thighs and see red underwear.

"You were hoping to get lucky tonight?" I say, pulling her underwear down.

"Something like that," she says before bringing my

mouth to her wet heat. Jaclyn's dripping with need on my tongue. "Oh!" she moans and puts her hands on my head. She pulls me closer to her while grinding gently against my face. "God, Hayden that feels..." she trails off, in a bliss before moaning softly. I play with her clit and press two fingers against her opening. "Hayden!"

I look up at Jaclyn as I shove those two fingers inside. She moans while biting onto her bottom lip to quiet down the sound.

I swirl my tongue around her sensitive folds and move my fingers in and out of her slowly. My cock is throbbing against my pants and I almost come undone just from touching her like this and hearing her moan uncontrollably from my touch.

"You make me fucking mad, princess. You have no clue what you got yourself into with me," I say while making her see stars and scream my name out.

She tenses and clenches around my fingers while coming. I look up at her, throwing her head back and gripping my hair tightly.

I taste every drop of cum from her and stand up, pressing my mouth against hers.

She kisses me back with urgency and trails her hands down my waist to my pants.

I pick her up and take her to the bed. I take off her dress and the bandana and she lays on the bed in front of me, with hungry eyes, bare naked.

I take my shirt off all while she stares at me. When I take my pants and briefs off she clenches her thighs together and stares at my cock with awe as it touches my stomach.

"Hayden-"

I get on top of her and her legs wrap around my waist, desperately trying to grind against me. "You know the best part about fucking you is?"

"What?" she whispers, her eyes closing lightly from how she rubs herself against me.

I lean down, my lips next to her ear. "When I first thrust inside of you." I push myself into her in one go and Jaclyn moans and scratches my back. I hold her legs against the bed so she doesn't move. "Your fucking reaction, princess. The way you hold onto me and make that little noise, makes me come undone." I say before pulling out and pushing back in hard. "Fuck," I say, my lips against her neck.

Jaclyn lets out moans and screams making sure the whole city knows my name like I promised her. I drive into her faster and harder.

Her voice fills the room with her moans and screams. "Hayden, Hayden, Hayden."

Her breasts move against my bare chest with every thrust and I lean down and take them into my mouth. She arches into me and holds onto my shoulders. I give attention to her breasts, biting and kissing them all over before moving to the next one, all while still pushing into her fast and hard.

She feels fucking amazing. She feels like she's mine.

"God, there is no one in the world I can love more than you, princess. I swear," I mumble while kissing the valley between her breasts and up until we are only a breath away from between our lips. "I will always love you. Whether it's this life or a million others. Whether you love yourself or not, I will love you enough for the both of us. Nothing in the world will ever make me stop loving you," I say to her, without mentioning proposing to her, in her ear.

I literally have the ring in the side table next to the bed.

And she has no fucking clue.

"I love you," she says softly.

"Say it again." I lean down and kiss her everywhere I can. "Say it again, please princess."

"I love you."

"Say you're mine," I say, one of my hands reaching towards her neck.

"I'm yours," she says with a lustful look in her eyes.

I thrust a few more times before we both finish, my semen seeping inside her as I move in and out at a slow pace.

Jaclyn moans and wraps her legs tightly around me while scratching my back with her nails, which will most definitely leave a mark.

We both kiss while coming down from the high and I stay inside of her, enjoying the feel of her around me.

"I love you," she whispers against my lips. "I love you so much it scares me."

"I know, baby. I know."

We kiss and forget about everything else.

We enjoy the feel of us wrapped in one another, not moving.

Fifty-Seven

Jaclyn

I wake up before Hayden.

He is still sleeping with his arms around my waist and his head cuddling into my chest. I've just been staring down at him while tracing the features on his face.

I can't stop smiling down at him and my heart is beating uncontrollably fast.

Being with him always feels so unreal. It feels like everything is a dream, like one of those really good ones that you never want to wake up from.

Then adding Junior to the mix makes everything better.

But when I wake up, I'm back to the reality of us and what it's really like.

I'm still terrified of everything ending up in a disaster and going terribly wrong.

Because good things never last forever, I've learned that the hard way.

"What are you thinking about?" I hear Hayden say, making me look down at him. He's awake and looking up at me with concern. My heart warms over how he knows without me telling him. "You're stuck in your head?"

I lean against pillows behind me and Hayden moves up so that his face is close to mine. "I'm just thinking about what's next," I answer honestly. I look down at Hayden and he looks like he's thinking, but about what? I run my hands through his hair and he closes his eyes for a good second, enjoying the feel of my hands in his hair. I know Hayden always loved when I touched his hair, so much to the point where he got hard off it. "What are you thinking?"

Hayden leans in and his mouth ghosts over mine. "Right now I'm just thinking of how I want to make you cum so many times you'll see stars, princess." My hands freeze in his hair and Hayden chuckles. "So if you want to wait on that for later tonight then I would stop touching my hair."

I smirk and take my hands out of his hair and instead hold his jaw in my hands. "So what is next, Hayden?" Hayden licks his lips and looks at the table next to me before looking at me again. "What?"

Hayden leans up on his knees, straddling my hips and he reaches towards the side table next to me. I slide down and lay completely down on the bed instead of resting against the pillows. Hayden opens and closes the drawer and I see him bring a red box labeled Cartier in front of my face.

He lays back on top of me and opens the box showing me a ring with two huge diamonds on the band that's filled with more diamonds. One of the diamonds is light pink in an oval shape and the one next to it is a regular clear diamond that is a little bigger.

I let Hayden take my hand and I watch as he takes the ring out of the box and slides it on my ring finger. I stare in awe, not knowing what to say or do.

"Hayden-"

"We don't have to get married anytime soon. I know we still have a lot of things we need to work on together but I want to marry you. If I don't marry you, I won't marry anyone. It's you. You're it for me, Jaclyn. You'll be the only girl I want to be with and love for an eternity. There is no one else and will never be anyone else. I'm giving you this now to show you how serious I am about you. I'm not leaving you, not unless you really really want me to. I'm not going to leave you like you left me last time because I want to be there for you. I want to be there for you when you're going through shit, I want to be there when you get pregnant with my kid again, and I want to be there for all of your accomplishments because you will have so many," Hayden says while I try not to cry. I try my best to contain my tears and just ease my mind and calm my heart down from beating so much. "I love you. More than I love myself and anyone else in this fucked up world. If I don't have you then I might as well just die because you and Junior are the only thing worth living and dying for. I told you many times before, my heartbeats are dedicated to you and that is still true even after so many years," Hayden says and he rests his forehead on mine. "So please, I'll literally go on my knees if you want me to, but please accept the ring and promise to marry me."

I hold Hayden's jaw in my hands. He looks at me with pleading eyes, as if he is desperate for me to say yes to him. A tear finally falls from my eyes after holding it in for so long. Hayden wipes the tear away and he leans in and presses his lips to where the tear fell.

He trails the kisses all over my cheeks and face before going to my lips.

I've always hated how my cheeks were so full and made my face look round but Hayden has always loved them. He loved all my insecurities enough for me to learn to love myself.

Hayden grabs my hand, the one with the ring, and he holds it while kissing me, going lower. His lips are on my neck now instead of my lips. I part my lips, wanting to tell him 'yes'. I want to scream it and then tell him to show me how much he loves me because I love the way Hayden loves.

Hayden sucks on my skin and whispers. "Please say yes, baby. God, I'll do anything."

"Yes," I moan and then grab his face to pull him up to meet my lips. "Yes, Hayden."

Hayden smiles into the kiss then grabs my hips before pushing inside me and making me see stars like he promised.

Epilogue

Jaclyn

Five Years Later

Patience always told me that if I loved myself enough, I shouldn't worry about how others saw me. All that mattered was how I felt in my own body and with the people around me.

Being with Hayden made me learn to love myself. Loving myself while being alone was hard because how could someone ever love me if I was always alone.

That's what I explained to Patience and she understood why I needed Hayden. Why we both needed each other.

After I got pregnant with our second son, Easton, I developed the same evil voice in my head.

It's a constant battle with myself but Hayden made things easier.

Every single night he would show me why he loved me and how he still loved me even when I didn't look how I did before all the baby weight.

My biggest enemy is myself and I've known that for years, since my freshman year of high school. The only person who's really able to quiet down the voice is myself but Hayden being around helps.

Easton and Junior always bringing me flowers with notes helps too but I know it's because of their father.

Patience says it takes time. Being happy with yourself is one of the hardest things a person can do.

And I'm still learning.

"Mom!" Junior calls out to me, making me focus back on the boys. All three of them are on the sand, throwing a football to one another. But Junior takes a pause to run up to me. "I'm thirsty."

I pass him a water and he takes huge gulps, to the point where the bottle is almost empty.

It's my birthday today. Hayden and the boys woke me up this morning with breakfast in bed. They made crepes, eggs, and bacon. I taught Hayden how to make crepes a long time ago so he taught the boys this morning.

They turned out good and we all ate in bed before the boys started tackling each other.

Hayden takes them to training so that they can learn even though Junior is only ten and Easton is four, turning five soon.

We are going to Rowan's house for dinner later to celebrate my birthday.

We live in Italy now. Lombardy to be specific.

Hayden and I had a long conversation about it because he said he wanted to be close to Killian instead of traveling back and forth so much since a lot of his work was in Italy.

I didn't want to take the kids, especially Junior since Easton didn't really go to school and was a baby, because then he would have to start fresh while also learning new things in a new country. It was a huge culture change and I thought it'd be scary for them.

But since we moved to Italy, things have been easier. Hayden is home more and we still visit the US whenever we have time. Hayden has fights out there still but he's thinking of retiring and starting a clothing company called Night Apparel.

It's something in the works.

But at least we get Hayden every night and we spend more time as a family.

The kids like the school and had an easy time adjusting to everything.

Hayden taught us Italian so that we'd understand things. It took me a good year to fully understand it since I had a little trouble with adjusting to a new language.

"Thanks, mom," Junior says before giving me the water bottle and running back to Hayden and Easton.

Junior doesn't have any resentment towards his father like I thought he would. He loves Hayden and being with him all the time. Hayden loves him just as much and hangs out with him a lot. They are both so alike while Easton is calm like me but looks like his father. Junior is just like Hayden, both in looks and personality.

They spend time together in the gym and Hayden shows Junior how to control his anger.

Easton is still young so he's mainly calm for the most part.

For the past five years, things between Hayden and I have been good. Obviously there were ups and downs but that mostly had to do with me and my constant overthinking. Hayden was still there, even when I tried to push him away because I thought he didn't love me.

Patience was there with me to help as well.

Whenever Hayden would see me deep in thought, he would distract me because that would be the only way to quiet down my mind.

He knows whenever I'm overthinking and helps me through it.

Like now, he turns his attention to me instead of the boys.

He immediately walks over while the boys keep playing. Hayden sits down behind me and pulls me closer to him.

His mouth is next to my head as he whispers, "You

okay?" I nod my head and turn to look at him. "What are you thinking?"

"Just how far we've come," I admit. "We've been through a lot."

"And you're still here as strong as ever," Hayden whispers before kissing my neck softly. "What else?"

"I'm thinking about how lucky I am to be able to have you and the boys."

And in the future, another addition to the family.

"You'll always have us. No matter what," Hayden says and he turns me around so that I'm facing him. "You never have to worry about me leaving, trust me."

"I know," I whisper before leaning in and kissing him gently. Hayden of course takes control and dominates the kiss. I close my eyes and breathe heavily into his mouth desperate for more but we're on a beach with our kids. Plus I have news to tell him. "You won the bet by the way," I mumble against his lips and Hayden freezes.

He pulls away and looks at me with an excited but also confused look on his face.

Hayden and I made a bet about a month or two ago. He said he wants more kids and I told him if he could get me pregnant while I'm on birth control, then it'd be a sign to have more. He told me he wants to keep trying until he has at least one girl because he wants to have a mini me running around for him to love.

And he won.

"You're joking," Hayden says, his smile widening. "You're pregnant?"

I smile and nod my head. "I took a test last week and saw my doctor right away."

Obviously me being pregnant always causes health issues upon health issues but it makes Hayden happy and seeing him happy makes me happy too.

With Junior, the pregnancy was difficult because that was my first one. Easton was a bit easier since I knew what to expect. This one for some reason makes me nervous but I don't know why.

Easton came out completely healthy, thankfully. And Junior's VSD is gone after all the medicine he was given.

I'm glad Junior doesn't have to live with that anymore.

"I'll be there every step of the way," Hayden says before leaning in and kissing me. "I love you but God, I'm so happy you lost." I laugh in the kiss and hold his jaw in my hand.

"I bet it will be a boy," I say, teasing him because I know how badly he wants a girl.

"Watch it be a girl. Wanna make another bet?" Hayden asks, smiling into the kiss too.

I'm about to answer but then I hear one of the boys start to gag, probably Junior.

"Ew! Gross."

Yup, sounds like Junior.

I remove my lips from Hayden and look at the boys walking up to us. "Boys, you're going to have a little sister soon."

"You don't even know if it will be a girl," I exclaim to Hayden, but he just smiles down at me.

"But I'll be so goddamn lucky if I have one because then she'll end up looking like you."

The boys get excited about another addition to the family as Hayden and I stare at them with smiles on our faces.

My mind is quiet.

There are no voices to ruin the moment.

It's times like this when I wish the world would stop.

THE END

Thank You

If you enjoyed this book please feel free to leave a review as it would mean a lot to me.

I always enjoy reading good reviews and I always love reading reviews that have criticism in them. Criticism makes me a better author and I always love knowing what I can work on as a writer.

A simple, "Great Book" would be amazing.

Appreciate your love and support so so much!

Acknowledgments

This book felt like a good way to close off Jaclyn and Hayden's story. As I said on my instagram and in Blinded By Love's acknowledgments, this series (duet) will always be close to my heart because of Jaclyn's character and how Hayden treats her.

Closing this story off with an happy ending after many ups and downs between Hayden and Jaclyn felt right. Adding another book to the mix would be too much for me and also for the characters. Jaclyn and Hayden deserve this kind of ending after everything they both have been through and what I put them through.

In this book you really focus on Jaclyn's character development since Hayden already grew into the best version of himself when he was with Jaclyn in college. So during the book you see Jaclyn go through many struggles that some people in real life struggle with. I wanted to include her addiction with the antidepressants and her body image because that's what I went through in college.

I use to take antidepressant, not because I was feeling shitty or overthinking but because it made me think I was losing weight when it was just really damaging for myself. So I think that me including that part of plot was important because I know I'm not the only person who has gone through that.

If you or anyone you know is going through that or anything worse please go to the trigger warning page and call those hotline number. I'm always a message away too. I always answer my DMs on Instagram.

To my editor Antonia for making this story better with her amazing editing skills. I appreciate you for always helping me and giving me advice on how to make my writing better. To Ama, my cover designer, who created the PERFECT cover. I never loved a cover so much and haven't been so excited and in love with a cover. You made my vision come to life. This cover looks so amazing next to Blinded By Love's cover.

To my readers, THANK YOU. I have no clue how lucky I got with you guys. You guys are incredible and so supportive of me. I can't ask for anyone better to stand by me. I have no clue what I would do without you guys. You make my dreams come true every single day.

And to myself again, since Jaclyn is also you in this book. You're so beautiful, please always remember that. Be kind to yourself, you deserve that for how much kindness you show others. If you're still worried about love, don't worry the right one is out there. Don't worry about the outside world. Just focus on you and you'll be okay.

About the Author

Jaclin Marie is a Self Published Author who lives in Southern California. When she isn't writing a compelling story or reading, she either spends her time at the gym or watching Disney Animation movies.

Jaclin started writing at the age of sixteen but she has always been a book lover. She started writing on this writing platform called Wattpad before she decided to publish her debut, Ace De Luca. Although that was her first published book, it wasn't the only book she has written. Since she started writing, she couldn't seem to stop and just like she found her passion.

Darkness evades Jaclin's mind and it demands to be heard. Writing darkness down on paper is something she loves doing. She makes her readers not only think about her plots but completely sob over them.

Her current works published are just a taste of what goes on inside her head.